ACCORDING TO MY SCIENCE

a novel

JEN SINCLAIR

wjb press
St. Augustine, Florida 32092

Printed in the United States of America
First Printing, 2025

Library of Congress Control Number: 2024927015

ISBN-13: 978-1-965014-02-8 Paperback

ISBN-13: 978-1-965014-03-5 eBook

ASIN: B0DSGDVYWC

Copy edits: LZ Edits

Proofreading: Kate Underwood

PROLOGUE

You don't have to live in the gray, Elle. You just have to see it.

Dad drilled those words into her head from the time the test results came back in kindergarten and explained everything wrong with her. From then on, he worked hard to remind Elle that while it might be difficult for her brain to work in anything but absolutes, she had to remain in the middle of things and reprogram herself to not be so this or that—so *scientific*—or else she'd never survive in a gray world.

There was no gray here, in the cracked and faded hunter-green of the lecture hall door. She'd walked through this very one hundreds of times over the last five years she'd taught here. Though today was the first time she'd been back since campus security escorted her out almost two weeks ago.

After guiding space science students forward in the universe, it took the recent unraveling of her life to discover she'd stopped moving. Though Dad had trained her to remain present by focusing on things like the scuff of her feet across the concrete, or the warmth of the August sun washing over her,

Elle still managed to miss what was right in front of her more times than she cared to admit.

The chatter and creaking of risers leaked out from the door seams. The lecture hall wasn't occupied by her students today, but a hundred-plus strangers. Thousands more were accessing the livestream.

One last lecture. One final shot to impart some bit of wisdom and share her excitement about the possibilities that exist beyond the atmosphere. Elle acknowledged she'd done at least one thing right since she'd come to the university. Her students respected her enough to orchestrate this Worldwide Lecture. Without it, she might still be in bed, hungover or drunk.

Will he be inside?

"Of course," she said to the door, a wave of anger scorching her throat.

How did she ever let herself get so wrapped up in him and give away so much of herself?

There was no gray in trusting someone. You either did, or you didn't. You either put too much faith in others—like her mom and brother did—or you learned not to trust anyone. You took the stones of past betrayals and regrets and built a wall to keep others out and yourself tucked inside. Fortify it, adding layers of brick and mortar every time a new crack appeared. All in an effort to protect yourself, because at the end of the day, you were the only one who could.

It was a process Elle had stopped ever since Dad's last rattled breath grazed her right cheek. His death had made her weak and vulnerable, two things he'd fought to protect her from becoming.

She swallowed the lump rising in her throat as the door handle jiggled and turned.

The world changed when someone you loved left you.

The world changed when someone you trusted betrayed you.

And the world changed when you decided to do something about it.

CHAPTER ONE

A new semester started with the withdrawal list. On a drab and frigid January morning, as the icy sludge from Elle's boots scattered across the brown construction-grade carpet in her office, she learned three of her upper-level students weren't coming back. One had left for an internship at Space-Tech, and two more for undisclosed reasons, though Elle suspected burnout.

The demanding curriculum at the National University of Science and Technology could get the best of even the brightest. Some left because they were no longer the best. That was the hardest lesson for students to learn.

Elle typed out a short congratulatory email to the now-former student about the internship. She had been beyond excited when she landed hers with the American Astronomical Society. It was an impossible feat, or so said her then-adviser Dr. Edgar Linton when she broached the subject of applying. But she went for it anyway. Not only did it give her access to some of the most high-end scopes and data, but it also allowed her to stay on the West Coast for the summer, far away from her family.

Life was something to be lived back then. The whole universe spread wide, or so she believed. She had started her journey much sooner than most, graduating with her PhD at the tender age of twenty-three, largely thanks to Edgar's guidance. The possibilities seemed endless. Oh, how dumb she'd been despite her advanced intelligence.

She reached down into her bag and withdrew the single envelope slipped between the pages of her notebook. She feathered her fingers across the bright yellow star logo that dared her to reread the rejection she'd already memorized:

Dr. Conroy,

Thank you for taking the time to apply. The fellowship pool was even more competitive than in previous years and garnered over three thousand applicants for four spots. Unfortunately, you were not among the final candidates, and we are unable to continue with your application. Best of luck for your continued success in the space science field.

Sincerely,

The Space Technology and Aeronautics Research Institute

She tossed it in the trash.

Her life's work, started when she was just a girl on a beach with Dad, down the drain. It was the third rejection she'd gotten from STAR, the most prestigious space science agency on the planet. She sighed the air out between her lips and shook off the weight of disappointment that affixed itself to her, which at this point had morphed into apathy. Five years ago, when she moved back to D.C. after Dad's diagnosis, he had warned Elle it was a mistake. She was better floating from one grant to another rather than anchoring herself. He didn't want a little old thing like his cancer to sideline her. She didn't want to come back, especially since Edgar opened her eyes to what an injustice Dad had done to her.

But Elle couldn't let Mom and Pete take care of him alone,

and Edgar's offer of an associate professor position felt more like kismet than pity. It gave her the chance to come back into the fold of the single most positive influence on her life.

"I can't believe you beat me," Janet said from the doorway, unfurling the deep red wool scarf that swaddled her throat. "Coming?"

Elle remained unmoved. "I have no idea what you're talking about."

"If only there were some magical way messages could get electronically beamed to your computer or phone." Janet shook her head full of tight black curls and shuffled away, the whisper of her puffer jacket growing quieter.

Elle dug her phone out from her bag and scrolled through the text messages.

Dennis Piedmont: THIRD REMINDER. Mandatory Department Staff Meeting at 9:00 in the Conference Room. No late admittance. No excuses.

Apparently, she'd missed the other two messages. She grabbed her empty "Born to be Spacey" mug and the box of mini coffee cake muffins she'd whipped up last night and shuffled along to the break room. Janet and Carson simultaneously checked their watches, and Carson placed a flat palm towards Janet.

"What's this all about?" she asked, moving past them to the coffee station, the cacophony of her coworkers dying down as they trickled out for the meeting.

She took the last of the coffee without remorse and turned to find Carson fanning himself with a fresh ten-dollar bill.

"Really." Elle leaned against the counter. Carson's crooked grin beamed in stark opposition to Janet's exaggerated eye roll. "Let me guess: I'm on time for a meeting you were sure I'd miss, *or,* I got stuck with the last of the coffee."

"The former." Carson gave an extra waggle in his already arched black brows.

"You didn't even know we had a meeting until I stopped by your office. I should have kept my mouth shut and walked right on past." Janet reached for a coffee cake muffin. "But you did bring my favorite muffins, so I guess I'll forgive you."

"First—they're all your favorite, and second—if you didn't feel the need to bet on my comings and goings—"

"Or your sayings and moanings." Carson retrieved a bottle of hand sanitizer from his pocket and began his thirty-six-second ritual.

"I'm so glad I'm here to amuse the two of you."

"In all fairness, you probably entertain more than just us." His lips continued to silently count.

"However, *we're* the most appreciative." Janet flashed her toothy smile.

The three of them fell into step through the hallway, muted by the absence of a full staff and students. Janet and Carson chatted beside her while she mulled over the obvious reason for the meeting. Dean Piedmont must be finally announcing Edgar's replacement. Dread soured her stomach.

The conference room was packed with colleagues Elle hadn't seen since the second week of December. Unlike the unexpected student changes every semester, Elle enjoyed observing the metamorphoses of her coworkers. Mortimer from chemistry, who underwent a midlife crisis at least once an academic year, was now attempting to pull off a Fu Manchu mustache. Greer, the physicist who let his latest younger flavor-of-the-semester dress him, was now firmly in his Western phase, sporting a blue-and-black plaid snap shirt. And Navara from environmental appeared to have stopped practicing hygiene (again), no doubt for a study about air quality.

Elle took the furthest chair away from Navara. Carson also

appeared to note their colleague's ripeness and opted to sit against the wall behind Janet and Elle. He withdrew his sanitizer bottle again. Carson's beginning-of-the-semester OCD ritual was at its peak.

The science department at NatU was more collaborative than most. Various science specialists combined skill sets for lectures, research, and studies. Elle was slated to start working with Carson and Janet, and several others from botany and environmental, to study whether the ozone could be repaired by accelerating photosynthesis. The prospect of being part of a team to develop a breakthrough of some sort brought a flicker of excitement back to her otherwise apathetic spirit.

Dean Dennis Piedmont stepped into the room, his presence hushing the chatter, his smile welcoming. Then Lance Dunwoody strutted in behind him.

Carson leaned in from his chair behind and whispered in her ear. "Maybe it isn't as bad as you think."

She was one hundred percent sure he was wrong. That sniveling grin plastered on Lance's long and sallow face said it all. He was doing that head shake thing that screamed, "I'm important! Look at me!" Even his suit—something he had never worn before, opting usually for nicotine-stained yellow polos and khakis—acted as a billboard for the ultimate reason for this meeting.

Dean Piedmont stood at the head of the table, not even bothering to sit down. Elle fixated on the scrunch of her toes along the nylon sock inside her leather boot so she would remember to remain present and control her face.

"Welcome back, professors. I know you all didn't want to come in so early on the first workday of the new semester, but this will be brief."

Dean Piedmont had a kind way about him, though he had aged noticeably since his appointment to the position four years ago. He had more lines pitting his face. More gray wove through his raven hair. But the sincerity in his brown eyes still remained.

Under him, NatU had climbed six spots in the national rankings, with the Department of Space Science and Aeronautics making the biggest leap, from twelve to nine. Of course, that was due in large part to Edgar's leadership, too. He'd been a prominent part of her life for over two decades now. Ever since Elle's first week at Stanford when he had tucked her under his wing. So, when he abruptly retired in September without confiding in her, she had been gutted. Messages to Edgar went unreturned for weeks. She had assumed he was dead, or at least dying. When he finally reached out, he had assured her in his soft way that all was well. He needed to tend to some things back in California.

Janet nudged an elbow to her side.

"...so it is my great pleasure," Dean Piedmont said, "to announce that Dr. Dunwoody has agreed to take over the helm of space and aeronautics."

Elle squeezed her hands together under the table while the rest of the room clapped. Lance Dunwoody was the most infuriating, least intelligent person in the room. He looked over shoulders for answers and rode coattails to get what and where he wanted.

Now, he had ascended from annoying colleague to boss. Wonderful.

"This is my worst nightmare," she grumbled.

"My condolences." Carson placed a hand on her shoulder. He and Janet as botanists didn't fall under the fascist regime Lance would surely institute.

"Thank you, Dean Piedmont, for that lovely introduction. You're too kind, old friend." Lance said, a holier-than-thou expression fixed across his face. "I have big shoes to fill. I cannot hold myself up to Edgar Linton. It's an impossible task, so I won't even try."

That was the most honest statement Lance had ever made. Even so, Elle had to fend off a reflexive eye roll. He was obviously trying to soften the blow of some kind of sweeping change.

"However," he continued, "Dean Piedmont and I have discussed at length the goals we have for the space and aeronautics department. We both agree that this is an opportunity to move in a new direction."

There it was. Elle crossed her arms to brace herself.

"My first act as chair is to announce that NatU be hosting the thirty-first International Space Science Symposium here in D.C. this April."

"I thought it was being held in Frankfurt?" Steven said.

"It seems they hit a bit of a snafu with permitting. The board was thrilled we were willing to take it on with such short notice."

Lance raised his arms up as if he'd delivered a winning political speech or, more fitting, announced the start of the first departmental hunger games.

Heat moved up Elle's chest and into her neck.

"What the hell is he doing? We can't pull this off in four months."

"Uh-oh," Carson said. "She's approaching nuclear."

She shook her head. These things took a year, sometimes more, to plan, between vendors, sponsors, speakers, and student projects. Though Elle had never spoken at the symposium (Edgar encouraged her to wait until her acceptance at STAR), she'd attended her fair share.

"Because of the expedited time frame," Dean Piedmont said, as if reading her mind, "the university has hired a professional planning firm to handle logistics. The tech department is building the website and developing the necessary software."

"That leaves *my* department to handle speakers, projects, and sponsors." Lance beamed. "*My* assistant Pam will be scheduling a meeting ASAP."

Elle wanted to throw up.

"I know you all have a lot to do before classes resume tomorrow, so I'll let you get back to it. Congratulations again, Dr. Dunwoody. I'm sure you'll lead the space science department in an even better direction." Dean Piedmont led another round of applause.

Elle sprung to her feet, drawing Lance's attention from the front of the room. She didn't attempt to hide her disdain.

She knew exactly what direction Lance was going to lead them in—down.

Dear Edgar,

I hope you're well and that your trips have gone smoothly. Did you get a chance to read the piece about the cryovolcano on Pluto? I'm not sure if I agree with the journal that it's a significant find.

Lance got your job and is bringing the symposium here. He said there was a permit issue in Germany, but counterparts at the University of Berlin said there was a misappropriation of funds and resources. Regardless, this seems like an all but impossible feat to pull off, but it's not my responsibility. I'll keep my head down and do my thing.

I got my third rejection from STAR. I know you'll tell me it's a huge universe and something I do will get me where I want to go. But it's frustrating that what I want is still so unattainable, even after working so hard to get it. Maybe now I'll (finally) take your advice and pivot away from my black hole research. It's been my life's work, and so hard to let go of.

Maybe you'll be back in town by April and can join the symposium. You'd make an excellent speaker.

Yours,

Elle

CHAPTER TWO

Elle closed her laptop and leaned back into her chair. She'd been working on black hole theory since she was in elementary school. She should have been in a lab with award-winning colleagues by now, not wasting away in academia.

Every rejection from STAR brought the thundering truth: She had failed. Frustration filled her every time some of her former peers and classmates ascended higher, while she remained at this mid-level rung of professor.

A knock on her door drew her out of the perpetual melancholy that had descended since Edgar left. She doubted she'd hear back from him anytime soon, but at least she had sent something out into the universe aimed at him.

"Come in." She stiffened, thinking it might be Lance, but then relaxed as one of her fourth-year students came in. "Darsha, you're here a day early."

The young woman tucked a piece of her bobbed chestnut hair behind her ear, her chin bent by shyness.

"I wanted to get a jump on my project at the library. It's been nice having it all to myself today."

Darsha was one of the elite students Elle had the pleasure of teaching. She was intelligent, thoughtful, and diligent—three things that would get her into the graduate school of her choice next fall.

"How can I help?" Elle clasped her hands on the desk, consciously melting away the frustration and tension of the morning at the prospect of being useful to someone.

"I'm so embarrassed." Darsha brushed a hand down her cheek. "I can't make sense out of one of these stellar evolution studies. I've read it four times and I'm lost."

Elle nodded, empathizing with Darsha's frustration.

"It's hard sometimes to get to the bones of some of these studies." She reached her hand out, prompting Darsha to hand her the packet. Elle started flipping. "I can tell you right now, even without reading the whole thing, the author of this study is known to ramble and bury the real research under unnecessary narratives."

Darsha's eyes widened, and Elle noted the lingering red left behind by the young woman's tears, shed, no doubt, in frustration.

"Sometimes you just need to figure out a way to cut through the fluff." She slid open the top drawer and dug around until she found a black marker. "And this will do the trick. You'd think they got paid by the word the way some go on. Shoot, maybe they do. In which case, I need to start paying attention."

Darsha smiled and her shoulders melted.

Elle redacted the needless and confusing verbiage from the study. She worked quickly, blacking out a word or two, and then a sentence or three. After a few minutes, she handed the packet back.

Darsha flipped through it, scanning the pages. Slowly, her cheeks rose under a smile. She moved her gaze back to Elle.

"Dr. Conroy, this is amazing. Thank you so much."

"Of course. But before you dive into what's left, you should get a good meal and maybe a nap. My mom still asks me if I've eaten and slept every time I see her." Elle didn't tell Darsha that she didn't do enough of either.

"I'll try." Exhaustion pulled at the young woman's eyes. She stood and hefted her bag onto her shoulder. "I wouldn't still be here if it wasn't for you, Dr. Conroy. You're *different* from the other professors. You always make the impossible understandable for me. Thank you."

Elle's chest bubbled and she swallowed against the discomfort rising in her throat.

"I'm glad that you're still here, Darsha. You've got a bright future." She shifted in her chair to shake her unease in the aftermath of the compliment. "See you Wednesday."

When the girl shut the door behind her, Elle exhaled. Darsha was every professor's dream. While her compliment was lovely, it wasn't the praise Elle wanted or needed.

ACCORDING TO MY SCIENCE
FIRST SPRING EDITION—JANUARY 8TH

NatU School of Science

Welcome back, NatU Students!

Dean Piedmont is honored to announce that Dr. Lance Dunwoody has accepted the Department of Space Science and Aeronautics chair position vacated by Dr. Linton in the fall. Dr. Dunwoody is well qualified, having worked under Dr. Linton for six years. Dr. Dunwoody is kicking off his new role by announcing that a team of delegates has asked NatU to host the 31st International Space Science Symposium in April. More information about this exciting opportunity will be forthcoming.

There will be a celebratory cocktail reception for Dr. Dunwoody tomorrow, Wednesday evening at 7:00 p.m. at Dean Piedmont's home. Students are encouraged to drop in whenever your schedule permits. ***Department faculty and staff are required to attend.***

Research Opportunities:

**Dr. Mortimer has a few openings for his Periodical Round Table. Students who are interested in digging into alkaline earth metals won't want to miss it. Message Dr. Mortimer or stop by during office hours for more information.

**Dr. Navara is looking for people to participate in her Live Free of Dyes study. Any student willing to forgo the societal norm when it comes to hygiene and go au naturel should contact Dr. Navara.

Nominations Due:

Every year, the Universal Science Instructor Society chooses one science professor out of thousands of nominations to give a lecture that is live streamed in classrooms worldwide. NatU has never had a professor in the running. What do you think about changing that? Nominate your favorite NatU lecturer before the **March 1st** deadline.

CHAPTER THREE

Elle had made the mistake of asking Jim in meteorology if she should wear a heavier coat to the cocktail party. This turned into a seven-minute diatribe on weather patterns and atmospheric pressure over the North Atlantic and how the dry air would give them a welcome reprieve from the snow.

She grasped the bakery box with bare hands and stepped along the cobblestone to Dean Piedmont's house. Venus should be visible in the west, but the blanket of low-lying clouds and the light pollution would keep the Evening Star hidden. Elle would kill to be stargazing instead of going to this stupid party to honor a man she despised.

After Monday's announcement, she spent the bulk of the afternoon with her department colleagues trying to get ahead of Lance's agenda. Unlike her, most were happy one of their own had risen to department chair rather than a transfer. Elle neither agreed nor disagreed, even when they asked. She steered the meeting to other matters, like who was going to take over the two intro courses Lance had decided he was "too busy" to teach.

In a shock to no one, she wound up with both sections, only giving up one third-year class on particle acceleration she didn't really care to teach anyway. This still gave her six classes and three labs compared to the department average of four and two. There wasn't enough time in the day—or night—for Elle to do it all: lectures, labs, office hours, tutoring, the photosynthesis project with Carson and Janet. She was also the department liaison for the student-helmed newsletter she had started five years ago.

Rounding the corner, she followed the trail of jazz notes spilling from the Colonial at the end of the block. She'd attended other events at Dean Piedmont's, but this would be the first without Edgar. She never went unless it was mandatory, or it involved prestigious scientists, like James Peebles. Elle had been so excited and nervous that she'd baked enough truffles for the entire department.

She had spent that night enamored with Dr. Peebles, and even got a chance to bend his ear about her dissertation on cosmology and quantum gravity. He was surprised when she said she didn't consider herself a physicist, but an astronomer, her real passion—and the first of her two PhDs. Edgar interrupted and explained her situation in his cavalier way. She was an anomaly, a once-in-a-lifetime student who had accelerated at a very young age and attained by thirty-two what most merely dreamed of.

Dad used to do that, too. Step in and talk for her when her tongue got tied. When her brain couldn't translate her thoughts into words the outside world understood, Dad figured out a way. He had spent enough time listening to her chattering that he'd figured out enough to bail her out when she froze.

The day after Dr. Peebles's reception, she had visited Dad in the hospice center and told him about the party. He had asked, words slurred and voice raspy, if she'd talked about her black hole project. She hadn't, of course, still wanting to keep everything close. Dad had lifted his head atop his thinning neck and asked her to tell him about it the way she used to before she went off to college.

She suspected it hurt him to be replaced by Edgar. But Dad could never understand her the way Edgar did. Before college, she had believed Dad knew everything and always had her best interests at heart. She listened, for example, when he encouraged her to remain silent about quantum physics in her fifth-grade class and, instead, talk about how her Tamagotchi was doing. "Be like the other kids there, and come home and be yourself," he said when she'd started to protest.

Edgar first made her realize that Dad had stunted her growth by making her shut away her intelligence, and therefore herself. Dad had held her back, likely out of shame. It made her so angry toward him she intentionally stayed away—until she couldn't anymore.

But that day in hospice, her anger broke like a fever. Maybe because it was the first time in a long time she had opened up to him the way she used to. Maybe she recognized Dad's time was growing short as the bones of his face and chest pushed through his skin more by the day.

Maybe deep down, she knew it would be the last time he ever spoke to her or anyone else. He fell asleep after that, his breath sounding more and more like boiling water as the days went on. On the fourth day, she stood across the bed from Pete and Mom. When she bent to kiss him, the rattle that had been seared into her memory fell silent and he slipped away.

"DR. CONROY, YOU COMING IN?"

She looked up from the bottom of the steps to Dean Piedmont's. At the top was Noah Declan, a fourth-year student and a legacy cosmology major. His father ran the prestigious Aero

Lab in upstate New York, and Noah was joining him there after graduation.

"I suppose I should, thanks." She met him at the top of the stoop. As he held the door, his gaze immediately shifted from her face down to the floorboards.

"It's kinda crowded, which is good for Dr. Dunwoody, I guess. But I hate cramped spaces."

"Me, too. But I have to be here. You don't."

The young man gave her a shy smile, his olive cheeks ringed with a hint of pink. He pushed his jet-black mop top out of his eyes, though it wouldn't hinder his view if he held his head up.

"I'm only staying a few more minutes."

They both went inside, the air thickened with breath. Noah was right; there were a lot more people than Elle anticipated.

Janet waved from the far corner. Relieved to find her friend so quickly, Elle booked it over. She was five steps away when her forward progress was stopped by Dean Piedmont.

"Elle, I've been waiting for you," he said.

Busted for dragging her feet.

"One of the labs ran a little late." Not the truth *exactly*. She lifted the bakery box, which was the real reason. "I brought scones." Stalling by baking was unlikely to be a great excuse for her tardiness.

"You always do go above and beyond for the students and for us." Baked goods held power, so Grandma had always purported.

"I don't know any other way to be." Since STAR was off the table for the foreseeable future, she might as well continue to make good with the university.

He moved a half step closer and bent his head towards hers. "I'm sorry I didn't speak with you before the announcement Monday. Everything moved kind of fast. There was a lot of pressure from the higher ups to get a new chair before this semester. If I had my wa—"

"Ellery." Lance inserted himself into the space between her and the dean. He wore his smug expression like a badge. "I thought for sure you'd be a no-show."

What she wouldn't give for a calculated meteor strike right now. Not anything huge, though even a rock a few inches in diameter could take out a city block or two. Fine. Maybe not that extreme. But something. She settled for curling her toes inside her boots.

"Elle had a lab that ran late." Dean Piedmont tipped the box toward Lance and smiled.

"Of course she did."

Elle needed a drink if she was going to get through this, though admittedly, she might only want to throw it in Lance's face.

"My course load increased this semester. Quite unexpected-ly," she said.

Dean Piedmont furrowed his brow. "Oh? How so?"

Lance didn't show any signs of discomfort. Damn.

"I took on two of Lance's classes. On account of him now having these new more important duties." There was no hiding the ire that flew out with each word and, quite frankly, she wasn't trying.

"You know, Dennis, if I hadn't landed the *symposium*, I would have been able to continue with my normal course load. But being that *we* wanted to get some more exposure for the *department* and really for the *university*, that took priority." The corners of Lance's mouth twitched. "To be fair, Ellery took the *easiest* courses."

Easiest. Elle scrunched her toes so hard her left foot began to cramp.

"Yes, but I also have other obligations with inter-department research projects..."

Lance stopped her with a wave. "That ozone study? I'll need you to bow out of that."

Her skin pricked. "What? I've been committed since last spring."

"You'll need that time for the symposium."

Here it comes.

Lance continued. "I...well, *Dennis* and I...think you'd be the perfect person to head the student portion of the symposium."

"What does that entail?"

"We'd like you to put on a workshop and assist students with their applications. And then coordinate student volunteers to ensure everything goes off without a hitch day-of."

He rocked back on his heels, and there was a second where Elle could've reached out and knocked him flat on his ass without expending much more than a finger poke to that puffed up chest. Could she claim temporary insanity? No. It would fall under heat-of-the-moment, and thereby a crime of passion. She didn't want *passion* in the same sentence as her and Lance. Yuck.

"Before we get ahead of ourselves." Dean Piedmont raised a hand. "Are you planning to present at the symposium, Elle? We don't want to overload you."

She shook her head. "I have no intent—"

"Splendid." Lance clapped his hands like a seal.

"You won't have to do everything alone, Elle." Dean Piedmont's calm voice momentarily quelled the fire. "Lance found you a TA who can help."

"He's from your alma mater, Ellery. A PhD candidate who you have a lot in common with." Lance turned and called to someone behind her, bushy eyebrows raised. "Spencer, come and meet your mentor."

A young, rail-thin, barely-man, awkwardly ambled into their circle. His glasses were the stereotypical thick black-rimmed scientist type. His wheat hair was slicked away from his high brow and a cowlick feathered from the crown of his head.

"Spencer Draisson, meet Dr. Ellery Conroy, your mentor for the spring."

Spencer had been a frequent flyer in The Loop alumni newsletter over the past two years. He was a genius, entering as an undergrad at sixteen and now at twenty-two, a PhD candidate.

"It's nice to meet you, Spencer," Elle said, taking care that the ugliness aimed at Lance wouldn't come out toward the young man.

"I've studied up on you and am pleased Dr. Dunwoody saw fit to appoint you. I believe you are worthy. Enough."

Well, then. That was one hell of a way to start a mentor-mentee relationship. But Elle was used to dealing with ultra-intelligent people who were confident because they'd genuinely never failed before.

However, not everyone had a family like she did that kept her from being too much of a genius. Dad had pointed out her social failures and built skills to keep her grounded.

"It's always nice to meet a fellow Stanfordian." She smiled hoping to soften him.

"You should know that I actively worked on disproving your theory of star cluster formations in outer Andromeda. Which, coincidentally, I succeeded in doing." His cowlick waved with each sharp jerk of his head.

Lance's fangs fully displayed in some semblance of a smile, his lips twitching at the push and pull between her and Spencer. She would not give him the satisfaction of seeing her rattled by this...kid.

"We wouldn't be very good scientists if we couldn't take a

dose of our own medicine once in a while, right? Besides, here at NatU we're all about collaboration, innovation, and exploration." She plastered on her most generous smile and even added some high eyebrows to sell everyone, especially Lance, on her pleasure.

"I knew this was going to work out." Lance turned to Dean Piedmont. "I told you Ellery could handle anything and everything I heaped on her."

That gleam in his eye and the subsequent resigned nod from Dean Piedmont meant she was sunk. She'd not only be stuck with the extra course load, but now she'd have to drop the study, take on helping students apply to the symposium, and mentor Spencer. At this point, he might prove her biggest time suck of the semester.

"I never doubted Elle from the minute Edgar brought her on board," Dean Piedmont said. "Now, if you'll excuse me, I'd like to borrow Spencer for a minute and introduce him around."

Spencer stiffly followed the dean's steps so closely, he almost caught the older man's heels. The moment the two walked away, the fake class drained from Lance's face, and his smug, arrogant, authentic self returned.

"Say, how's Edgar doing?" He pinched his gaze. "It's a shame how he left the way he did. Without telling his prized... student. Here everyone thought you were so close." The fake empathy radiating from his face and the tsk tsk hissing through his lips sparked a raging fire in her chest that roared even as he turned his back.

The tips of her ears burned, and she tensed her feet so hard her arches stabbed. Elle didn't bother searching for Janet or Carson, or anyone else. She uncurled her toes and shuffled her feet on the hardwood for a beat or two to stop the clenching. Now that her mandatory attendance requirement was fulfilled, she made a fast getaway, knowing where to get the drink she desperately needed.

CHAPTER FOUR

Pete's bar was dead, which was exactly what Elle had hoped for as she pushed through the doors. Aside from a trio of older guys at one of the high tops near the dartboards and two men tucked into the dark corner of the bar, she was the only other one here. She took her customary seat at the far end, away from the door and the chill.

She had walked the mile from Dean Piedmont's, hoping the activity would expend some of her frustration. She had considered going home and whipping up a few batches of peanut butter blossoms, but then she remembered she had used the last of the butter on the scones. So Pete's won out.

He came waltzing out from the back room shortly after she sat. His brown eyebrows cocked high, folding the sun-kissed skin under the muddy waves that tickled his forehead. He had hair like Dad's—thick and effortless. The kind of hair that always looked good no matter what. Even shaved it had looked better than Elle's limp dishwater locks she inherited from Mom. Hair so paper-thin she'd be doomed to chop it into a pixie as Mom had done or wear it up, so it didn't string down her shoulders like angel-hair pasta. Elle stocked up on hair ties, opting for the latter.

"Everything okay?" he asked.

"What do you think?" She shed her pea coat and laid it across the bar. Pete squinted at her shimmery silver sweater.

"Special occasion?"

It wasn't too crazy, but it was definitely out of the norm for her day-to-day wear.

"Mandatory cocktail reception. And before you ask, no, I didn't have a drink there, so you don't need to worry about me mixing liquor."

He pulled down a pint glass from the rack above the taps, but Elle shook her head.

"Not that. Stronger. Vodka and cranberry. Please." She craned her neck one way, then the other and considered removing her boots and shaking her toes. She'd have to soak her feet in Epsom salt tonight or they'd ache tomorrow.

She watched how much vodka Pete added. He was still a protective big brother even though, at thirty-eight, Elle didn't need him to be.

He set the highball on the coaster and leaned against the back bar, crossing his arms, stacking the *This We'll Defend* scribed across one forearm over the soaring eagle on the other.

He stood with the authority of his former life when he'd carried a rifle and led soldiers across scorching desert sands. But here, he was simply Pete the bar owner.

The vodka took the edge off the cranberry. It was smooth, a perfect balance. Elle appreciated her brother's bartending skills. She needed balance, especially when she felt like the whole world was anything but.

"Wanna talk about it?" he said.

"Not particularly."

"You sure?"

"I'm letting it go. It's fine."

He scoffed. "You aren't letting go of shit. I bet your toes are still balled up."

She put her glass back on the coaster and wiggled her toes inside her boots. Pete was one of the only people who knew she did that, something she really hated at the moment.

"There's a lot going on at work."

"Already? Didn't the semester just start?"

"Yesterday, but..." What could or should she say? That her new boss was a pompous asshole who didn't know a nebula from a supernova? That he had stuck her with hours and hours of extra work because he could?

"It's a lot of change, that's all." It was the nicest way she could put it without weighing her already overburdened brother down with anything else.

He ran this bar on next to nothing. His was the only income since his wife, Tabitha, couldn't keep a job. She always clashed with management and disagreed with their policies, like their insistence she show up on time.

"You never were great with change."

She brought her gaze up to his, the same olive green as Dad's. Elle had inherited neither Mom or Dad's eye color, but a blend that made hers almost turquoise. The retort she was trying to concoct died when the three older men loudly yelled their good nights to Pete on their way out.

That left her and the two men in the very dark corner. The one closest to her looked large, his back a barrier tucking his companion into the wall. The only other thing Elle could glean was they were wearing dark baseball caps.

The bar fell quiet, and she allowed the vodka to act as a salve, relaxing the muscles in her feet, and elsewhere. She wondered why she didn't drink more often. Maybe she should start, get ahead of the dumpster fire this semester was surely headed for.

Pete stared at his phone screen, tapping away and pausing for what were obvious return messages.

"How's my favorite nephew?" she asked.

"Giving his mother a hard time."

"Ah, who is, in turn, giving you a hard time." She tipped her glass back and wondered when Pete would cut ties with Tabitha. She was a leech, using Elle's four-year-old nephew, Brody, as a tool to control her brother.

"How's the letting go thing going?" Pete asked, eyes narrowed.

"How's the happy family thing going?" Her retort rose up without much thought and landed heavily across her brother's face. Hurt edged his eyes.

"You don't get to be an asshole because you had a bad day, Elle."

He was right and wrong. She didn't have to be an asshole and, in fact, she never wanted to be, at least usually not to Pete. This wasn't about a single bad day, but a horizon full of them with no end in sight.

The guy hugged to the wall gestured Pete over, though his friend shook his head and tapped his watch. Pete flipped the tops off two fresh Coronas and swapped them out for the empties. The guy by the wall dipped his head, giving Elle a clear view of the white "Navy" emblazoned on his cap.

That explained the pensiveness. They're probably on leave, or about to redeploy. Either way, Pete's on a Wednesday night seemed a weird choice.

The vodka continued to work its magic and she entered the stage of bravery. She wanted to fire off a message to Dean Piedmont about how unfair all of this was. How she shouldn't get stuck with more work than everyone else. How it would leave her with little free time.

She scoffed into her glass. What difference did it make when nothing she had done thus far seemed to be enough? She worked circles around so many others who had ultimately attained what they wanted. Meanwhile, she was stuck spinning her wheels being average.

She choked down the rest of her drink and resolved to leave it alone. Staying silent when all she wanted to do was scream was a blessing and the worst curse. People often mistook silence for a lack of understanding when the opposite was true. Like when she was in kindergarten, the teacher and administration had called a parent conference and suggested Elle would be better served in special education classes because she hadn't spoken. Along with that, she had started scribbling "nonsense" on the outer edges of all her work. Her kindergarten teacher proffered page after page of this troubling evidence that Elle was not ready for the rigors of a regular curriculum.

Her parents had listened intently, Mom clutching Dad's hand on one side while Elle sat on the other. His size extended beyond the chair, and when she looked up at him, she could only see the side of his shoulder and the tip of his ear. She didn't need to see his face to know the lines etched around his eyes and mouth would remain rigid while he listened. He, too, often stayed silent. For him, it came with being a cop because the less he talked the more those he suspected of a crime would. Was she a criminal?

Dad placed his heavy hand atop her head like he sensed her unease. It brought immediate relief and grounded her. When she angled her gaze toward him, she met his green eyes, slack at the corners, telling her without words it was safe to come out and do what needed to be done. She could share a secret he couldn't possibly know about, yet somehow did.

So, when the room grew quiet, she cleared her throat and told them all she could talk; she just didn't want to. She leaned forward and rearranged the pages on the desk, explaining the marks on the sides were patterns of stars and planets in the sky each night. She drew them because the worksheets were too simple, and she didn't see the point in wasting time or energy on busy work.

Dad wrapped his burly arm around her bony shoulder and nestled her into his side—the safest spot in the world.

The school didn't know what to do with her after that. They tested her three times before admitting she had scored above everyone in the district, adults included. The counselor suggested she attend a special private school or move up to the eighth grade, but Dad refused to put her in more of a box. Eventually, they reached a compromise. She would join the gifted program and jump up into third grade, one grade behind Pete.

"How long you serve?" Wall Guy asked Pete. The sharp steel of his voice cut into Elle's trip down memory lane. She still couldn't see his face, which was beginning to annoy her. But the hand that swallowed the bottle looked nice.

"Twelve years. You?"

"Twenty. You get hurt?"

Wall Guy was astute. Pete's limp was subtle these days, a far cry from what it had been.

"IED along the road to Fallujah. Took out three men in my unit. Left me with a permanent souvenir and a nice disability check, though. Can't complain. Lots of guys had it far worse." Pete only talked to other military people about the service.

"I understand that."

"You ship or soar?"

"Both," Wall Guy said.

"Frogs?"

The two dipped their heads. Elle didn't know what any of it meant, but Pete seemed impressed.

"Beers on me," he said.

"Can't let you do that. But I appreciate it."

"Wasn't asking. My bar, my rules."

Pete walked back and started refilling her drink, heavier on the cranberry this time.

"What was that all about?" she asked, a tad louder than she planned.

"A little professional courtesy."

She wanted to know more, but a rustling from the men caught her attention. Wall Guy stood, prompting the other to follow suit. Wall Guy patted him on the shoulder, willing him back down into the stool. After some cajoling, the guy sat as Wall Guy walked toward her on his way to the bathroom. She fixed her gaze on the mirror behind the bar; it was her best shot at checking him out. Something about his voice and his mystery piqued her interest. Which was ridiculous because Elle, historically speaking, didn't do *that* kind of thing.

Pete's phone rang at the exact wrong moment for her scouting mission, drawing her attention away as the air behind her filled with a delightful mix of wood and citrus. He lifted the phone to his ear and lumbered out of sight. Poor Pete. His night was about to get worse.

CHAPTER FIVE

"Is your boyfriend going to get mad if I throw cash on the bar before I walk out?" Wall Guy said in a voice the perfect blend of smooth and stony, like a paved road winding through the woods scattered with gravel.

"First of all, gross. He's my brother," Elle said, face puckered. "And second, Pete doesn't get mad. Just offended. Which is probably worse."

The hand that landed on the bar beside her, looked as capable as it had from the other side. Her mouth went dry, so she very casually attempted to sip her drink. But as with any other time she was on the verge of flirting, it went wrong. She underestimated how full the glass was and tipped it too far, sending a decent amount down her chin and onto her chest.

"Damn it," she yelped. Hopping off the stool, she caught her left foot on the rung, sending her mouth on a collision course with the bar. Before her enamel made contact with the wood, though, she was swept back and set upright by two strong hands.

"You okay?" he asked.

She covered her mouth, the prospect that she had almost lost her front teeth terrifying. Until she gazed up into the face of the man who steadied her, and the terror about what might have happened morphed into another kind altogether. Wow.

"Ma'am?"

She jerked her head. "I'm not *that* old." She brushed her hand over her soaked sweater. Before she could reach for the stack of napkins, her handsome savior offered her some.

She took them and swiped at the sweater. Great. This stain would not come out and the sweater she had splurged on because she might need it someday was ruined. All because of Lance and his stupid cocktail party that would never have happened if Edgar had warned her he was leaving and then just never did...

"I'm sorry. Old habits die hard," he said.

She huffed, not because she was mad at him for having manners. How many times had Pete called a woman ma'am and Elle had laughed because it made him sound like he was trying to come off as a rancher from Oklahoma.

The napkins weren't fixing the sweater, so she threw them on the bar.

"I didn't mean to...snap like that. I don't do that."

"Snap or try to give yourself a concussion?"

A laugh slipped out, taking the tension away from her body.

"Both, I guess." Her gaze drew up to his face. The bill of his hat was pulled low, but even with that, the image she had conjured shredded like an asteroid getting sucked into the atmosphere. He wasn't good-looking—he was magnificent. The square set of his jawline met in the middle of his chin, split by a subtle cleft that begged to be traced. She didn't, *obviously*, but her thumb pad itched to do it. The cut of his jaw was dotted with the beginnings of stubble, a five o'clock shadow a few hours late. The sprigs of hair were a mix of dark and light.

"I don't want to offend your brother," he said, stepping back into his space. "But at the same time, I don't want to take anything from him he can't afford. Is this a typical night?"

"Maybe? I'm not sure, but..." She let the thought disperse throughout the air between them. This was Pete's baby, and while she would like to continue a conversation with this very friendly, and now that she was standing near him, very tall and wide-shouldered stranger, she refused to reduce it to gossip or suppositions about her brother's business.

"Understood." He dipped his head and moved to rest both elbows on the bar. A strong line cut up from his watchband, disappearing under the rolled-up sleeves of his black fleece pullover. No wedding band, which literally meant nothing. People took those off all the time when it might be convenient to do so.

"What brings you here then tonight?" A line she'd rebuff if anyone else had asked.

A groan slipped out. "Work stuff."

"Same," he said and then without warning, walked back toward his friend long enough to grab his beer. "A toast to forgetting a shitty day."

A resigned feeling, like a surrender, overtook Elle. The toast turned into simple chatter about the weather, as strangers making small talk do (something she hated usually). He said the reprieve from the snow meant he could run before work again. She said the only way she'd run was if she was being chased and had no other choice. He smiled. Wow. Megawatt.

His voice was deep, but his tone light, and laugh lines jumped across his face at regular intervals throughout their easy conversation. Elle didn't talk this much to strangers unless they were scientists. She normally remained guarded with anyone else, in case she fell into scientific speak Dad had warned her would draw too much attention.

"Where'd you go?"

She shook her head clear of the nonsense she had folded into. Her cheeks burned. People usually didn't pick up on her internal wanderings unless they knew her.

"I'm sure you're sick of hearing me drone on." She grabbed her now third drink, much weaker than the first two. "I don't think you've said much."

"I prefer it that way. And besides"—he shifted his head so close to her the bill of his hat tickled her forehead—"I don't think I could ever get tired of listening to you. You're the most fascinating person I've met."

If a black hole sucked her in after having those words said to her by *this man*, Elle would happily tumble into the abyss until she was crushed.

He slid the hat off his head and brushed the light brown hair back from his forehead. This was the first time she'd had a chance to really see him. The eyes that had been shaded were the most enchanting shade of gray. But with that came something else...

"Do I know you?" she said.

For a half-second, he paused before he replaced the cap and turned his head toward where his friend sat at the other end of the bar. He seemed to give him a small shake of the head, almost imperceptible, before casually swinging back to her. The man stared back at them, eyes hooded under his own hat, his only distinguishing feature a white zigzag that ran down his chin.

"I would definitely remember you," he said. His eyes were back under cover, but the tilt of his head and the proximity of his hops-breath sent a shiver through her.

She cleared her throat and gazed back into the mirror. Maybe she'd seen him at a conference. But the build Elle imagined existed beneath the understated clothes did not seem to fit a scientist. Neither did the silent confidence or quiet authority he exuded. He seemed like the kind of man others wanted to be, but in their attempt at emulation would often come off cocky. And then, it hit her. He looked just like...

"The president!"

He casually swung his attention toward her and grinned. "What about him?"

"That's who you remind me of. President Ben Foster." The first unmarried president elected in two centuries, though no one in the media could figure out why he was still single. He was the total package: smart, tall, ruggedly handsome, humble, and genuinely kind, something D.C. had been lacking for far too long. The fact he was single seemed to overshadow his bigger achievement—being the first Independent elected to the White House.

"You think the president would be at a bar?"

His breath seared across her face, his mouth so close she had incontrovertible proof it was sprigs of gray, not blond stubble, peppered through the brown along his jaw.

"Well... no. I don't think *you're* the president. You look like him. A lot." Wow, Elle could be such a master with words in the presence of a handsome man. Shocking she was still single.

"Wait a minute," she continued, widening the expanse between them. "Are you his body double? They must have those. I mean I always assumed they did. For photo ops and trips that the real president doesn't want to do."

Amusement danced around the shadows on his face as he dragged a long index finger across his lips and winked.

Before Elle had a chance to ask him for details, Pete skulked over. He clanked bottles loudly and aggressively rubbed down the bar top. Something had pissed him off, most likely, Tabitha. Though Fake Ben Foster hadn't had the pleasure of dealing with her brother through the throes of every age and hormonal stage of his life, he, too sensed a shift.

"We should head out," he said, looking down at his watch.

His buddy was up off the stool before he finished the words and the two moved back toward the corner.

Disappointment choked the words out of her throat, so all she could manage was a nod. He tossed a hundred-dollar bill on the bar and nodded at Pete before both men turned to leave. A surge of courage coursed through Elle. She opened her mouth and—nothing. The fear of being wrong and looking stupid, two things she detested, took away any chance she'd ask him for his number.

A man like that didn't go for a woman like her. She'd not dated too much, mostly because she preferred a lab or scope to the company of the men she'd met. To be fair, they were almost always scientists who had their own agendas, most of which involved ensuring she didn't come off smarter than them.

"Earth to Elle," Pete said.

"Mhmm?"

"I was saying that I'll drop you off."

"I'll walk."

He crossed his arms again. "It's almost midnight."

Really? When did that happen? The weightlessness of the past few hours left her and gravity returned with a vengeance.

"It's a few blocks." She put on her coat as she slid off the stool.

Her brother was behind her as she pushed out the door. "If you think I'm letting you walk..."

But he stopped talking, prompting Elle to follow his puzzled gaze to the sidewalk where Fake Ben Foster stood.

"Sorry," he said, and his posture dipped just a bit. "I couldn't help but hear." He shuffled his feet back and forth, all confidence appearing to have left him. "I can walk you home. If, uh, that's okay with you?"

He spoke the offer to Elle, but slid his eyes to Pete for permission. What big brother wouldn't want a complete stranger, a man who could probably wrestle a bear, walking his little sister home on a Wednesday night?

Amusement flashed over Pete's face. He shook his head and threw both arms up in surrender.

"I don't own her, man." His boots squeaked backward as he pulled the door closed and clicked the lock into place.

"May I walk you home?" His manners were beyond ridiculous, and a whole other level of chivalrous.

"Where's your friend?"

"Oh, he's waiting back there in the car." He tilted his head towards the blacked-out Charger on the opposite side of the street.

Not alarming. At all.

Dad's voice banged around in her head. *Don't trust someone because they look nice, Ellie.*

She didn't always listen to that voice, and in the last fifteen years of his life, she had stopped listening to Dad altogether.

"Let's go," she said, taking the first step toward uncertainty.

CHAPTER SIX

"So, this isn't strange," he said.

They had been walking through the quiet street in a comfortable silence. Elle couldn't help but feel an inexplicable pull toward him, like there was something in the air, a point of gravity drawing them together.

"Which part?" she said. "The one where my brother gave me to you, or the one where I agreed to walk a strange man to my door?"

Now that she said it aloud, it was a really bad idea. The beginning of a *Dateline* episode or a Lifetime movie.

"I swear I won't kill you," he said.

"Not tonight, you mean."

"Exactly. Too obvious. I'll come back some other time."

"You've got a great cover with a twin in such a high place."

Fake Ben chuckled as they passed some brownstones that remained decorated with white twinkling lights.

He cleared his throat. "I still don't know anything about you except that you had a bad day. And that you seem to know a lot about the weather patterns."

"Afraid I'm the killer?" she said.

"What are the chances there'd be two of us?" He shrugged and smiled, a mischievous and sweet pop of his cheeks painted pink by the chill. It made her laugh. Like, really laugh.

"I'm a science teacher."

"That explains the meteorology."

"No, that was from a colleague. I deal in space."

"Whoa, that was my favorite." He touched his chest, the megawatt smile lighting up his face. "The best field trip ever was Lowell Observatory in seventh grade."

"Flagstaff, yes. That's a great scope."

His cheek popped under his grin again, adorable and insanely hot at the same time. It sent a flow of heat sputtering up inside her, but not the bad kind.

What underwear did she have on? It was definitely not sex-worthy because she didn't own anything that even remotely qualified. Did it at least match? When was the last time she'd even had sex?

"I lost you again."

She shook her head. "Sorry. It's a bad habit. I do a lot of talking to myself."

"Me, too, especially when I'm trying to solve a problem." He tapped his temple. "I give the best advice. You should try me."

"With what?"

"What's bothering you. Tell me what you were just thinking about."

She was not about to tell this man he caught her pontificating about the condition of her bra and panties and the status of her non-existent sex life. They stopped outside her brownstone *where she had just brought him of her own accord.*

He hung back as she walked to the door and punched the code to open it, fingers trembling, and stepped inside.

"Thanks for walking me home." She turned in the doorway, looking at him standing at the bottom of the steps. It was lame, but what else was new. Elle wasn't going to suddenly become awesome at this.

"Thanks for letting me."

"Good night," Elle said, willing her voice to remain steady.

"Good night, science teacher with no name." He winked and turned away.

"Do you want to come in?" Her voice surprised them both. Before she knew it, he was standing in her living room.

"You have a lot of books." He scanned the floor to ceiling bookcase filled with a wide variety of texts. The soft glow of the floor lamp gave Elle the opportunity to examine him. Her insides quivered when he dropped into a squat to peruse the bottom shelf.

"Teacher, remember?"

The impulse to reach out and touch him was hard to fight. Without realizing it, she had drifted so close that when he stood, he almost knocked her over.

"Sorry..." He grabbed her softly by the shoulders to steady her. Again.

Before she could step back, his hands folded over either side of her face, tracing her cheeks with his thumbs. She closed her eyes and angled her face up, giving him silent permission. Then she braced for impact.

The collision wasn't hard. It was soft. Purposeful. Tender. His lips shook against hers, or maybe it was her insides. His mouth devoured hers with deliberate hot strokes. She reached up to trace the sharp edge of his jaw dotted in stubble.

She pulled away, breathless. The wanton part of her, a place so deep and dark she had forgotten it had even existed, cried out wordlessly for him. Begged her to let herself go.

She slid the cap from his head and buried her fingers in his soft brown hair. This reckless abandon was not a trait anyone, including Elle, would have ever believed she possessed. But something about this handsome stranger with the rugged face and soft confidence felt safe.

Before she could analyze any further, he wrapped her in his arms and pulled her to him, bringing his lips back to hers. She aligned her body so closely that every inch of her ran along all the inches of him she could reach. His kiss was a contradiction to the rest of him, his lips like warm cashmere compared to the hewn granite pressed against her.

She lifted up the pullover, and he removed his hands from her long enough to finish what she started. The flash of cobblestone abs as he slid it over his head elicited another pulse of heat from her core.

My god. He was breathtaking even with a T-shirt. His arms were tan, his biceps bulging against the sleeves of the plain black cotton. The voracious desire radiating from every pore of him threatened to disintegrate her.

"Are you sure you're not the president?" she gasped.

"Would the president do this?" He lifted her and in two long strides, she was on the couch. His substantial weight pressed down on her. With delight, she buried her nose into the heat of his neck and inhaled the citrus, wood, and spice of his skin.

She'd never had the pleasure of touching anything like him, all carved and edged, but warm and soft in all the right places. They moved together, his tongue lapping her neck, her hands gripping his arms, a tender push and pull. As he moved the neck of her sweater down to gain access to the tender skin beneath, she caught a tattoo peeking from beneath his right sleeve. A trident, spanning his sizable upper arm.

"You are so beautiful." He breathed it into her neck with such passion, like he meant it. Like they were going to spend the next half hour or hour or hours on this couch, touching, taunting, licking, lapping, and every other measure of heat they ignited. She would forever have his fingerprints seared into the soft skin of her belly as he worked his hand under her sweater. A permanent reminder of how capable she was of letting herself go, after all the years of staying locked up tight against outside forces like him. He groaned into her mouth when his fingers met the underside of what was likely a very practical cotton bra, something not at all groanworthy.

She had never been this connected with another living soul, and here she was now on her couch, on the most recent worst day of her life, about to maybe have sex with a man who didn't know her name (to be fair, she also didn't know his).

Then ringing blared from his jacket.

"Shit." He rolled off the couch and swept up the jacket in one single move. He cleared his throat. "Yes," he said very authoritatively into the phone. He stood and smoothed down his hair, turning away from her. "You're sure?...Give me fifteen."

He plunged his arms into the pullover and affixed the hat back to his head.

He turned, his beautiful gray eyes shrouded. "I'm sorry, but I have to go." The authority was gone from his voice.

All she could do was nod.

He hesitated before moving away. Likely trying to come up with something. How he didn't want her number. How he was married and this was all a huge mistake.

Men who looked like him wanted young and perky woman with average intelligence and above-average cup sizes. Not the other way around. A bitterness rose up inside her chest, but she wouldn't let it get any further. Once he left, she'd whip up a batch of three-chocolate chip cookies and tuck herself into bed with one or two.

She stood and tried to regain her dignity while he turned back toward her. A pitter-patter punched her gut at just how much he looked like the president.

"You never did tell me your name," he said.

She swallowed a scoff because it didn't seem to matter. But his eyes seemed rimmed with sadness that choked off a sarcastic retort.

"Elle."

"It was *really* nice meeting you, Elle." The way he said it gave rise to a fluttering in her stomach. Like he actually meant it. "Full disclosure: I wouldn't leave right now if I didn't have to."

When he opened the door and slid out into the night, for some inexplicable reason, Elle believed him.

CHAPTER SEVEN

———————

"Did you stay up baking all night?" Janet took another cookie from her plate, a peanut butter dipper.

"Not all night." Elle stared at the news headline glaring back from her laptop.

Late last night, Russia launched the beginning stages of an invasion into Ukraine. President Foster was informed of the incursion just after midnight, and spent the early morning hours holed up in the situation room, meeting with advisers and allies to devise a plan.

That was one thing. But the picture of President Foster around a table in his black fleece pullover and Navy hat was another.

The man in the bar last night was *the* president. Every modicum of logic—of which she had plenty—screamed it wasn't possible. He was supposed to be the most heavily guarded person in the world aside from the pope. He couldn't travel anywhere without a team of Secret Service and press.

Yet, somehow, he had been on her couch.

"So you started baking after you bailed on the party?"

Her friend's voice demanded a return to the present. Elle leaned forward and closed her laptop.

"Something like that. Did I miss anything?"

Janet shook her head and filled her in. It was a dull event, as she'd predicted, meant only to puff up Lance's ego even more than it already was.

"The kid you're mentoring seems like he's going to be interesting..."

"Yeah, that's not going to be easy. Especially given my extra classes and the symposium work." She released her hair from the clip. She shook it out and let it fall down her back, finger combing it. As if letting it loose would ease the burdens plaguing her.

From across the desk, Janet scrutinized her.

"What's up with you today?"

"I just told you. Mentee. Extra coursework. Symposium. Does there need to be something else?"

Oh yeah, and the President of the United States got to second base with me last night on my couch. She forced away the thought and twisted her hair back up, adding another item to her to-do list: publish an update about the symposium in the newsletter.

Janet took a calculated bite of a brookie. "You want to talk about Lance?"

"God, no. I'm trying to will him into nonexistence."

"If you can figure out how to do that, I've got a few other candidates."

Elle appreciated her friend's support and frequent attempts to loosen her up. They had drifted together during Elle's rookie year, partly because they were two of only four women in the entire science department at the time (the number had grown to six since) and because Janet had an insatiable sweet tooth. Over a tray of blueberry muffins, the women connected about photosynthesis and the prospect of it existing on Mars—a common belief among space scientists devoting their lives to making the case that the Red Planet was a suitable replacement for Earth.

"Maybe I'll drop the project I've been working on forever and start that one. Some kind of quasar technology that would allow one to simply zap another being out into the stratosphere somewhere."

A knock at the door interrupted their fun revelry, and Elle tried not to let her posture change as Spencer made his way in.

"Dr. Gibbons." Spencer addressed Janet before turning to Elle. "I was hoping we could go over the list of duties, expectations, and responsibilities Dr. Dunwoody shared with me last evening."

Janet shot Elle the side-eye that made her famous around a meeting table.

"I'll let you two have at it. I have to check on some earthworms." It was a lie, Elle was sure, but she wasn't going to challenge her at the moment.

Spencer rocked forward and back, looking down at his iPad. After Janet closed the door, the only sound left was his light tapping on the screen.

"Have a seat," Elle said.

He plopped down into the chair, still never raising his eyes from the screen. Elle waited, fixated on the feather cowlick bobbing as he continued tapping an electronic pencil.

This lasted much longer than it should have, but Elle exercised great patience with people like Spencer. They had systems, as she had, that helped them process the world in a way that differed from others.

"Dr. Dunwoody mentioned that you might assign me to the first-year sections."

Elle eased back in her chair and put on her best neutral face.

"That isn't necessarily the case."

He pursed his lips and tapped back on the tablet. If she had to admit under oath, yes, all of his tapping was driving her absolutely crazy.

"That isn't ideal for my particular skill set, anyway. I would better serve you in upper levels or graduate levels. Which is what I proposed to Dr. Dunwoody."

She regretted wearing the thicker wool socks today because it made scrunching that much harder. But she could concentrate on the scratch and thickness of the fabric. Under no circumstances could she let Lance get under her skin by way of this kid.

"I think we need to get a couple of things straight." She slid some stapled packets across to him. His face soured as he flipped through them.

"These are all wrong," he said. "I just informed you that 1100 is too beneath me. Dr. Dunw—"

"Dr. Dunwoody isn't your mentor. I am. And while he's my boss, he can't dictate how I utilize a PhD candidate who needs time in the classroom." The words came out harsher than she intended, but they didn't seem to faze the young man. "My plan is to have you present in all my classes and labs for the next two weeks. That should give me a good read on where you'll best fit in."

"I can save you the time. It will be the higher level."

"We'll see."

He did nothing to hide the huff whistling through his lips. He tapped again.

"What about the symposium?" he asked, not pausing to meet her gaze.

"I'll spend a few days hashing out a plan. I'll likely need your help in the long run."

This stopped him and he puffed out his chest. This appeared worthy for him to be a part of.

"For now, I want you to study my syllabi, put together your own CV—"

"I emailed it to you. Along with my references and publication citations."

"Great. 1113 starts in ten minutes. It's also my biggest class thus far, so it'll mean a lot of grading."

"I'm happy to judge people's work."

She forced the scoff to die in her throat.

He jumped up and tucked the tablet and papers under his arm. He didn't bother waiting at the door for her, and she didn't expect him to. She grabbed her "I Love My Space" mug and made her way to the kitchen. Lecturing was one thing she could do without much preparation. Dealing with Spencer, however, would require a whole other level of astuteness only three hours of sleep hadn't afforded her.

CHAPTER EIGHT

The line at the bakery hadn't died down yet, though 11:00 a.m. mass at St. Luke's across the street had started. Elle bypassed the line of waiting patrons outside and went around back to the kitchen entrance. Immediately, she was rewarded with chocolate, cinnamon, and apple dancing in the air.

She hung her messenger bag and coat on the rack and picked up a broom. The floor was dusted with flour, sugar, and every other measure of ingredient. Mom and Ida, her assistant, had been busy, as usual. The industrial fridge housed six cake boxes, three with the same name, which likely meant a tiered wedding cake. Elle paused her sweeping to admire framed photos of the family through the years on the wall behind Mom's workstation. A picture of her and Dad hung at the top of the grouping. Mom had snapped it upon their return from the beach the morning Halley's Comet made its appearance. Dad had taken Elle out of bed in the dark to see it. He'd even bought a telescope. Whenever he'd told the story, which was often, he swore up and down she'd squealed and screeched with delight as the comet streaked past, thus cementing her love of space.

But she had been four months shy of her third birthday, so the likelihood of that being true was slim.

The doors thudded open and Pete pushed in, his arms piled with empty trays. They both stared, startled by the other's appearance. She leaned on her broom and opened her mouth.

"Don't ask," he said, then proceeded to the back counter to deposit his armload. "Mom didn't mention she called you in."

"She didn't. I just stopped by."

He grabbed three coffee cakes from the warmer and set them on the cutting counter.

"She's slammed."

"I guessed by"—she swept her arms about at the unusual messiness of the kitchen—"this."

He used the square cutters and within seconds had thirty-six slices of cake. Elle lined a tray with parchment and arranged the pieces for the display case out front.

"She'll be glad you're here in any case," he said, hefting the tray in one move. "Maybe you can help us out there."

"No, I'm good cleaning up. I'm not the one with the cute dimples that can woo women young and old."

"Still jealous, I see. It's good that some things don't change." He smiled wide, the dimples making their obligatory appearance. She tossed a towel at his retreating back.

She went back to work, using the busy time to lay out her plan for how to break up the work for the symposium. Spencer had been kind of a disaster in her 1100 classes. During her lecture, she caught him rolling his eyes more than once. When she called him out on it afterward, he said she had acted like a simpleton.

She couldn't respond the way she wanted, (the word ass might get her fired), so she simply stacked him high with weekend homework and sent him packing to labs. Not hers, but

Nate's, Lance's self-appointed "second in command," who had taken on the two graduate labs she'd taught last spring.

She didn't have the energy to shove her nose up Lance's ass to get those back. It didn't matter. She would teach her classes, get her symposium work finished, and then figure out her next move over the summer.

She could go after a position at MIT. She'd considered sending them her CV after Dad died, but Edgar said it wasn't a good idea when she was so close to perfecting her theory. Then she could put teaching in the rear view where it belonged.

Time passed, and Elle had just finished wiping out the mixing vat when Mom's familiar singsong greeting met her.

"Ellie Belly!" she said, arms and smile horizontal. Her embrace engulfed Elle in her signature sugar and lily scent.

"Hi, Mom."

"Pete told me you were back here, but this is the first break we've gotten. I can't believe how crazy it's been." She adjusted the headband that kept her gray and blond pixie away from her face. "Did you get something to eat?"

Elle's stomach grumbled.

"Not yet, but I will now."

Mom pulled out another coffee cake, the last in the warmer, and handed Elle a spoon with a wink.

"All I'm saying is he's a damn fool if he lets that asshole get away with this," Ida said as Pete held the door for her.

"He's definitely not a fool. He's a SEAL. He isn't afraid to get his hands dirty."

"We'll see," Ida continued. "This will be his first test with that manipulative power-hungry"—she stroked Elle's chin—"I won't use that kind of language around you, sweetie."

"I'm not Brody, Ida. I work around college kids." Colorful language was practically part of the curriculum.

Pete swooped in and gouged a chunk of the coffee cake with

a spoon. An avalanche of crumbs fell onto the workstation, and Elle tossed them at him.

"What are you even talking about?" she asked, digging into the cake before her brother ate the whole thing out from under her.

"Politics. Again." Mom piped up from the sink.

"The president can't be a wuss when it comes to Russia. Too much of my family is back in Ukraine." Ida wagged a finger at Pete who raised his arms up in surrender.

"All I'm saying is I don't think he will. He's not the typical politician."

The bite of cake got caught in Elle's mouth, and she hacked until Mom handed her a glass of water.

"Sorry," she said between sips.

"See, Elle doesn't want to hear this, either," Mom said.

Right. *Politics* was what Elle didn't want to hear about. The image of a trident and a bicep raced through her head as she took a long draw of water.

"Did you get the text I sent last night?" Mom asked, eyebrows high on her face.

Elle sighed. "Yes, Mom."

"He seemed like a good prospect, don't you think?"

Why did they have to do this dance? Mom was always trying to plug a hole in Elle's life that didn't exist.

Mom slid her readers up over her nose and pulled out her phone. "He's an accountant with a stamp collection. He likes stargazing! I thought that sounded like something you would have in common."

Pete snickered. If Elle hadn't cared about the cake, she would have thrown it at him.

"I didn't really notice."

"Honey, you're never going to find someone if you don't start noticing."

"I don't *need* to find someone. I'm happy being alone. And besides, I don't have time." She was ready for this round of relationship interrogation to be over, especially since Pete was having such a good time at her expense.

"You're too young to be alone. Put yourself out there."

She opened her mouth to argue. Putting herself out there had never worked out before. She was too different from almost everyone else and therefore, as Dad had said, it was better that she blend in and do anything but stand out. But Mom was never going to underst—

"She put herself out there Wednesday night. How'd that go?"

Elle's gaze shot to Pete's wide smile and eyebrow waggle. It was a good thing there were no sharp objects nearby.

"What is this about?" Mom said.

Dying on the spot wouldn't be a bad thing.

"Pete?"

She shook her head firmly at her brother, but this only served to brighten the glimmer in his eye.

"Elle came to the bar Wednesday and had quite the conversation with a Navy guy. He even walked her home."

The heat threatened to melt the skin from her neck. First, for bringing this up at all and second because he wasn't exactly *just* a Navy guy...

"Ellery Lincoln Conroy!" Joy painted itself across Mom's face. "Details, please."

"It wasn't like that." She swallowed hard in a poor attempt to stall. She couldn't tell the exact truth because, well, they would likely commit her on the spot. Pete didn't seem to recognize the Navy guy as the president, either, but he had been distracted.

"I love watching this." Pete chuckled and Elle decided to finally sacrifice the rest of the crumb cake—now really a piece—

and hurled it in his direction. He ducked and it hit the wall. He nodded his head, seemingly impressed by her aim.

"Look, nothing happened. He was nice and polite and walked me home. He left a few minutes later." The truth was the best way to go, even if it was only part of it.

"Wow, that's quite a standup guy. Can't stay more than a few minutes aft—"

"PETER!" Elle realized her mistake and Pete erupted into full-hearted laughter. Damn it, she'd fallen right into his trap. "I didn't mean that. I meant a few minutes after he came inside..."

Pete paused his laughter long enough for Elle to hear what she said.

"Stop making this a thing when it wasn't!" She started cleaning up the remnants of the crumb cake, its path of destruction marked by trickles of brown sugar and cake on the floor.

The bell from the front door saved her from further humiliation. Both Pete and Ida went to tend to the customers, which left Elle and Mom alone with only the notes from the old FM radio drifting in the air between them.

She and Mom hadn't been like other mothers and daughters growing up. Her interests were far outside the typical girl things like makeup, tea parties, and boys. But they did do their best bonding in the kitchen over mixing bowls and icing bags. Mom never tried to change her. Not like Dad.

"Can you come back here for a minute, Ellie?"

Mom understood, more than most, how she tended to recede into her head.

"It was nothing, Mom. Just a couple of drinks and a walk home." Her last attempt at a relationship had been over a year ago with a visiting professor from Germany. It lasted six months, but not a moment of it had been as memorable as Wednesday night.

Mom trickled her fingers beneath Elle's chin, forcing her gaze to Mom's blue eyes, bright like Regulus.

"If you want something to happen with a man, it will. But you need to be willing to let him in. Don't wall yourself off from the possibility that life exists beyond what's up in the sky. Or inside that beautiful and brilliant head of yours." She tucked a piece of hair behind Elle's ear and stroked her cheek.

Mom was right about a lot of things. But not this. Walling herself off was the safest thing she could do.

But still, what happened Wednesday night was unfathomable. Never had Elle connected with anyone so freely. It was as if there had been something invisible straddling the space between them. Despite who he was.

"Anything else, Ellie?"

Mom wanted to understand. She loved Elle and would take whatever she had to say in confidence. But Mom was so stressed. The bakery was going strong, but it left her little downtime.

She refused to pile anything else on Mom. Instead, she plastered a fake smile and shook her head.

"Nothing, Mom. Promise."

NatU School of Science

Greetings Students,

As the new Department of Space Science and Aeronautics chair, I was able to bring the 31st International Space Science Symposium to our university this April. After thinking long and hard about a relevant and impactful theme, I've chosen Innovation, Collaboration, and Exploration. As with everything I do, I'm working diligently to assemble a powerhouse of world-renowned space scientists and sponsors to ensure the symposium is a rousing success. To do so will require a team of student volunteers who will work the various sessions and areas on the day of the event. If you have an interest in volunteering, contact Dr. Ellery Conroy.

Yours faithfully in science,
Dr. Lance Dunwoody
Department of Space Science and Aeronautics Chair

SYMPOSIUM PROJECTS:

Do you have a research study you would like to feature in the poster gallery? Dr. Conroy is holding a meeting at 9:00 a.m. this Saturday in LH115 to go over the application requirements and some of the foundational elements each project should include to give you the best shot at being accepted. If you can't attend Saturday, make an appointment to see Dr. Conroy during her office hours. Applications close in one month. Good luck!

RESEARCH OPPORTUNITIES:

Dr. Slade is looking for three students who played a contact sport for a minimum of four years. Visit him during office hours this week to sign up and participate in a financially lucrative study.

REMINDER:

Nominations for the Worldwide Lecture are still open. Don't forget to add your favorite instructor to the candidate pool before the window closes March 1st.

CHAPTER NINE

"**Y**ou should give me the upper-level lab."

Spencer didn't understand boundaries. He tended to forget, quite often, that he was not the mentor in this relationship. It wasn't all his fault exactly. Lance bore a great deal of the burden by empowering him so much.

"I have a better idea," she said, packing up her bag from the lecture hall. "How about I give you the notes for 1101 next week. Have a draft of the lectures to me Friday afternoon, so I can look them over and give you feedback."

She did her best to give him an encouraging and enthusiastic smile, but he wasn't having it.

"That's filler work. I'm better suited for the upper levels, as I've told you."

Yes, that he did. Every chance he got. Bombarding her with the argument that he was better suited to teach the advanced students than she was.

This push and pull—him both pushing and pulling—was wearing on her already and it had only been a week. His arguments didn't make her more prone to do what he wanted. In fact, they had the opposite effect. She pulled back when she normally would have given slack because he irritated her, *and* he wasn't nearly as capable as he believed.

Spencer was on her heels as they approached her office door. She noted there were six names on her afternoon office hours sheet already, the first starting in less than twenty minutes. Exhaustion pulled at her. Between the lack of sleep, the avalanche of work, and the barrage of challenges Spencer threw at her, she stayed up too late and awoke too early.

"Listen." She stopped before the closed door, hand poised on her handle. "I appreciate that you have a very strong belief in yourself. But remember, you're here to learn from me, not the other way around."

He didn't like that answer. He pushed up on his glasses and wrinkled his nose. She figured he was about to fight back, but instead, he went back to his tablet and mumbled something.

At least, he was quiet for now and for that, she was grateful. She pushed into her office and was startled to find a rather sizable man standing inside.

She closed the door again and turned, barring Spencer from entering. "Uh, so go ahead and take a crack at the lectures. I'll see you later."

"Fine, though you're wasting my intelligence on this drivel." He rushed away down the hall, his short, exaggerated steps clacking.

She took an extra beat to gather herself before opening the door again to see if she had imagined the man inside.

He was still standing. Still staring. So not an illusion. Check. He was gargantuan, his neck swallowed between his mountainous shoulders. His hair was cropped so tight, and the little bit on top was almost as pale as the skin around it. But it was the scar that zigzagged down his chin that, ironically, put her a bit at ease.

She sidestepped behind her desk and gestured toward the chair.

"You recognize me?" he said.

She nodded and they both sat.

"I never told anyone, if that's why you're here," she said.

"It's not."

She squeezed her hands together on top of her desk and waited. He seemed collected and in no hurry. He also struck her as a man of few words, so whatever he did say would mean something.

"My friend sent me," he said.

"Your...friend."

"He wanted me to extend an invitation. He'd like to see you."

She squeezed her toes. "Really?"

He nodded. His almost reddish-white eyebrows ticked up a beat. He had a Nordic quality about him, with what she assumed was an eternal blush of red across his pale face.

"Tonight at his place."

"And that would be"—she leaned forward over the desk—"the house that's comprised of all colors, not devoid of them. It only appears...white...because of the way the wavelengths all reflect into the eyes at once?"

The corner of his mouth twitched. He didn't strike Elle as a man with a sense of humor, but what did she know?

Wait. Maybe this whole thing was a ruse. A joke to lure Elle in and make her feel like an idiot. It was the very thing Dad always swore she would be prone to if she didn't protect herself.

Irritation rubbed along her ribs like knuckles. She didn't want to be the butt of anyone's jokes.

"I don't know who sent you, but I'm not falling for it."

He remained unmoved.

"It was Pete, wasn't it?" she continued. "Sometimes my

brother can be such an asshole. Let me guess. You guys all served together and he put you both up to this." Pete was a jokester and Elle had always been his favorite target because it was part of being a little sister. But this was too far. Nordic Beast here would probably go back and report the whole thing to him. *I thought you said your sister was smart.*

"I don't know what you're talking about, ma'am."

"Sure you don't. Listen, I have too much to do... A new boss who is a total egomaniac and asshole... A symposium for which I am somehow doing way more than I should... A slew of new classes I have to teach... A mentee, who is proving to be more work than help... All of which can be traced back to the aforementioned asshole boss. So, run and tell Pete that, yes, I fell for this"—she gestured wildly toward the man—"pensive, hulking, Secret Service act. The nondescript black suit is a nice touch, but you're missing the outdated ear wig, which, let's face it, the government can do better with at this point."

The air rushed out of her lungs and the weight it carried with it surprised even her. She sank into the cushion of her chair falling back against the headrest.

"Feel better?"

She glanced around the office and nodded. "I think I do."

"Good." He stood. "If you're free tonight, come to the southeast gate at Hamilton and East Executive anytime after twenty hundred. Hand this"—he reached inside his pocket and withdrew a business card—"to the first checkpoint you come to. Or that comes to you." He set the card face down on her desk.

Her gaze remained fixated on his movements from his buttoning of the jacket to his respectful nod, and then his steps out the door. He was quiet and swift for such a large man. She imagined that might come in handy if he was someone who needed to remain in the background.

After he was gone, she tapped the keys on her laptop,

searching for pictures of the president out and about. She scrolled, not really interested in the president himself (though, wow, what a specimen). It was the man lurking in the background of most shots in the nondescript black suit, his head almost shaved except for cropped white-blond hair at the top. And a scar down his chin.

If this was a joke orchestrated by her brother, she had to hand it to him: he had outdone himself.

She pulled the business card across her desk and flipped it over. The man had written a sequence of numbers next to the name Theodore Brockovich, Secret Service.

CHAPTER TEN

Elle didn't have a clue what to expect as she inched down Hamilton Place. The wrought iron railings atop cobblestone columns appeared extra daunting the closer she got. She had tried, and failed, to talk herself out of going on what seemed to be some sort of suicide mission. Though she probably shouldn't even think that word this close to the most heavily guarded home in the United States.

Her bones rattled beneath the full-length black wool coat belted around her, but it wasn't the cold causing the shake. Her nerves were off the chart, and no amount of heat would counteract the shiver at the prospect of what—*who*—was waiting behind the gates.

"Ma'am?"

She startled upright and met the brown eyes of a young man in uniform and heavily armed. Elle opened her mouth, but the attempt to explain...what exactly again?...failed. Instead, she withdrew the business card and proffered it with a shaky hand.

The young soldier took it without breaking his gaze. He was probably trying to gauge whether she was unhinged or not. She definitely felt like she was.

He flicked his eyes down to the card, used his flashlight to illuminate it, and then lifted his gaze back to her. He pocketed the card and put his hand up to a radio on his shoulder.

"Base this is SEVEN-O-FOUR. Be advised I'm transporting one to the house. Over."

He stared her down again, then nodded to some unseen voice giving unheard orders through his earpiece.

Was it too late to run away? What if that card was some kind of trap meant to lure her here so they could lock her up on the spot. She'd probably be tossed in some underground cell or shipped off to a black-ops interrogation site she'd seen in a documentary. Or—

"Follow me, Dr. Conroy," the soldier said, stepping forward. Another man assumed the position he'd occupied moments ago.

She hesitated. They knew her name. Not a great sign. Maybe she should have paid more attention to Carson's conspiracy theories.

"Ma'am?"

A week ago, she met a man at the bar who also called her ma'am. When she balked, he smiled and said it was an old habit. Now that man, who she admittedly hadn't stopped thinking about when her mind had any kind of chance to relax, was waiting somewhere inside the imposing house ahead. All she had to do was be brave and put one foot in front of the other.

"Sorry," she stammered. "I've never done anything like this before." She smoothed her coat, shook her feet from side to side to wake up the toes she'd been scrunching, and inhaled some courage. This was the stupidest thing she'd ever done...and that said a lot.

THEY JUMPED into a waiting golf cart and took off down East Executive. If Elle thought her heart would pound out of her chest at any other point in her life, those instances paled to this one. She gawked at the grounds illuminated by sweeps of light.

Fake Ben Foster... Ben Foster, probably. No. President Foster. *Mr. President.* Yes, that was the way she'd have to address him. Unless she never made it inside. They'd put her under bright lights to ensure she never talked about a man with riveting gray eyes drinking Corona at her brother's bar on a random Wednesday night... Of course, he didn't have a tattoo... How would she have seen that?

When the cart stopped, she slid out on trembling legs. Two more uniformed soldiers stepped in front of her. This was it. This was the end.

"Good evening, Dr. Conroy," the taller one said. "I need to search your bag. Corporal Estelle will pat you down."

She gave away her bag as if it was nothing. Damn it, her phone was tucked inside. Now she wouldn't be able to call for help.

911, what's your emergency?

I'm being kidnapped by the White House.

It's a crime to prank call 911.

No, I swear! I'm being held captive because I made out with the president a week ago.

"Unbutton your coat and stand like a starfish, please." Corporal Estelle's tight bun swirled at the bottom of her head. Elle could never wind her hair that tight, though she'd tried. The woman ran her hands all over Elle. Though was petite, Elle was confident the corporal could hold her own against any of the men here. She was compact, lean, and her fingers were strong.

"I need to unzip your boots," Corporal Estelle said with a

stout nod. Elle bent over to do it, but the woman held up her palm. She dropped to the ground and examined the inside of Elle's boots one at a time with a flashlight. Elle had to work hard not to grip her socks with her toes, afraid the corporal would think she was attempting to hide something beneath her feet.

The woman stood and nodded to someone behind Elle.

"We're going to lock up your phone until you leave." The man in charge handed her back the bag. "Follow me," he continued and then set off. Corporal Estelle faded into the lawn area, flipping around the gun from her back to her front.

A familiar scar—and face—met Elle at the bottom of the steps.

"I'll take it from here," Agent Brockovich said. The man escorting her peeled off, no doubt to return to his post. "I'm glad you made it. He's inside."

Her feet stayed stuck to the walkway, eyes fixated on the glass double doors, and the soft light seeping out from beyond.

"Do you need help?"

"Wha—, uh, no. Although. Maybe." The chill in the air nipped at her nose like Brody's little fingernails when he was trying to honk it. "I don't know how I got here."

"You walked, I assume."

If this had been her brother, she would have smacked him in the arm.

"So are you going to make it, or do I need to ca—"

"I'm fine. Geez. Nothing like a little old-fashioned peer pressure." She willed one foot to move until she'd made it. Then Agent Brockovich was opening the door and urging her with a sweep of his arm to go inside.

She paused and leaned over toward him. "Is this the part where someone jumps out and kidnaps me?"

His eyes crinkled slightly and then went slack. "I can see why he likes you."

"That isn't an answer."

"Take it up with my boss," he said, and raised his almost invisible eyebrows. "He should be down the hall by now."

Before Elle realized it, she was across the threshold and the door was shutting softly behind her.

CHAPTER ELEVEN

Elle moved past the vacant desk, her boots clacking over the gray and white tile floor. Crystal dripped from the three chandeliers illuminating the stretch of hall toward the steps at the end. Her attention drew to the painting on her left and the regal gaze of Nancy Reagan staring toward the door she had just walked through. Mom always did love that red dress.

"I can have the overheads turned on, if that would help."

His voice called to her from the steps. She tightened her grip on the strap of her bag as he drew closer. His light brown hair was styled with some kind of gel, slicked back and stiffer than last week.

"I hope they didn't rough you up too bad out there." He stopped a few steps away and gazed down at her. The stubble was emerging from its day of hibernation, though this was probably about the same time she had met him at the bar. Only tonight, the pullover had been replaced by a light blue button-down with the top two buttons undone and the sleeves rolled to his elbows.

She drew her gaze back up to his and softly shook her head.

"Good." He shifted and continued to stare, but it wasn't crushing or intimidating. More like uncertain.

"I really appreciate you coming. I wasn't sure you would. In fact, when Ted said you were here, I sprinted down from my office"—he gestured behind him—"in case you changed your mind."

She nodded. Maybe. Maybe not. She was woefully unaware of much, except she was somehow standing in the East Wing of the White House at 8:30 on a Wednesday night. Holding onto the strap of her bag like it was a lifeline she couldn't afford to let go.

"Right. So you probably want to know why I asked you to come here. I mean, you already know why I wanted you to come *here*, but... Let me start over."

He inhaled and placed his palms together. "I'm really sorry about what happened. I don't know what got into me. I shouldn't have..."

Right. Because how could a man like *him*, gorgeous and important, possibly ever go for a woman like *her*, plain and wildly unimportant, under non-desperate circumstances. She shifted her weight to one leg.

"That didn't come out right." He paused and wiped a hand down his face. "I'm sorry I let you think I was a body double, which, by the way, isn't a thing. I checked." His chuckle was full of nerves and he cleared his throat. "It's just, I wasn't exactly supposed to be at that bar. Or meet you. I strong-armed Ted into taking me. Well, I called in a favor."

She glanced up to Nancy, imploring her to step out of the painting and slap her or shake her.

He continued to gaze straight into her eyes so intently she thought it perfectly logical two holes would open in the back of her head. She swallowed. Her knees trembled from cold or fear, or perhaps because she had balled her toes up so tight it was rippling up the muscles of her legs.

She quaked like she had for her first book report presentation in fourth grade when she was seven. She had chosen *A Brief History of Time* because it was her favorite, though Dad had suggested she choose something more in line with what her classmates read, like *Black Beauty* or *Because of Winn-Dixie*. In the end, she had done what she wanted, and he correctly predicted it would not go well.

Her presentation started off strong. But then came the deadpan stares and the furrowed glances. Her knees shook. Her lips stuck together. Her head grew light. When she couldn't take the judgment a second longer, she flung her report on the teacher's desk, dashing to her seat in the back and sat ramrod in her desk, willing herself *not to cry*. She was already a freak. Crying would make it worse.

That was the day she had accepted Dad was right. The disparity between her brain and the world around her was vast. She made a vow to believe Dad and let him help her bridge the gap between the two from then on.

"Elle?" Ben asked, his voice barely above a whisper. "I can't tell if you're about to scream or cry. I hope it's the first—I can handle that better than the second." The concern spread about his face was palpable.

"No. Sorry. This is all just...odd."

He nodded. "Right. Okay. Odd is manageable." He gestured toward the hall he had come from. "Want to get some air?"

"That's a good idea."

She followed him up a few stairs. At the top, her footfalls changed across the terracotta floor. He led her ahead and opened a door, the blast of cold air snapping her back to life.

The quiet stroll along the brick-paved walkway gave her time to unclench. A bank of windows looking back into the building formed the barrier on the right, while trees and shrubbery diminished by the winter lined the field to their left. Elle tipped her head back toward the sky at the half-moon peeking through the low clouds.

"This is weirder than the last time," she said as they approached a white rectangular pergola with a bench and chairs. He waited until she sat on the bench and pulled a chair facing her.

"A little, yeah."

"You have an unfair advantage, what with all this security. I can't exactly come back and stalk you properly."

His smile warmed her, and that's when she realized he didn't even have on a jacket.

"You must be freezing."

"I can hang for a bit. I'm tougher than I look."

"Considering how tough you look..." A warmth flushed her cheeks as the words she'd meant to keep inside rushed out. She folded her hands on her lap and eased into the cushion. "I already told Agent Brockovich that I never told anyone. About you."

"I wasn't worried."

"Because you thought I didn't recognize you?"

"More like I figured no one would believe you." The left side of his cheek popped up.

"Right. Meeting the president at a bar sounds like the beginning to a bad joke. Or a delusional fantasy concocted by a lonely old spinster. I don't have cats, by the way."

His smile faded, but the hope raised in the corners of his eyes remained. "I really am sorry, Elle. For all of it. Mostly because if things were different..."

She breathed out her nose and paid attention to the way it whooshed through her head. She needed to ground herself in reality and not in fantasy, though he was making that hard. That pull between them was real. It begged her to leap off the bench and jump on his lap. Considering what might happen if she did, she shook off these very un-Elle-like urges.

"I'm not mad. And I do appreciate you saying that...the apology. Thank you," she said.

His face softened. "Good. Glad to hear it."

She let her gaze travel again and wondered what this garden would look like in a few months when it was kissed by spring. It probably burst with color and the perfume of roses and gardenias. When she tilted her head up, the stars were too faded to see.

She wouldn't have much time for stargazing or anything else for the next few months. Edgar would know what she should do. He'd be able to talk her down. Dad used to be able to do it, too. Though he suggested she do *normal* things, like walks and breathing exercises, while Edgar had encouraged her to dive deeper into her research.

"Still got work problems, I see," he said. His hands were plunged into his pockets, and his breath fanned out into the dark before him.

Elle felt an unsubstantiated desire to tell him everything. To unload and rattle through the laundry list of all her problems, past, present, and future. But she didn't.

"I should get going," she said and stood.

"Of course. I'll walk you out."

The silence back inside was burdened by the weight of her thoughts. Overwhelm threatened to swallow her, even as they walked into the warmth of the hall, down the steps and past Nancy.

"I don't know as much as a rocket scientist," he said pausing at the door. "But I'm a pretty good listener. If you ever need someone to help you unravel whatever is tying up your head."

The soft light of the chandelier dripped down in circles over

his skin. He was an intelligent man, but he had far more important things to worry about than anything as ridiculous as once-
in-a-lifetime research fellowships, catty bosses who were only
out for themselves, and know-it-all mentees. The president
certainly didn't have time to deal with nonsense.

"...again next week?"

Elle moved her focus to him.

"Sorry?"

"I was wondering if you might be free to come back next
week."

Confusion clouded her face. "For what?"

He laughed and rubbed the back of his neck. "I was hoping
you'd want to have dinner. With me."

Of all the scenarios she'd imagined since Agent Brockovich
—Ted apparently to his friend *THE PRESIDENT*—came to her
office, this one had never entered the realm of possibility.

"Why would you want to do that?"

He shifted his head, searching her face with what felt like
real intent. "I want to get to know you. I meant it when I said
you're the most fascinating person I've met."

The sincerity floated from his voice and wrapped around
her like a warm blanket. He was good at making her feel seen
and heard. Two things lacking since Edgar's departure.

"I can't." The words barely choked from her mouth. "I've
got work."

"Of course." He grinned, but it was smaller somehow. Was
he disappointed? He looked like he might be. But that was probably a ridiculous notion. "Another time."

She nodded.

"Thanks again for coming." He walked a little past her and
opened the door where Ted waited outside.

"Thank you, Mr. President," she said.

He placed his right palm across his heart. "Please don't call me that. It's ridiculous. I'm just Ben."

She hesitated because it felt like she would be breaking some kind of protocol, committing some act of treason. Then again, considering what she was doing with him last week...

"Thank you, Just Ben."

He flashed that megawatt smile and laughed. The sound continued to swell her chest even as she walked away.

CHAPTER TWELVE

Feeding all the students who showed up to the Saturday workshop turned out to be easy, in large part because since Wednesday, Elle had spent most of her time outside of the university baking.

She wouldn't say she was on cloud nine after she left the White House, exactly. The meeting wasn't *that* big of a deal. Not that she had expected it to be, with the exception of believing she might be kidnapped. Other than that, it had been just...not much. He'd talked. She'd...choked. He'd asked her to come back. She'd turned him down. The end.

If she had told anyone, they would have admitted her to the hospital that very second. Even Mom and Pete would have been hard pressed to believe she hadn't snapped after decades of internalizing her stress. A pressure cooker with a hairline crack that finally exploded.

So when she got home from the White House (ridiculous, right?), she started baking. She wiped her work surface. Laid out her ingredients. Pre-measured everything. Lined them up in the order they went into the bowl. Just like Grandma Ellery had shown her thirty-plus years ago.

While she mixed, she let her mind wander without rhyme or reason. She replayed the conversation. How short it had been. How disappointed she thought he looked when she turned down his invitation. How she was really good at making something out of nothing. How long she'd stood there and said *nothing* while he stumbled over an apology he hadn't needed to give her. On and on, her mind had unraveled. For three nights straight.

Grandma Ellery would be delighted her namesake still baked in the fashion she'd been taught. Though Grandma had died suddenly when Elle was only twelve, all of those afternoons and weekends baking together in her warm and cozy kitchen remained imprinted. The process had always been a safe haven for Elle, and in many ways, something she could wrap her busy brain around, while also letting it unwind. Putting together seemingly unconnected ingredients to create something magical appealed to her. It was a lot like science—putting elements together until the end result turned out.

Now cleaning up after the workshop, she noted there weren't many leftovers. The cinnamon rolls (pure perfection, if she did say so) and coffee cake muffins (a little too dry, but no one seemed to care) were wiped out. Most of the other muffins, too. Random lemon poppy seed, blueberry, and chocolate chip remained.

"Dr. Conroy, what do you want me to do with the extras?" Noah had stayed behind to help clean up.

"Do you know anyone who might want them?"

"My roommates, for sure. Thanks." He flipped his bangs out of his eyes and smiled. "Hey, how many student projects are being selected for the symposium?"

"No idea. That'll be up to Dr. Dunwoody. This is as far as my involvement with it goes."

"I'm not sure I'm going to do it." He shrugged and tucked the box under his arm.

"How come?"

"It seems like too big of a place."

Noah had always been unassuming. Reserved. A little on the shy side.

She nodded. "It is, but remember, you won't be standing on the main stage. Think middle school science fair. Only more professional."

"So me and my trifold in a cafeteria. That was a nightmare." He chuckled.

"I've seen what you can do. You have strong research. Be proud of how far you've come. Not scared."

His olive cheeks reddened. "I guess when you put it that way."

"Excellent." She broke down the last of the bakery boxes and gathered up her bag. "And if you do apply and get picked, I'll be there cheering you and your poster on."

The door to the lecture hall opened, and before Elle could steady herself, Brody came bounding towards her.

"Aunt Lelly!" he cried, taking a leap and rushing into her arms. She had just enough time to drop the folded boxes and catch him. He wrapped his arms and legs around her as she stood and squeezed.

"This is just what I needed." She inhaled his little-boy scent of dirt, sugar, and coconut. He rested his head against her shoulder and his flyaway hair tickled her face.

"I missed you," he said, patting her shoulder.

"I missed you, too."

He lifted his head and pushed away. "Why have you been gone?"

"I've been busy."

"Why?"

"Because I have a lot of work. Just like your daddy."

"But he still sees me. Why can't you?" Brody was, if nothing else, persistent.

"I blame you for this," Pete said from the doorway. "You encourage him to question everything he doesn't understand or like. Turns out he's a natural."

Noah closed his lips around a laugh.

"You are not blaming me for that." Elle put down the tot, and he trotted up the risers of the lecture hall.

Pete turned to Noah. "Is she or is she not teaching you to question everything?"

"It is kind of fundamental for science, Dr. Conroy." He shrugged.

"I did not come here on a Saturday morning to be attacked," she huffed. Before she could grab the broken-down boxes, Noah rushed over and took them.

"I'll drop these in the recycling bin on my way out." He rocked back and forth for a beat and cleared his throat. "I should go. Thanks for the information and the encouragement."

"Not a problem. Just don't be too afraid to put yourself out there. It might turn out better than you think."

Brody's footfalls up and down the risers echoed as the door shut behind Noah.

Pete cocked an eyebrow. "That kid's got a mad crush on you."

"What! Why would you even say that?"

"Because I was his age once."

"Yeah, so was I...like seventeen years ago. That's gross." She shivered and drew her sweater closer around her, like that would help. "So what's up? You were very vague in your message about needing to come by."

Her first reaction was to believe that he might be ready to

tell her what was going on with him. But now with Brody running about, she doubted that was going to be the case.

"Two things. One, Brody's been asking about you. And two, we've got to clean out the storage unit. We told Mom we would do it *last* winter."

"Ugh." She let her head fall backwards. "Can't we just pay someone to go in there, box it all up and toss it?"

"You know Mom would never let that happen."

"I'll take over the rental payments." The prospect of adding one more task to her infinite—and still growing—to-do list was beyond overwhelming.

"It's not about that, and you know it. It's been three years, Ellie. We promised Dad."

Pete didn't ask or insist on much. He was the archetypal big brother. Always taller, stronger, and popular. The complete opposite to his too-smart-for-her-age little sister. He had loved to tease her every waking second of their childhood, and even now he still ribbed her every chance he got.

Then there was this serious older-brother side. The one that would snap into action if he got wind of someone making fun of her. The one that had called her back from the West Coast and convinced her she needed to come home, not just for Mom and Dad, but for him.

It was this second version of Pete before her now. She so badly wanted to tell him she'd pay *him* to do it all. But the pull on his face, and the exhaustion etched in the dark circles under his eyes, said so much more than his words ever could.

She sighed. "When do you want to start?"

CHAPTER THIRTEEN

Three years after your dad dies is a strange time to find out he had a hoarding problem. It seemed like something Elle and Pete should have known about before they were standing in front of a tightly packed storage unit.

"How big is this again?" She stared at the wall of boxes.

"Ten by thirty." Pete's voice sounded as defeated as she felt.

"Did you know it was this bad?"

Pete shook his head. "I knew it was a lot. But not like this."

"Didn't you move it here?"

"No. Dad started moving it himself years ago. Then he arranged for some of his buddies to move the rest after." He stared into the space. The lines around his eyes were deepening. He was nodding slowly, no doubt replaying the past inside his head. Elle remembered the group of Dad's old cop friends carrying boxes out of the house after the funeral while Mom tended to their wives and the rest of the guests.

"I thought they were taking things he left them. Not moving them here." She gestured into the storage space packed floor to ceiling with white, brown, and yellowed boxes.

Pete let out a hefty sigh. "Welp, the only way to do this is to start." He took a few steps and slid out an entire column of boxes.

"Wait, we need to have some kind of a system, or this is going to go sideways real fast."

"Okay. How do you want to do it?"

Elle *wanted* to pay someone else to load it up and haul it away. What website would that be—Hoarders "R" Us? There was nothing in here they needed or wanted, and if there was, who cared? If they didn't know it existed at this point, they wouldn't miss it when it was gone.

Pete would not be on board with this. He took their promise to Dad very seriously. Plus, he was a softy and, no doubt, wanted to hang on to more of the past than she did.

"We each take a box and decide if it's work, family, personal, or garbage. We move them around accordingly. Hopefully, most of these are garbage we can toss or case files we can shred."

Pete put his hands on his hips. "Dad worked some pretty cool cases, though. I might want to take a look at what's here." Her brother had clearly inherited the hoarding gene from Dad. Great.

"Can we agree to at least not go through anything until we've got them marked?"

"I'll try. But no promises." He tossed her a rueful smile and she rolled her eyes.

They started making their way through the first stack, which seemed to be mostly cases. Pete grabbed a couple of markers to label the boxes. Since they didn't have much space to work with inside the unit until they could throw some out (a prospect that was looking less likely with each, "oh cool" Pete exclaimed), they needed a way to know which box belonged where.

About an hour into their work, Mom sent a picture of Brody

in the apron and hat she'd ordered special for him. They both paused to ooh and aww over how adorable he looked. Pete replaced the phone into his back pocket and opened another box.

"So why were you at work this morning?" he asked.

She slid a work box out of the way. "Meeting with students about a symposium."

"On a weekend?"

"There aren't enough hours during the week." She pulled down another box, popped off the lid, to find what appeared to be an album of baseball cards. Thank god she found it and not Pete or else he'd never make it through another box. She labeled it "personal" and set it aside.

"I thought you did your own projects on the weekend."

She stood up and sighed. "Not for the foreseeable future." Though what would she work on at this point? Her lifelong pursuit had turned out to be a total dud in the eyes of the most prestigious space association in the world. Did she have it in her to go back to something else she'd worked on, or find a new corner of the universe to delve into? Only time would tell. Something she lacked at the moment.

"You gotta stop volunteering for stuff that takes away from your work, Ellie."

"I didn't. I was voluntold. Or rather just told."

He stopped and rubbed the back of his hand over his forehead. "Is it something you want to do?"

She shrugged. "Under normal circumstances, it wouldn't be bad. But throw it on top of a very tight timeline, extra classes, and a mentee who I was also assigned to deal with, and it's a bit much."

"Jesus, Elle. I don't know what half of that means, and I still somehow know it's a lot of work. Tell them you can't do it."

"Won't work."

"Why not?"

She sighed. How could she explain something inexplicable? She could do it when it came to space. Human nature was much more difficult.

"My new boss won't hear any of it. He knows how much I've got on my plate and doesn't care."

"And he's in charge of this symposium?"

"He's in charge of"—she swept her arms wide—"everything."

Pete cocked his head. "Then it's on him if shit goes wrong. Not you."

"I wish it was that simple."

He shook his head. "Nothing complicated about it. I had a buddy who was in logistics back in the army. His boss was a real peach. A little guy who needed to make himself feel big by stomping on everyone who worked for him."

"Was his name Lance Dunwoody by any chance?" It sure sounded like it could be.

"Anyway, there was this huge movement of supplies that Little Guy put himself in charge of. Touted to all the higher-ups that he'd be able to get it all done in half the time as any other unit. Thing was, he wasn't planning on doing any of the work. He assigned it all to my buddy who knew there was absolutely nothing in it for him. Little Guy was gonna take all the credit, as usual, and my buddy was going to bust his ass twenty hours a day to do the work."

Elle's interest was piqued. "So what happened?"

Pete's left eyebrow ticked up. "That's the best part. My buddy said fuck it. Since it wasn't his ass on the line, he backed off. Worked his designated number of hours and left on time every day. And when the supplies weren't there on the day the boss promised, Little Guy took the fall. Not my buddy."

"But how did your friend not get in any trouble?" If she dropped any of the dozen balls she had up in the air, Lance would be sure they crashed down on top of her.

"He did exactly what his job description said he *had* to do. No more. No less. Little Guy could accuse him of slacking off all he wanted, but the official documentation said otherwise. When shit goes sideways, the leader should take the fall. But a good one doesn't let it get that far. They step up and do the work themselves."

Elle leaned back against the column of boxes. She had a hard time justifying someone intentionally failing or letting someone else fail. It wasn't within her to do that.

"And," he continued, putting what Elle suspected to be something that could be trash in the personal pile. "As a person who's known you every day of your thirty-eight years—"

"Fourteen thousand and fifty days." She rattled off without hesitation.

He chuckled. "Of course you'd do that in your head. Anyway, as someone who's known you your entire life, I know slacking off isn't in your nature." He started rearranging the boxes into their designated spots. "But it is possible to do what you have to do, and not all the extra an unappreciative prick gives you. Otherwise, they'll keep having you do their work the rest of your life, Ellie."

Her breath caught at the way his hair fell across his eyes. He looked and sounded like Dad. All those years ago when she came home for the holidays and explained she needed to go back to school early to start a project for Edgar, Dad had the same sincere look about him as Pete did now. And his advice was almost identical.

Pete glanced at his watch. "I gotta get the bar ready. I think we did pretty good for an hour."

"Not exactly great though," she said, gesturing down to the only two boxes marked garbage.

"Yeah, but it's better than when we got here. Let's take the win, little sis." He winked as they stepped out and he slid the door down. "I think you could use one."

ACCORDING TO MY SCIENCE
FIFTH SPRING EDITION—FEBRUARY 5TH

NatU School of Science

SYMPOSIUM UPDATE:

Dr. Dunwoody is pleased that six department faculty members and two visiting professors will display their research at the symposium leaving room for 52 student projects. The deadline for applications is today.

DEADLINES:

**Sign up to volunteer at the symposium with Dr. Conroy. All science disciplines are welcome and encouraged.

Nominations for the Worldwide Lecture close **MARCH 1.

CHAPTER FOURTEEN

This whole semester, thus far, felt like a series of Mondays strung together. And not the good ones after she'd spent the weekend on her research or hanging out with Brody. These were the Mondays she dreaded. The ones that came too quickly.

Elle gazed around the conference room. It was especially gloomy. Snow clouds had settled in last night and held the city hostage in an eternal gray haze of occasional sleet. The lights in this room seemed particularly yellow, which only made it easier for her lids to get heavy.

Lance was ten minutes late to the mandatory meeting he had called yesterday. When Greer asked her if she had any idea what this was about, she shrugged, not bothering to postulate. What did it matter?

"You look exhausted," he said to her. "Are you having trouble sleeping? I heard about this new app..."

She'd stopped him with a wave and lied. "I'm fine." Between classes, labs, Spencer, helping students with symposium applications, and coming up with a system for student volunteers, she planned on not being fine until the summer break. Luckily, the deadline for student applications was yesterday, so she could recapture that bit of time.

"Thank you all for being here." He sounded like he'd started developing a British accent. She could imagine him standing before his mirror in the morning practicing.

Elle crossed her arms and dug her nails into the crook of her elbow. It didn't do much because of her sweater, but at least it kept her aware. She'd left Spencer in charge of the 3215 class, but didn't feel right about it. She hoped whatever this was ended quick enough, though she also knew nothing with Lance would end "quickly" (except for one thing that made her want to vomit thinking about).

"I'll keep this brief."

"Wait," Greer said, turning his head. "Where's Rachel?"

"She didn't feel comfortable leaving a TA to proctor a quiz."

Elle had to grind her teeth to keep her mouth from opening. Not mandatory for pets. Check.

"So I've run into a bit of a snag, and I need my best and brightest to help me out." He cleared his throat and one of his student assistants (he somehow needed three though he taught one class) opened a bottle of water and handed it to him. Lance took his time sipping and Elle was certain she'd have bruises on her arms from squeezing so tight.

"I am having difficulty securing enough speakers and sponsors. It seems some of them made other arrangements after the event was moved. I was hoping my superstars of space science" —he gestured around the table—"would be able to pull some strings and get an excellent lineup going."

"How many do we have?" she said. And immediately regretted it.

"Four have confirmed. We need at least six more."

Six?

Around her, people dove into their phones, undoubtedly

going through contacts, as they freely shared names and ideas. Elle didn't feel the need to help things any more than she already had. She'd contributed enough. Let everyone else chip in. No one here taught more than four classes and two labs. They all had TAs of their choosing. Their chatter in the break room about weekend trips, evenings out, and the progression of their own research, pissed her off because she certainly hadn't had the same opportunities since the semester started.

"Ellery, do you have something to add to the conversation?" Lance said.

The smug bastard left campus by 3:00 p.m. and didn't roll in until close to 10:00 a.m. Meanwhile, she was lucky to get out before 9:00 p.m. after a full twelve-hour day.

"No, it sounds like you all have it figured out." She kept her arms tight.

He stared her down and his right eyebrow twitched. "That's all well and good. I need you for something else."

"I'm still coordinating the volunteers."

"Yes, but the student applications—"

"Those were due yesterday. My part in that is done."

He sipped from his water, his pinkie raised like he was at high tea with the queen.

"Not quite. I have to reshuffle tasks to spend more time on the sponsors and speakers."

Her colleagues stopped and looked at her like she was the only woman on the prison block. Technically true, since she was the only one in this room, and it did feel like a prison at the moment.

"Since you're in the unique position of having educated and helped some of the students with their applications, you're already that much further ahead of things."

She gripped the crook of her elbow. "That doesn't make me ahead of anything."

"You've seen some already. You're more familiar with what to look for in terms of quality. It makes more sense for you to choose the best fifty-two projects. I'd be starting from zero."

She swallowed back the frustration rumbling in her chest. She had helped quite a few students already, so the process would likely go quicker. If she could choose fifty-two, it meant probably having to sift through maybe an additional fifty or so. That wouldn't be too bad.

"How many applications came in?"

His eyebrow twitched again. "As of yesterday afternoon, there were 238."

Scratch that. "Are you kidding me?"

"Wow, that's a great turnout." Steven leaned back and seemed very pleased until he read her face, which disagreed with him. He cleared his throat and went back to his phone.

"I'll have tech send over the login information so you can get started." Lance leaned forward and slapped the table with both hands as he got up. "I need the list of accepted projects the Monday after spring break so I can inform the students. That gives you about six weeks. You should be able to handle it."

Greer raised a hand to speak. He and Steven exchanged glances. Then Greer's hand went down, and Kal shifted in his chair until he was sitting as far away from her as possible.

Lance left while Elle was still processing how she had somehow been put in charge of a major part of a symposium that was already impossible to pull off. She was expected to shoulder it all. Plus do her actual job, which also included most of Lance's.

"Hey, Elle, I'd love to help, but I've got so much going on..." Steven said. Kal and Greer looked similarly regretful.

She didn't bother attempting to acknowledge them. Their department had been a team not long ago, when Edgar was in charge. He made sure they all had a voice. That things were fair.

That she had time to focus on her life's work, and not turn *this* work into her life.

Pete's story about his friend came rumbling back in her head. Could she do the minimum for the first time, maybe ever? Could she free herself from the burden and perhaps, even better, stick it to the man clearly planning to take all the credit without doing any of the work? The prospect warmed her insides in a good way. She'd have to figure out how, though. She needed plausible deniability. Maybe taking this approach would be good for her in the short and long run.

When she left the room, the glimmer of a thought sparked. She felt a little lighter, perhaps because it was so unlike her. But she was turning over a new leaf. If she was stepping out of one comfort zone, she might as well not stop there. As she walked down the hall, she wondered how hard it would be to get in touch with a Secret Service agent.

CHAPTER FIFTEEN

"Dr. Conroy." Agent Brockovich stepped out from behind the barricade at the Southwest gate not far from New York Avenue. "Do you mind walking?" he asked, wearing a long black coat to match his generic suit.

"Lead the way." The snow flurries floated through the air like confetti, and she pulled her knit cap down over her ears as they set off toward the White House. She suspected Ted had slowed his pace to match hers, but she appreciated it, considering she had been in an all-out sprint to get here. She'd gotten stopped in the office by Spencer groaning and grumbling about a student in 1113 who had looked at him like he had two heads after Spencer answered a question. Elle was already familiar with the exchange. That very same student had appeared at her door in tears hours before.

She wasn't sure what to do about Spencer. He was highly intelligent but lacked the social skills to make an effective instructor. His ultimate goal of becoming a tenured professor someday shocked her. She didn't want to discourage him; it had only been a month since they'd been forced together. But she had hoped he'd be a bit more adapted to teaching than he was at this point.

Agent Brockovich moved from one side to the other, and Elle realized it was so he could block the wind from pelting her. His chivalrous gesture touched her.

"Any more field trips since I was here last?" she asked.

A flicker of a smile twitched the corner of his mouth.

"That was a one-time thing. He's lucky I didn't get fired over that."

"But isn't he your boss?"

"Yes and no. The protocol is clear, and I broke it. If something would've happened…"

She nodded. He didn't need to tell her how bad things would be if something had gone wrong that night. But this was personal for Agent Brockovich since it was more than an assignment—it was his friend.

So many questions burgeoned in her head, things like how long they'd known each other, and which had come first, Ben's presidency or Ted's Secret Service job. She thought better of asking, assuming he wouldn't answer. She turned her attention toward the idyllic setting around them: The uncleared footpaths through the famed rose garden. Even blanketed by a thin layer of fresh powder, it was still magnificent. She almost hated leaving prints in it.

She shrugged as they approached the building and turned to walk alongside it. "You're welcome."

He angled his head down at her. "For what?"

"For not being an assassin or deranged lunatic. That wouldn't have turned out well for you… or him." She jerked her head toward the building rising up on her left.

He rewarded the joke with a smile. It softened the man's face, crinkling the skin up next to his eyes. He shook his head as he opened an unassuming door. "I can't believe I fell for that."

"I can. You're a serious guy."

"Aren't you supposed to be some kind of genius? I didn't think that came with a sense of humor."

"Touché, Agent Brockovich."

"Ted," he said opening a door.

Her footfalls echoed across the light gray tile. The room reminded her of the portico where she and Ben had sat during her last visit. The walls were covered in bright white lattice save for the oval cutouts that housed paintings that appeared to be old.

A door on the far side of the room opened, and Ben stepped out from beneath the arched doorway.

"Hey," he said with a little wave. Then he dropped the hand awkwardly.

She burst out laughing as embarrassment bloomed across his face.

Ted leaned close. "I swear he used to be a stud not long ago," he whispered not so quietly.

Her mouth fell open and Ben's cheeks reddened even more.

"And he used to be my best friend not long ago," Ben managed after clearing his throat. Ted shot him a devilish grin.

"We can all agree that the wave was uncool, but very cute." She turned to Ted. "Though I would like to hear more about this stud thing."

"Please don't." Ben stepped forward and held open the door. "How about we go inside and eat before I melt into the floor."

Ted shrugged. "That would be hard for me to detail in my report." He nodded at them both, then walked back out into the snow.

She followed Ben down a short hallway before stepping into a waiting elevator. It was small, the air steeped with wood, vanilla, and a hint of rosemary. Her stomach grumbled and she put her hand over it, hoping he hadn't heard. Her lunch had been a couple hard-boiled eggs and a side of leftover carrots from a veggie platter someone left in the break room. Hardly filling.

"I'll take that for you." Ben slid her coat off when they stepped out of the elevator. She pulled off her hat, static loosening the strands from her braid. She swiped her hand over it in a vain attempt to flatten it.

"I've got us set up in here." He ushered her into a dining room, hanging her coat and hat in a nearby closet. A very strange sensation rushed through her as she took in the space with its navy blue-and-cream striped wallpaper and dark wood furniture. This wasn't just any dining room; it was the White House. How many important people had stood in this very spot over the years? Her mind reeled with the possibilities, much like it had when she'd perched at a scope, gawking at faraway places.

The moss-green drapes over the windows were open, and the lights on the north lawn showcased the snow dancing outside. Traffic crawled past on Pennsylvania Avenue beyond the barricades. It all seemed a world away.

"I hope chicken parm was a safe choice." Ben charged back in with their plates. He placed them down and pulled out a chair for her. It was strange, this very formal-feeling dinner in such an intimate setting. In his *home*. In the White House.

She glanced at the dish. "It looks delicious."

"I've got a Riesling, a chardonnay, some reds?"

"Which do you recommend?"

His eyes pulsed for a beat, like he was considering something. "Full disclosure?"

She sat back. "Sure."

"I don't drink wine. Except when I have a meal with people who expect me to. And then I have whatever they're serving.

All I know about wine is that white is supposed to go with white meat, and red with everything else."

"I'm not sure that's accurate, but I can't prove you wrong."

He chuckled. "I'm a beer guy."

Something about him feeling comfortable enough with her to be so honest warmed her. It reminded her of that first night at the bar when the molecules in the air had connected so easily between them.

"I'd love a beer, actually."

He flashed that smile, then disappeared for what seemed like five seconds before returning with two bottles.

When he finally sat down opposite her, his eyes seemed to flicker. Maybe it was the way the corners crinkled when the apples of his angular cheeks lifted as he dipped his beer bottle toward her.

"Thanks for having dinner with me."

"If I knew you were pairing Kona Blue Wave with chicken parmigiana, I would have come back sooner." Attempting-to-flirt Elle was back tonight. Whether that was a good or bad thing remained to be seen.

"It's good to know I haven't completely forgotten how to woo a woman." His eyebrow lift and mischievous smile shuddered through Elle like a spreading wildfire. She took a sip of the beer, thrilled it was extra chilled.

The chicken was so tender her fork cut through it. The fettuccine noodles and creamy red sauce, with a perfect balance of oregano and garlic, tasted heavenly. She tried not to inhale it.

"This is so good," she managed between bites.

"One of my favorites." A piece of fettuccine slapped him in the chin and she closed her mouth over a laugh. "Obviously because I look so cool eating it." He smiled and sat back, wiping the line of sauce from his chin. "And of course I wore white, which guarantees I'll be wearing this at some point."

He swiped his napkin down the middle of the cream knit shirt that hugged his arms in all the right places.

They fell into easy conversation about everything and nothing. Arizona where he'd grown up. California where she'd gone to college. His mom's hair salon and her mom's bakery. It was comfortable, like she'd slipped into some alternate version of herself. One where she hadn't grown up a freak and wasted decades of her life on a project that would never get her the recognition or the job she wanted.

STAR was the pinnacle space agency—the best of the best. It spanned continents and every scope in the world (and beyond) was at its disposal. She had imagined so many times through the years where she would start off her fellowship. Perhaps, she'd get the much sought-after Mauna Kea in Hawaii. That's where she really wanted to go.

"... work going?"

She moved her gaze from her plate up to Ben's. Shit. She'd missed something again, lost in the space of her ever-winding brain.

"Sorry."

He laughed and cocked his eyebrow. "If you keep zoning out like that, I'm going to start taking it personally." He sipped from the bottle, and her eyes ratcheted to the way his lips sealed the opening. That definitely brought the moment thundering back into focus.

"Don't. I do it to everyone. Even my mother." Although Mom was usually rambling on about some customer who had a son who was smart and responsible and recently divorced. That was the territory she had now found herself in at the ripe age of thirty-eight—more men than not were going to be looking for seconds (or thirds). She shuddered and didn't even consider dipping a toe into that.

"I can start a fire if you're cold."

"Oh, no, I was just thinking... How are you single?"

That was not what she had been thinking. At least not consciously.

"Wow, out of the gate with a heavy hitter. I like it." He leaned forward and put his forearms on the table. "I'll tell you if you tell me."

"Tell you what?"

"How are you single? Was an astronaut forced to choose between you and deep space exploration that would keep him away from earth for decades?"

Ben had jokes. Good ones. She laughed and was rewarded with his smile.

"Nothing that dramatic."

He leaned back and held up a palm, inviting her to speak.

"I've spent a lot of time working. Personal stuff just seemed like an afterthought. It hasn't been a priority." Getting that fellowship was. Her work had been her first love. No one had ever come close to fulfilling her like it did.

He nodded, gaze locked onto hers.

"Plus," she continued, pushing what was left of her pasta around the sauce on her plate. "There aren't many men interested in someone like me."

"Men don't want a beautiful woman?"

She scoffed. "I don't think anyone would call me that. Besides my mom."

"I just did."

She swallowed hard and wiped her lips with her napkin. She cleared her throat. His gaze was intense, but not heavy. It did that thing again where he seemed to be peering deep inside her head, burrowing through with his eyes. She shook it off.

"You don't count. But thanks."

"Ouch. Friend-zoned before the first date is even halfway through. That might be a new personal best."

Her skin caught fire with embarrassment. She glanced to the window where the snow continued to flurry down and wondered if she would survive the jump.

"It's a lot higher than it looks," he said.

She cut her gaze back to his, mouth hung open. "Wh—, how... What?"

He let fly an uproarious sound that sent his body crumpling forward. His wide shoulders shook and his entire face lit from the exuberance escaping his mouth with each breath.

"I'm sorry," he managed between laughs. "But you have the cutest guilty look I've ever seen."

"Well, yeah, considering you caught me contemplating jumping out a window after embarrassing myself." She stood and dramatically huffed, dropping her napkin on the plate. "If you'll excuse me..." She marched toward the window, but before she could reach it, his hands were around her waist, turning her toward him.

"I wouldn't be much of a gentleman if I let you hurl yourself out a window. I appreciate the sentiment, though."

His breath singed the skin on her face, and that flame he'd sparked in her living room a month ago roared back, incinerating all the resolve she had built up, suggesting the only reason that had happened was because he was drunk, or desperate. The man who held her now was neither.

"That might be hard to explain."

"It would be." He brushed an errant strand of hair away from her cheek and tucked it behind her ear. The act was so soft and intimate, she inhaled the hops and rosemary from his breath mixed with the wood and citrus from his skin.

"Can I kiss you now? I haven't stopped thinking about it since last time." His whisper growled over her, reverberating through her chest.

She gulped and nodded. She gave into the charge between

them that grounded them in something nonsensical. She was a scientist who lived and breathed in black and white. What was happening between her and Ben was neither. It nestled steadfast in the gray, the part of life Dad taught her to keep a foot in with every suggestion she think differently about things.

Before their lips met, a knock at a door broke the spell. Ben glanced over his shoulder and back at her. "Let me see who that is. Be right back."

CHAPTER SIXTEEN

Ben's absence gave her time to come back to earth and talk herself out of doing anything else stupid, like kissing the president of the United States. In the White House. She killed the rest of her beer and gathered their dishes.

She pushed through the only other door and into a modest kitchen, unassuming in the scheme of things. It was pretty equal to her own—a reasonable size with all the modern touches. Nothing like she expected one at the White House to be.

Cleaning up the kitchen was a part of the baking process that had been drilled into her from a young age by both Grandma and Mom. Back then, it felt more like slave labor. But through the years, she found comfort in the routine. Making something messy better gave her a measure of control in a very uncontrollable world.

Wiping off the counters and scrubbing pans had allowed her time to think on more than one occasion. If baking soothed her, cleaning was the final step in a wind-down routine she'd adopted.

Ben came into the kitchen accompanied by a shorter man

wearing a three-piece tweed suit with a folder tucked under his arm.

Elle stopped wiping off the counter, feeling guilty about something she didn't have any reason to feel that way about. Ben shot her an apologetic look as the smaller man stepped forward.

"Dr. Ellery Conroy," he said, extending a hand. "Raymond Marshall, President Foster's chief of staff."

She took the hand and nodded. "It's nice to meet you."

"Likewise." He set the folder on the counter and spread his brown suit coat open, putting his hands on his hips. His pinched gaze explored her face. "Right, so I'll just come out with it." He clapped his hands together, opened the folder, then slid a packet across the counter. "This is a Non-Disclosure Agreement, Dr. Conroy. I trust you've heard of them before."

"Yes, of course."

"The president had a lapse in judgment last month when he left the security of his detail behind to engage in"—he gestured around with his right hand—"activities that put his life in jeopardy. Since you were a part of that, and apparently still are"—he moved his attention to Ben and shook his head—"we need your assurance that you will not disclose this information. Not about that night or the now two that have followed. The ones I had to find out about from the security team out front." His voice grew louder before falling silent.

"This is so unnecessary, Raymond," Ben said, shaking his head.

"Oh, no, it is. We discussed this."

"No. *You* discussed it. I listened because you cornered me and I didn't have a choice."

Raymond motioned toward Elle. "And apparently it warrants a third time because she's here. Again." Exasperation spread from Raymond to Ben, albeit for different reasons.

"Elle, you don't have to sign anythin—"

"To hell she doesn't. Do you know what will happen if any of *this* gets out?"

"Yes, Raymond. You've told me. Many, many times now." Ben's voice grew louder.

"And yet, here she is." He put his hands up in exasperation. Ben bent his head and turned away, walking to the small window at the back of the kitchen.

Elle lifted the papers and read through them. A bunch of legal jargon, which wasn't hard to figure out, but like so many of the studies she'd read, it contained a lot of unnecessary words to hide the real meat. In this case, it was about how she would never disclose, in writing or conversation, that she had ever met the President of the United States, Benjamin Foster, in any capacity other than an official visit, if applicable. If she was caught saying otherwise or disclosing the nature of their *relationship*, she'd be the subject of an injunction and lawsuit that could result in, among other things, any and all financial assets being seized, both those held individually and jointly. In other words, if it got out she and Ben were seeing each other (really, though, was that what was going on?), then he, or rather the government (she wasn't sure who exactly) would clean her out and leave her a pauper.

"I haven't told anyone," she said to Raymond.

"And this will protect President Foster if you change your mind."

"Jesus, Raymond, it won't cause World War III."

"No, but it will cause *other* problems you can't *afford*."

Ben shook his head and came back over. "You don't have to sign it, Elle. It's overkill, as far as I'm concerned."

Raymond did not like this interjection. "Mr. President. I implore you to rethink this course of action. As your chief of staff, I cannot protect you or maintain the integrity of your presidency if there is a danger that your private life gets exposed. It'll blow the lid off everything you're working toward accomplishing, including securing another term."

"That's almost three years away."

"It's around the corner. And if this"—he gestured towards Elle—"doesn't go well, you may not get a second chance."

Elle considered the pages in her hands. As if she wasn't overwhelmed with life enough, she was adding this into the mix. Sure, she had always been able to shoulder an immeasurable amount of pressure—it was second nature—but this seemed heavier. And it was unnecessary. It wouldn't get her any closer to STAR or help her figure out what to do about work, Spencer, or the symposium. In fact, it would serve as a distraction, much in the way Raymond likely felt she would be to Ben.

She opened her mouth to talk to Ben, but the sight of him looking so utterly torn and defeated took the words from her mouth. Was he, too, feeling the gravity between them as she had been? For her, it ran deeper than mere attraction, though that was definitely a factor. Who wouldn't want to roll around with a tall, sexy, chiseled (she imagined from their couch encounter) man who kissed her with a never-before-experienced intensity? Heat bubbled up from her core.

"Elle." Ben sighed. "I don't want you to have to go through all of this. I know it probably isn't worth it to you, and I don't blame you. It was ridiculous to think this could continue. I'm so sorry. You have enou—"

"I'll sign it."

He cocked his head and furrowed his brow. "Are you sure? Don't do it because you think I want you to. Because I don't."

She believed him. Before she could change her mind, or attempt to unravel what she was thinking, she had her hand out waiting for a pen.

"I've dealt with confidential information before with

research projects, studies, formulas. I know how this works." Raymond turned the pages and pointed to three spots where she had to initial or sign. She did it without another thought.

Raymond examined the pages and sighed the air out from between clenched teeth. He returned the papers to the folder and slid it under his arm.

"I think it would be best if we discuss expectations moving forward."

Ben raked his hand through his hair. "Jesus, Raymond. There's no *we* here."

"Everyone in this room has to be on the same page. You hired me to do a job—"

"That has nothing to do with my personal life—"

"Which you no longer have in the same capacity you once did, Mr. President. You knew the terms when you signed on. *All* of them."

Ben put his hands on his hips and dropped his head.

"My only concern," Raymond continued, "is to ensure that you have the best chance to leave your mark on this country and to do your job."

Ben scoffed. "Which I never wanted in the first place."

Elle held her breath. Ben never wanted to be president? That seemed like a revelation she shouldn't be hearing. When she thought back to the election, to the thoughtful way he spoke to people, and his genuine interest in them, all the empathy he displayed...it hadn't been an act. Mom had said more than once she didn't know why a man like Ben would ever want the burden of being president. And Pete had pointed out it was the exact reason why he would be perfect for the job.

Ben had an innate leadership quality. A quiet confidence. He was humble. A man who wanted to be president usually did so for the power and control. It was why so many chased it. Yet Ben, a man who came literally out of nowhere a couple of years ago, had bested all of them with humility, reason, kindness, and a moderate platform.

"I'm sorry. I shouldn't have said that." Ben laid a hand on Raymond's shoulder. "I don't want to argue."

The older man visibly softened. "But you know what's at stake. Are you willing to risk it? Your supporters..."

Something passed between the men. A quiet tension. Like Raymond wanted to say more and Ben needed him to say less. But neither could say all of it. It made her uneasy. It felt a lot like there was a secret, or at the very least, more to the conversation than what was being shared.

Ben nodded. Raymond sighed and hung his head for a beat before turning to face Elle.

"Do you plan on continuing to see him? Just tell me that. Because if you aren't even interested, then I'll walk you out, and we'll all go our separate ways. Pretend none of this happened."

Ben groaned from over his shoulder and dropped his head. "Not what I had in mind, Ray. Jesus Christ."

"I'm proactive and protective. It's what makes me good at my job." He readjusted the folder under his arm. "Dr. Conroy?"

Elle squeezed her toes and only then realized she hadn't been doing it all night. Not since she'd walked through the gate. Even during this conversation, where she was wildly uncomfortable, she hadn't been tense and her mind hadn't wandered. That didn't happen anywhere outside of her research, her kitchen, and the lecture hall. The three places she always felt comfortable. Guess this was now a fourth. Or at least being in Ben's presence was.

A weak smile appeared over Ben's face. Resigned. Accepting. His smile encouraged her to be honest. It was okay. He was letting her off the hook.

But that wasn't really what she wanted.

She met Ben's gaze. "I've never been on a tour of the White

House before. Maybe I could come back some other time, and you could give me one."

And that was the moment Elle chose to do something more insane than she'd ever done. She decided to sneak around and date the president.

Dear Edgar,

So much has happened since I last wrote. My mentee, Spencer, is giving me absolute hell. Did I do that to you? Challenge everything you ever tried to teach me? I don't think I did. I was more intimidated, whereas Spencer seems emboldened. Lance is certainly not helping. He's so far up Dean Piedmont's ass and too concerned with looking better than he is that he doesn't have time for things like actual work. He dumped the entire symposium on the rest of us.

We received somewhere close to 286 student applications for the 52 spots. I'm supposed to be the one who chooses. Me. I figured you'd get a good laugh at that given how I pull for every student to succeed. I'm trying to come up with a plan that'll get me through it without losing my mind. I've got some outside distractions that I want to spend time exploring, so I don't want even more work.

I hope to hear from you soon. Someone said they'd seen your picture in a post and that gave me some measure of comfort that you're doing well.

With love,

Elle

CHAPTER SEVENTEEN

She sent the message and thought maybe she shouldn't have included the distraction part since that alluded to a certain man she wasn't supposed to talk about. Knowing Edgar like she did, though, he would assume it meant something about her family or another research project she'd decided to take on.

She sighed and set her head back against the chair. Ben was leaving for a European summit today and wouldn't return for ten days. But when he bid her goodbye in the Palm Room the other night with a full-body, lingering hug, he had placed his soft lips against her cheek and promised he would get in touch soon about that tour.

The prospect made her heart lurch in all the good and wildly unfamiliar ways. She'd been in relationships before, though none had ever started out in quite this way. They usually involved another scientist whom she'd worked with. At some point, it morphed from simply collegial to dating. She couldn't recall any that had made her want to throw away her life. Ben wasn't doing that, but per the terms of the NDA, which Raymond had reminded her about at least three more times before she'd left, if anyone found out about them, it would certainly destroy everything she'd built.

Which was...what exactly? She'd been turning that over in her mind in the quiet space between lectures and meetings and sleep. Her research wasn't as groundbreaking as she had hoped, and her theory wasn't worth a damn. Her chances of ever landing at STAR grew fainter by the year, what with all the up-and-coming scientists, like Spencer, hot on her tail. Which is what she wanted and how it should be. Dad had always reminded her how infinite and unimaginable space was. There was room for her and for everyone else who came before and after. Though at the moment, it certainly didn't feel like it.

She would remain in this box of science professor. No more. No less. She had to start accepting she was not nearly as qualified as she'd once believed. She was mediocre. She wouldn't discover anything groundbreaking or be on the cusp of a brilliant breakthrough. Perhaps she should stick to helping others be what she couldn't. Dad would be disappointed, though really, as Edgar would remind her if he were here, it was not her place to please a parent who had kept her from reaching her full potential.

"What's up with you this week?" Janet walked in.

Elle shook the heaviness from her head. "Nothing. Just got a lot going on."

Janet cocked her right eyebrow. "You always do. This is different."

"It's really not. All this extra work with the symposium is bogging me down."

"Right, but you aren't baking." Janet put her hands on her hips.

"I've been sleeping more." Mostly true. She'd also been daydreaming about a certain man and what the rest of that tattoo might look like.

"Yeah, that's a good thing for you. But it means I've got to plan on getting breakfast elsewhere."

Elle smiled. "No matter what, I'll bring in your favorite muffins Monday. Remind me which ones they are this month?"

Janet stopped. "Something with chocolate. It's almost Valentine's Day." Then she waltzed out the door.

Elle went back to her email, intent on clearing out the unreads before Spencer came in. They'd had another chat yesterday about the way he handled a student question. It did not go well. It wasn't because he took it personally. That was the problem. He didn't. He couldn't fathom that she might be right, and he was wrong. It was new territory for him, not being right all the time. And that was proving to be a steep learning curve.

So when someone knocked, she assumed it was him.

"Did you get a chance to go through those short answers yet?" she said, and readied herself for battle while finishing up an email.

"I have no idea what you're talking about."

The tenor of the voice drew Elle's attention right up to Ted's face.

"Oh... I... Hi." She scanned his dressed-down appearance. Jeans and a Rolling Stones concert shirt that had seen better days. She glanced back toward her open door and stood up.

"Aren't you supposed to be traveling?" she whispered.

"I will be. In about an hour."

"You don't look like it."

He glanced down at his clothes, as if he didn't remember what he'd been wearing.

"How am I supposed to look?"

"Like you always do. The suit. The tie. The, you know"—she pointed to her ear—"phone cord."

He nodded slowly. "I'm not on duty."

"I didn't think you were ever off duty?"

"I don't live with Ben."

She glanced back at the door; Spencer could come in any minute. "Don't say that. What if people heard?"

"They'd think I have a job for someone named Ben. And they'd be right." He reached in his pocket and held up a phone. "This is why I'm here."

"To show me your phone?"

He closed his eyes and shook his head. "You know, for someone who's so smart—"

"I never said that. Everyone assumes it."

"It's for you and Ben."

Oh. She hadn't considered...

"You can't use yours because of security protocols and what-not. But this one is encrypted. No one can intercept the messages." He held it out for her to take, which she did, although very gingerly like it might—

"It's not going to explode," he said.

She grabbed it with more certainty and turned it over in her hand. "I knew that." But the short nod and little grin lifting the right side of his face told her he was not buying it.

"Set a strong password, something different from all your other ones."

"And then...we'll be able to, like, talk?"

He nodded. "That's typically what happens with a phone."

She rolled her eyes and groaned. "You're a real comedian."

"Been called worse. You can text, too. No email. No internet."

"It's practically archaic."

She hadn't considered it might be weird for two people who were kind-of-maybe-almost-dating to only talk on the rare opportunities they saw each other. Occasions arranged through a hulking third party whose visits to her office were going to become noticeable because he wasn't as invisible as he should have been. At least not around there.

Spencer cleared his throat from the door. She glanced past Ted to see him cradling his iPad against his chest, eyes wide and trained on Ted.

"That's my cue to leave." Ted dipped his head toward her.

"Thanks, Ted," she managed, and he walked out. His hulking stature cast a large shadow over Spencer as he passed.

"Who was that beast?" Spencer asked, dropping into the chair.

"No one." She put the phone down and sat. Spencer pulled out the folder she'd given him to keep his assignments in order. The one he complained about every single time she called him out for not having it. He produced it from his leather briefcase with extra flair, no doubt for her benefit.

"Why were you whispering to him?" Spencer cocked his head and squinted. "If it was no one."

The urge to rip the folder out of his hands was hard to fight against. Instead she merely put her hand out and waited for him to hand it over.

"Are these the short answers on the galaxy exam for 1101?" Ignoring him was her best course of action.

He scrunched his nose, something she'd noticed he did just before he was about to give an opinion she didn't want to hear.

"Yes, and they're horrible."

Of course they were.

"Be more specific. Like did most of the class answer a particular one wrong?" She flipped open the folder and scanned the first couple of answers. Spencer had marked them up so heavily she had to fight to see through the red.

"They don't understand anything. They're unintelligent as a whole."

He was marking them off for every single mistake, even little ones. The student who didn't capitalize Mars. The one who misidentified Hale-Bopp as Halle-Bop.

She closed the file and folded her hands on the desk.

"Spencer, if they didn't get anything right, then that's *our* fault, not theirs."

He shook his head and lifted his iPad and pen. "It's not my fault they aren't smart."

"You're not understanding."

"I understand everything on that test."

She sighed, but the exasperation drilled into her chest. "Spencer—"

A vibration from her desk startled her. The phone from Ted lit up with a message from "Just Ben." A smile tickled her lips.

"Do you need to get that?" Spencer asked.

She dropped the phone into her bag and cleared her throat. "No. But I do need you to put your iPad down so we can go over these one by one and see where I would have marked them differently than you."

He rolled his eyes and mumbled, "Spoon-feeder."

"Excuse me?"

"You baby them. And not just the freshmen. It's everyone. The upper levels don't understand the difference between a quasar and a quark unless you're there to give them some cutesy way to remember."

The frustration in her body became something harsher. Spencer was accusing her of not being a good teacher and letting her students flounder so she could, what? Swoop in and save them during a test or a quiz or project? No. This accusation was outside the bounds of his normal discourse; it was insulting and infuriating.

"I see by your reaction that you don't believe I'm right," he continued. "But I am. You have spent too much time making things easy for them, so when someone like me—someone more *advanced* comes in and challenges them, they shut down and don't make the grade. You're doing them no favors."

"Wow, that is a helluva thing to say to me, the person who needs to write you a recommendation after this semester." Her skin burned from the inside out. The fire alarms would surely start blaring at any second.

His nose wrinkled. "I think the students need someone willing to instruct them on a level that they believe they're getting, but aren't. From you. Perhaps you have been distracted with Dr. Linton leaving or your, what, *third* rejection from STAR. Or with your feud with Dr. Dunwoody. The symposium. Any number of factors that are impacting your judgment and ability to instruct the students in a manner they need to compete for upper-level educations and jobs."

She squeezed her toes so hard inside her shoes she was sure they'd burst through the soles. How dare this *kid* sit in her office, the one she'd *earned* and not been *handed* by anyone, and lecture *her* on the right way to handle *her* students. All measures of brevity and latitude she'd given Spencer over the last month were shot to hell. She no longer wanted to guide him or help him. She wanted to be done with him.

She stood, snapping up the folder. "Spencer, take the rest of the day off. I need to handle a few things."

"I don't want to take time off."

She scoffed. This little shit still believed she was just going to give him what he wanted? Even though she hadn't. Instead, she gave him what she thought he needed to guide him toward being a better instructor, and thereby a better scientist. But apparently she had been wrong.

"We'll regroup first thing Monday morning."

She set off out the door and waited for him to follow. He

huffed and rose, slinging his briefcase over his shoulder and tapping on his iPad.

After she locked her door, she set out for Dean Piedmont's office, hell-bent on this being the last time she and Spencer would lock horns.

CHAPTER EIGHTEEN

The lobby in the dean's building bustled with current students, parents and their prospective children, and professionals who were alums or hopeful future partners of the university. The three deans shared one administrative assistant and several work-study students who were working feverishly.

"Dr. Conroy." Darsha spoke up from behind a stack of mail.

"Hi, Darsha. Any chance Dean Piedmont is free?"

The young woman leaned forward. "He's between appointments, so you might want to move fast."

Elle tossed her a smile and set off, booking it down the hallway, as Dean Piedmont was closing his door.

"Dean Piedmont," she called from a few steps away.

He stopped and his face brightened. "Elle. What a surprise. I didn't think we had an appointment."

"We don't," she said. "I was hoping to catch you for just a few minutes."

He glanced down at his watch, then opened his door wide for her. She dipped her head and moved to the sitting area, sinking into a plush leather chair.

"What can I do for you?" he asked from the seat opposite.

His large dark eyes drooped at the corners, his tan face open and welcoming.

"I hate coming to you, but I'm not sure what else I can do…" She felt gross saying this, like she was some helpless child running to a parent. But she wiped that from her mind. "I'm having a lot of difficulties with Spencer Draisson."

He tilted his head thoughtfully, his brow wrinkling. "How so?"

She inhaled and then unloaded. She didn't hold back. Not about Spencer's constant undermining or his challenging of her authority. His complaints about the way she conducted her classes. When she proffered the folder as evidence, Dean Piedmont sifted through the pages while she wrapped up her diatribe. His face remained impassive, and she'd fallen silent before he closed the folder and handed it back.

He leaned back in his chair, crossing his ankle over his knee. "What would like me to do?"

"Reassign him to someone else."

"So you don't want or need a TA?"

"I do. But I would like to pick my own, just like everyone else." She'd had students lining up for years. She always had more volunteers than spots.

He turned his head and gazed out the window. The silver was winding its way through his wavy raven hair. "I think this might be more of a you issue than a Spencer issue."

His sharp rebuke hit her between the eyes. "How so exactly?" She had laid out all the facts in a precise, methodical, and logical fashion.

"You can't control everything, Elle. It's impossible."

She blinked and reared her head back. "No one knows that more than I do. That's not what I'm doing here."

"No?" he leaned forward. "It sounds like it to me. You're

indicating your workload is heavy, but you won't give Spencer anything meaningful to do."

"Because he isn't ready." Her voice was a little louder than intended. Frustration coursed through her chest.

"But his credentials say otherwise." Dean Piedmont's voice was even. "He is more than qualified and ready. I don't think you want him to be."

Had she failed in presenting her case...again? How was a reasonable, intelligent, and sensible man like Dean Piedmont not able to understand what was going on? She had given him the evidence, right there in black, white, and red! But somehow this was her fault? So many words begged to push out they clogged up her throat, making it impossible for her to do much more than stare back.

"You need to make a choice, Elle. You can either utilize Spencer and give him the responsibility befitting his intelligence. Or you can continue to keep him on a short leash and get dragged around until May. Sometimes, you have to let people be who they need to be and not try to change them."

"That's not... He doesn't have the social skills to connect with the students. He's alienating them and making me..."

When he glanced at his watch, Elle knew he had stopped listening. She stood and moved toward the door. He trailed behind.

"Thank you for your time," she mumbled, the disgust and defeat raw and sour.

"You may not believe this, but you're the best person to help Spencer through this transition. I think if you trust him a bit and let go, you'll see that he can handle it."

That didn't sound like a ringing endorsement of her ability and skills. In fact, it sounded to Elle like he was dismissing her as so many other men throughout her career and life had—too emotional and therefore irrational. This was why she never opened up. Didn't trust people enough to share real feelings in a male-dominated field where she'd had to work four times harder, faster, and longer than her counterparts to gain a modicum of respect or advancement.

Dean Piedmont fell in line with all the others who had dismissed her concerns through the years, acting as if she wasn't strong or worse, *smart* enough to handle it. *She* was always the one who needed to change. Dad had stitched that sentiment into her childhood heart, and it remained tender to this day.

If Dean Piedmont believed she wasn't up to the task of dealing with Spencer, she would have to do what she always did —prove him wrong.

CHAPTER NINETEEN

Elle sighed the heaviness from her chest, though all the breathing in the world wasn't going to magically take it away. She sat in her office, chair turned toward the night sky darkening her windows, attempting to do what she could to decompress. She should go home. Drag her old scope out of the spare room and escape the bounds of the world. Even that felt hard right now. It would only remind her of how her own life-long search for answers and purpose had failed.

It was hard to get lost like she used to when she believed in herself and her ability to find meaning in the chaos of space. She hadn't finished licking her wounds from rejection, and honestly, she might never. For now, all she could do was keep her head down and get through the next few months.

Her phone buzzed with a message.

Pete: Meet me at the storage unit tomorrow?

Elle: Do I have to?

Pete: Don't make me come over and get you.

Elle: Who says I'll be home?

Pete: Ellery…

The last thing she wanted or needed was to go digging

through Dad's things. So far they'd gone twice and hadn't made much progress. Pete acted like it was a treasure hunt while she preferred to leave it buried.

Elle: Fine. I'll meet you at 9:00. Bring the good coffee.

It was already 10:00 p.m. She shook the haze of a heavy day away and packed her stuff. Her phone vibrated again, but when she lifted it, there were no new messages. Odd. She dropped it into her bag and only then did she see a light at the bottom from...the other phone.

She slipped it out, her finger hovering before tapping the screen. Four unread messages. She'd never read the first, Ted's visit now a distant memory in an otherwise forgettable day. She pinched her lip between her teeth and dove in.

11:01 a.m. **Just Ben:** Hi! <insert awkward wave> I hope it's okay to do this. It means you'll have two phones, but hopefully people won't assume you're a drug dealer.

12:36 p.m. **Just Ben:** I was joking about the drug dealer thing. Unless, wait, are you? Juggling three phones seems harder.

2:47 p.m. **Just Ben:** Full disclosure: I'm not a scientist. So I need your expertise. I'm on the plane and there is a blue line on the horizon. Is that the atmosphere? (Please don't hate me for asking a stupid question.)

10:01 p.m. **Just Ben:** I hope you've had a busy day and haven't chucked this phone because you decided *this* was a bad idea or my dumb question annoyed you. Was it the drug dealer joke? Have you been arrested!? Know that I will miss you no matter what the reason.

She smiled, easing the pressure in her chest. She fired back a response before she could think too hard about it.

Elle: Hi. Sorry it's been a busy day. Full disclosure—I'm not a drug dealer. And I haven't destroyed this phone…yet. To answer your science question, which is not stupid in the least; the blue you're seeing is likely the reflection of the sun off the water creating a haze in the curvature of the earth. BUT the atmosphere does appear blue from a much higher height—like from space. Maybe your plane can fly that high. What do I know. I'm but a lowly science professor and not an aerospace engineer.

She hit send and slipped the phone in her pocket before heading home. She wasn't even out of the building when he responded.

Just Ben: Whew. I was really worried I'd lost you. Who else would answer my questions in such a thoughtful way.

Elle: I'm sure you could find someone.

Just Ben: Yes, but none will be as cute as you. <insert goofy look here>

Elle: Why don't you use emojis?

Just Ben: Is that something that a 42-year-old man does?

Elle: My brother crafts entire messages using only emojis.

Just Ben: I'll put it on my to-do list. Are you having a nice night at least?

Elle: I actually just left work.

She'd been so absorbed in their messaging she barely realized the bite of the cold as it nipped her ears. She pulled the coat around her tighter as the phone vibrated in her hand. Only this time it was a call. A fresh sprig of nerves lurched through her chest.

"Ah, hi," she said.

"I figured if you were on your way home this might be better." His voice against her ear immediately set her stomach fluttering. "With the dangers of texting and walking and all."

"Full disclosure?"

"Full disclosure."

"I walked into a pole a couple months ago texting a student. It was not pretty."

He laughed. Elle couldn't help but smile, with each resounding bellow that echoed through the phone. She could listen to his laugh all night.

"I'm sorry," he said, finally catching his breath. "But I can't believe you admitted that."

"I thought that's what full disclosure meant between us."

"It does. Total honesty, no matter what. Hang on. I'm in an elevator."

She'd wondered where he was. She only knew he was going to Europe. They hadn't had a ton of time or privacy to talk after Raymond barged in and never left.

"I'm back. I didn't want to cut out on you."

"Where are you right now?"

"Geneva."

She stopped short feet from her front walkway. "Switzerland?"

"Geneva, New York would be a strange place for a European summit. But it would be a lot more convenient." A rhythmic thud pattered through the phone.

"What time is it there?"

"Just after four—"

"In the *morning*?!" That thud continued. "Why are you up talking to me?"

He chuckled. "Well, for one I always get up around four."

"I can't imagine doing that intentionally."

"It's the best time to run."

He got up that early to *exercise*? That seemed like a waste of perfectly good sleep time.

"Are you running right now?"

"Yup. You don't mind coming along, do you?"

"You're barely out of breath." She pushed into her foyer, tossed her keys on the table and dropped her bag on the couch.

"If you stay on with me long enough, that'll change."

The prospect of him breathing heavy struck her as very sexy. She cleared her throat and made her way to the fridge, pulling out two sticks of butter.

"So you're just, like, trotting through the streets of Geneva alone right now at"—she pulled out three eggs and glanced at the clock on the microwave—"4:16 in the morning."

"Ted and some other guys are with me, but yeah. It's peaceful."

"The country is not paying those guys anywhere near enough." She shook her head like he could see her and pulled out the flour and sugars from the pantry. "You and I have very different definitions of peaceful. Why anyone would choose to run is beyond my understanding." She unstacked her mixing bowls.

"It helps me keep a clear head. Especially when I can run outside. You've got to have something like that, too, don't you?"

She looked down at her counter. Without any sort of conscious thought, she'd assembled baking ingredients.

"I do. But you can't laugh."

He exhaled into her ear. "I make no promises."

"When I need to clear my head or work something out...I bake." Did that sound as insane to him as it did to her?

"You're a stress baker."

"Yes. And I bring in what I make to work. Or in the case of tomorrow, to my brother."

"You work out your stress by doing something for other people. That's really cool."

Huh. She hadn't thought about it that way before. "I guess I do."

"Your brother... Pete, right?"

"Good memory."

He chuckled, his breath coming heavier. "The running works wonders. For my mind and body."

The whisk slipped from her fingers and splashed the egg wash back at her.

"Everything okay?" he asked

"Yeah, I dropped something. I can't do two things at once." *Like whisk eggs and think about your body...* "Meanwhile, you've already run, what, half a mile or something." She wiped at the splatters on the counter.

"A little more than a mile so far."

"It's been five minutes!"

"That's about my pace for the first three or four miles at least." He huffed. "So what are you making for Pete?"

"Cinnamon roll muffins. My grandma's recipe."

"God, that sounds amazing. Think you could make it the next time we see each other?"

The excitement of seeing him again bubbled up. A jolt of electricity shot up from the butterflies in her stomach.

"I'll make whatever you want." She was fairly sure that sounded desperate.

"It's a date. Full disclosure: I have a wicked sweet tooth."

"You certainly don't look like you do." A flame burned her

cheeks and she closed her eyes, hoping he didn't take it the wrong way.

"To be fair, you don't look like a rocket scientist."

"That's the second time you've called me that. I don't know what gave you that idea."

"Dual PhDs in physics and astronomy."

She stopped mid-sift and put her hand on her hip. "You've been checking up on me?"

He laughed, his breath coming faster. "You caught me. Actually it wasn't me who did the checking, it wa—"

"Raymond. Of course." The ultimate gatekeeper. She shook her head and sighed, resuming her work.

"I didn't look at the file. Told him to keep it to himself and walked away. He followed me out the door spouting off random things."

She stirred the sifted flour and the sugars. "Anything scandalous?"

"Just that there are signs you might have a thing for unavailable men."

She stopped mid-stir. She had nothing. Ben had just robbed her of the ability to speak. Unavailable men...was that true?

Then in between pants, Ben started laughing. "I can imagine your face right now with that cute red band streaking across it."

She swiped at her cheek. "You have a tendency to leave me speechless, Ben Foster."

"That makes two of us, Ellery Conroy. I haven't met anyone quite like you."

Women like her weren't exactly traveling in the packs that surrounded beefy military studs with tattoos and war stories to swap. That was more Tabitha's realm than Elle's.

It was getting a little harder for him to talk. She had the feeling he would not be the one to hang up. Not if she was willing to go along on the run with him, which exhausted her just thinking about. The man was a machine... and thinking of *that* was not so exhausting.

"I should go. I have to use the mixer."

"Of course, yeah. Hey, thanks for talking to me. It made my whole morning."

"Mine, too. Well, my night."

He chuckled. "Mind if I message you tomorrow?"

"Such a gentleman. I would love that."

"I don't know any other way to be."

Her heart squeezed. "Have a good night. No, wait. Have a good day."

He chuckled softly. "Goodnight, Elle. Sweet dreams."

She hung up and gazed into the muffin batter. That was a guarantee tonight.

CHAPTER TWENTY

Elle's weekend had looked a little different, in large part because she and Ben had texted and talked several times. On Saturday morning, during her time at the storage unit, he had sent her a picture of the Musée d'histoire des sciences in Geneva and she almost dropped her phone.

Elle: OMG did you actually go inside?

Just Ben: Not yet. Here at an event on the grounds. It's beautiful!

Elle: I did a book report in middle school on Jacques-André Mallet, and since then, I've kind of been obsessed with the place.

Just Ben: Don't mind me…just Googling who that is…

Elle: I'll quiz you on it later.

She giggled, which elicited the attention of her brother.

"Who's that?" Pete tossed aside another empty box.

"No one." She put away the phone and went back to shuffling through papers. More case files and notes. The usual manila envelope with mini cassettes labeled with matching case numbers and dates.

"Does Mom have Dad's mini recorder?" she asked Pete, not meaning to change the subject, but effectively doing so.

"Don't know. I haven't asked. I'm sure she does. He never went anywhere without it." The distraction worked and Pete started digging through more boxes.

Elle couldn't recall a time when Dad didn't have that little black recorder in his pocket or on a nearby table. "It was like a third hand. Remember how he used to pretend to interview us?"

"He only did that with you, genius."

"No, he didn't."

Pete stood up and brushed some hair off his forehead. The rings under his eyes were darker than even last week, and reminded her of the Black Eye Galaxy.

"Elle, he never pulled that recorder out for anyone else. Just you and the criminals."

Dad used to set that recorder between them and ask her about her day. He'd always start his pretend interview off with a date and time stamp, and then some variation of, "So tell me, Future Doctor Ellery Lincoln Conroy, what theory are you working on proving tonight?" She'd giggled when she was little and rolled her eyes when she was a teenager. That last day she talked to him in hospice, when she'd finally shared the details of her research project with him, he'd posed the same question. "Tell me, Dr. Ellery Lincoln Conroy, soon-to-be director of something important at STAR. What theory are you working on proving tonight?" And she'd prefaced her answer in the way she'd done since she could remember—

"Way to try and change the subject," Pete said.

She jerked back from her long-ago buried memories.

"I didn't! There's nothing to tell."

He chuckled. "You are so full of shit. You giggled at your phone, Elle. That's not nothing."

She opened another box, unleashing an errant piece of paper. She jumped up and stomped her boot down to catch it.

"It was a meme."

"It was a man. And I'm going to sic Brody on you tomorrow. He'll wear you down." He pointed his finger at her and grinned before stooping for another box.

That had been the end of the exchange with Pete Saturday. Though she could feel the phone vibrating in her pocket a time or two while they were together, she hadn't dared touch it, for fear her brother would reach over and snatch it.

Unfortunately, Pete made good on that promise with Brody. The next day at the bakery the little boy greeted her and commenced rapid-firing questions that all had to do with who she was talking to the day before. Elle swatted the baseball cap off Pete's head after he high-fived Brody, which drew Mom's attention.

"Aunt Lelly laughed at the phone yesterday and Daddy said it was at a boy."

Mom's face lit up, mouth parting with a toothy smile, and Elle, unable to contain the frustration and embarrassment aimed at Pete, grumbled louder than she should have. "It was a MEME. Nothing else. Stop picking on me!"

Brody stroked her hand with his lollipop-sticky fingers. "Poor Aunt Lelly. Daddy, leave her alone," Brody fired over his little shoulder to Pete who had doubled over laughing. Then Brody looked up at her, eyes full of four-year-old empathy. It eased her frustrated heart and turned her to putty.

She avoided her phone the rest of the afternoon except for stolen moments in the bathroom. She'd fired off a quick response or tried not to laugh at one of his attempts at impressing her with history and odd facts about Geneva, like a picture of the longest bench in the world (413 feet!) with Ted sitting alone in the middle doing his best Forrest Gump impression.

After a full afternoon and evening with her family (minus Tabitha, whose absence was noted a couple of times by Mom but shrugged off by Pete), Elle returned home to bake Janet's muffins and hopefully work out her Spencer problem. Ben had gone off to bed a few hours before, and Elle considered sending him a message about her situation to get his opinion. But then she discarded the idea as quickly as it had come. She would figure it out herself, as she always did.

A few minutes after 10:00 p.m., she had flipped off the lights in the kitchen and was headed upstairs to bed when the phone rang from the charger.

She scurried back and snatched it from the counter.

"Good morning." She tried to keep cool, like her chest wasn't heaving with the nightly wave of excitement brought by his phone calls. This was the third night in a row, and Elle realized she had been looking forward to it, but didn't want to admit it.

"Hey, care to join me on my run again?" The cadence of his footfalls across a sidewalk on the other side of the world pattered along with her heart.

"Sure. But know that when we're back in the same time zone, this no longer works for me."

He laughed. "Understood. So tell me about your day."

So went most of their conversations. She talked about her family, leaving out the incessant teasing at the hands of her brother and by proxy, Brody. Ben asked thoughtful questions, and then shared a bit about his day with her.

Elle lay in bed, tucked in under the covers. She'd cracked the window, a practice she'd done forever in the winter to keep her room as cold as possible. "I like it close to meat locker, but with lots of blankets," she'd told him.

He'd agreed that sleeping cold was way better, and then filled her in on the suite in the hotel where the walls were so thin he could hear his detail burp in the next room. She laughed harder than she probably should at that, picturing Ben lying in bed and being unable to sleep because of bodily noises.

Before she realized it, an hour and a half had passed, and Ben was making his way back up to his room. He'd opted to take the stairs, which she said was ridiculous for someone who'd been running for so long. But the squeak of his shoes and the huff in his words turned her on way too much.

"You probably want to get to sleep since you have work tomorrow," he said.

She groaned in response.

He continued. "That's not a ringing endorsement."

"I'm sorry. I didn't used to be like this."

"So what changed?"

She sighed. So much. If she started spouting all the things that were wrong, she might never stop and he would surely never ask again. He was the president—his job issues outweighed hers by a solar system.

"Did you make it back to your room yet?"

He chuckled as a beep and then a door closing echoed through the phone. "You like to change the subject a lot."

"No, I don't." Even she couldn't feign outrage.

"You never want to tell me about your job, or what's really on your mind."

"It's nothing important, that's why. No big deal." To him or anyone else. "Especially compared to what you're doing."

"I guarantee that's not true," he said.

"You're delusional."

"Okay, fine. I'll prove it to you." Something muffled against the phone and then he was back. "Check your messages."

She pulled the phone away and opened their text string.

She gasped and the phone flew out of her hands tumbling onto the bed and landing on the floor. She scrambled to retrieve it, but the call had hung up. She opened the string again to the picture of him, standing in the middle of a bathroom, hair wild and wet with sweat, a thick layer of stubble blanketing his jaw. A black long sleeved dry fit shirt clung to every curve of every muscle (and there were a lot) over his arms and chest. She was breathless until the phone rang and made her jump.

"Hi...hey...I—uh. I dropped the phone." She closed her eyes and pinched her lips between her teeth.

"That was one hell of a way to change the subject." He chuckled. "But as my picture demonstrates, I am doing nothing important. So hit me. What is it about work that's changed and makes you dread it?"

His logic was only slightly flawed. "You know I wasn't talking about right now. Your job as a whole is, like, bigger than anything else."

"That doesn't mean your problems aren't important to me."

"Ben." She shook her head and climbed back into bed. "I'm not dumping anything out on you in the midst of a summit that has something to do brokering peace between Russia and Ukraine. Warring countries trump professor's stupid work issues all day every day."

She wouldn't apologize for trying to spare Ben the mundane details of her life. In the process, she'd also be sparing herself from the humiliation that followed in the wake of any openness. Recent example: Dean Piedmont.

Ben sighed in her ear. "Full disclosure?"

"Full disclosure."

"You make me feel like I have a normal life, and that I'm not carrying the expectations of an entire country on my shoulders. I know, it's stupid because I had to chase this job, but it wasn't one I ever wanted."

She swallowed hard. His voice seeped with sadness and, maybe, regret? She understood that all too well.

"So why did you do it?" she asked. She'd been wondering since he made that comment to Raymond.

"Because how could I not? This country was so divided. It still is. Everyone against each other in a way that we haven't experienced since the Civil War. So much hate. I spent twenty years on active duty, fought around the world, lost a lot of friends, all to preserve an ideal that was crumbling. I couldn't sit back and let it keep happening. Someone needed to step up. I never in a million years wanted it to be me."

His sacrifice—then and now—and the sincerity with which he spoke touched her. He didn't turn away from the path he was called to walk. He doubled down.

He continued. "My dad lived, breathed, and eventually died for this country. He never wanted me to serve. Military life is hard and he made me promise when I was eight that I wouldn't do it. But, after he was gone, I had to break that promise because it was what I needed to do. To grieve him. To honor him. He'd shake his head and tell me, 'I told you so,' if he was here to see me now."

Elle choked out a laugh. But she understood what it meant to grow up with a parent like that. Who devoted themselves to serving others. Who only wanted better for their kids. But did Ben's dad also try to change who he was out of shame like hers had?

"I'm sure he'd be beyond proud. And that isn't just about the job." She swallowed hard. All she'd ever wanted to do growing up was make Dad happy. She did, in some ways, but also knew she had disappointed him in many others.

"Yeah, well. Anyway. That's why I want you to share more of your world. Or any of it. I like hearing you talk about what matters to you."

Interesting, since she no longer knew what mattered anymore.

"But you're off the hook for now. I've got to get ready for the day. Raymond will be here soon, so if I don't take a shower now, I'm afraid he'll jump in with me and keep talking."

She laughed at the thought of Raymond reading from a yellow legal pad while Ben was in the shower. The water dropping down over every ripple and bulge. And the suds...

"That's a very interesting visual to leave me with." She cleared her throat.

"I hope that's more about me being in the shower than Raymond."

"I—...uh..." She sunk down lower under the covers like he was there, seeing the red creeping up her neck at being caught absolutely thinking about what he looked like naked and wet.

She closed her eyes as the sound of his laughter washed through her.

CHAPTER TWENTY-ONE

Sleep didn't come easy that night. She kept staring at the picture Ben had sent while replaying their conversation. How personal he'd gotten. How much she'd avoided doing the same. Opening up to anyone was hard. There was the surface Elle, the easy stuff, that made up most of her side of their conversations. But then there was the rest of her that she could not delve into with him or anyone else.

Her thoughts eventually turned to her conundrum at work, and she drifted off ruminating about how she could fix it. On her way to work Monday morning, she turned over the prospect of giving Spencer the two upper-level classes and the respective lab that he wanted. Most of those students had been with her from their intro classes and would still come to her if they had issues.

But that made her heavy with guilt. She believed he wasn't ready for that, and so as she walked down the hall toward her office and saw Spencer's wiry frame looming, she put that thought out of her mind.

"Morning, Spencer. Did you have a good weekend?" She flicked on the lights and stripped off her heavy coat. Jim from meteorology had sent a message that morning to the group of weather-interested faculty members (she didn't remember joining the list) warning of the bitter freezing temps the city was in store for that afternoon.

Spencer nodded stiffly but said nothing. He stood next to the chair by her desk as she sat down.

He wrinkled his nose. "Dr. Conroy, I'm very unhappy with the way you have been handling my concerns."

"I'm sorry to hear that." She wasn't. As she tried to escape into her head to review all she had on her plate that morning, an idea finally sparked that might solve all of her problems.

"And I've been thinking." She leaned forward and folded her hands. "I agree that you should be taking on more responsibility. That's why I want you to take the student applications for the symposium."

He blinked. A lot. His feather cowlick danced.

"I was not expecting that." He sat down and pulled out his iPad.

"Maybe I haven't been fair to you. You are an extremely intelligent person, and I can accept that I've been thinking about this the wrong way."

She'd been worried too much about doing what was best for Spencer, rather than following along with the department status quo instituted by Lance, namely, doing what was best for *her*.

"All of those statements are true. Your mishandling has been troublesome."

He was not making it easy to maintain her poise. She curled her toes and pressed on.

"The applications will give you a larger sample of the students in the department. And it'll really help Dr. Dunwoody and the reputation of the university." She threw those last two in to sweeten the pot. It worked.

His eyebrows arched high and he gripped his iPad, but he didn't tap it.

"Excellent." He nodded enthusiastically. "I will get on it right away." He went to move but she stopped him with a wave.

"We have room for fifty-two student projects. Maybe choose an additional four as alternates."

He tapped on his screen while she continued. "They should have something to do with theme of innovation, collaboration, and exploration. You'll have latitude with how to interpret that."

She scrawled the name and number of the tech professor on a sticky note and handed it to him.

"You'll need to get your own username and password for the symposium portal from Dr. Patel. You can either drop by his office or send him a text."

Spencer snatched the note and set it on his screen. "May I be dismissed? I'd like to get started right away."

She smiled and nodded. "Please, go right ahead. I won't expect you in classes today."

"Or the lab tonight," he said, already halfway out the door.

"Have a good one," she called after him, smiling at the prospect of the first normal day of the semester.

CHAPTER TWENTY-TWO

Elle skirted the line at the counter after spotting Janet's frantic wave over from the corner of the coffee shop. She sat and Carson nudged a cup towards her.

"Thank you for this." She took a sip of the way-too-hot but delightful coffee. "That generic break room coffee was not cutting it today." She spied a piece of strudel on Janet's plate and ripped off a very small piece. The pastry was flaky and plenty sweet, but it wasn't Mom's.

"It's dry, I know," Janet cut in before taking another bite. "But I'm stressed out of my mind, and all the cookies were gone."

"Because you ate them," Carson chimed in.

"I blame you, anyway."

"What did I do to stress you out?" he asked, brushing an errant crumb from his gray sweater vest. Carson always dressed the part of college professor.

"Not you," Janet said and waved toward Elle.

She moved her gaze between the two of them. "Me? What did I do?"

"You bailed on the research study, which, in turn, prompted

this one"—she pointed at Carson—"to ask me to loop Greer in. That man is smart, but he is not *smart*."

Elle bobbed her head, knowing exactly what Janet meant. She'd worked with Greer for a couple of years. Much like Spencer, he could be very difficult to get through to, and he lacked social skills. But not on the same level as the young man.

"That's part of what I wanted to talk about," Elle said. "I want back in on the project."

Carson's eyes widened along with his mouth. "Are you serious? You better not be teasing me."

She shook her head. "I wouldn't do that to you."

"How are you doing this? Didn't Lance dump all the student projects in your lap, like, last week?"

She sipped her coffee, unable to stop a grin from breaking across her caffeinated lips.

"He did. But as of yesterday, I found a solution."

Her two friends exchanged curious glances and leaned in.

"You figured out a way to, you know..." Janet moved a finger across her neck.

"What?! No, I'm not killing him." The coffee shop noise had deadened in time to hear her proclamation, eliciting curious and concerned glances from several people.

She rolled her eyes and leaned back in her seat assuring them she wasn't attempting to hide anything.

"I'm taking a step back is all."

"Oh, my god, you *quit*?! That's worse!" Carson's eyebrows arched up almost to his hairline.

"Why do you two go straight to worst-case scenarios?"

"We're botanists. It's what we do," he said.

"Besides, what else could it possibly be if not one or the other?" Janet finished her pastry and brushed her hands together.

"I handed it off to Spencer."

By the looks on her friends' faces, telling them she concocted a plan to off Lance would have been more plausible. Their eyes bulged.

"And you're...okay with that?" Carson asked.

"I wouldn't have done it if I wasn't. I did come up with it."

Sort of. Yes, she had arrived at the conclusion, with a very swift kick by Dean Piedmont's refusal to act. That still burned in her belly. When someone she thought was on her side turned out to not be, or failed to consider her feelings, it had reminded her she was better off not even expressing them. Better to stay quiet and deal with things herself than be let down by someone else.

"So," she continued, smiling at two people she felt more at ease around, but still didn't let in completely. "I have some time. I'd really like to get back in if you'll have me—"

"YES." They both spoke in unison, drawing the crowd's attention once again. The three exchanged glances and melted into laughter.

Elle sipped her coffee while Carson and Janet filled her in on how far they'd gotten (not much) and the upcoming schedule and lab reservations. They promised to share all the documents and invited her to the team meeting at the end of the week. She asked them questions they didn't necessarily have answers to, mostly because neither was a physicist, but she reassured them she would table them until she got into the meat of the research.

"You made my whole semester." Carson sat back, breathless.

"Mine, too. And I don't mean to be a Debbie Downer here, but..." Janet cocked her eyebrow and leveled a gaze at Elle. "Are you sure you can let the applications go?"

She bucked her head back. "Of course I can. Why wouldn't I?"

Carson and Janet exchanged a look.

"You've never not done something all the way," Janet said.

True, but this time in her life was unlike any other. Edgar was gone. Lance was in control. Dean Piedmont was not on her side. Spencer was sucking her energy dry. Maybe they all needed to learn the hard way. Or perhaps *she* did. Though, she already had. She'd been through plenty of failed experiments and lots of trial and error through her life. The burdens left by those moments still plagued her.

"You've been acting strange the last few weeks." Janet examined her from across the table. "You've slacked off with baking. And now you've handed off a huge task you never would have if Edgar was here."

"Well, he's not, so all bets on what former Elle would've done are off."

"And," Janet said, "put those together with that very mysterious, very large man who's visited you *twice,* and I'd say maybe you have something else cooking in your kitchen other than my sugar fixes."

Fight. Flight. Freeze. These options cycled through Elle's nervous system rapidly, as was the purpose of the body's most basic survival response.

Fight—deny and get angry at the implication she was not performing her job to the best of her ability.

Flight—slide her coat off the chair back, toppling it in the process, and dash out the door, never to be heard from again.

Freeze—sit open mouthed and look as guilty as possible.

"We have a winner." Carson proffered a fist that Janet promptly bumped.

Damn the sympathetic nervous system, which seemed like an oxymoron because it was anything but.

Elle cleared her throat and scrunched her toes.

"Whatever you think is happening, you're wrong."

"I know what I saw last week...and Pam out front knows what *she* saw last month."

"You're talking about this with other people?"

"Pam brought him up a few weeks ago in the break room and asked who he was. I didn't have a clue what she was talking about and told her she was crazy. And then much to my surprise last Friday, I happen to run straight into him rounding the corner from your office. Pam did *not* do him justice in her description, by the way." Janet leaned back and waggled her eyebrows.

"So are you going to fill us in or keep this one under wraps, too? You'll fail, by the way, like you did with Dr. Lichtenstein," Carson said.

"I hate you both right now." Elle crossed her arms. "And it isn't what you think. He's barely an acquaintance."

"He's definitely not your type." Janet chuckled. "I mean he is the furthest thing from Dr. Lichtenstein—"

"That wasn't his name!" Elle shot up, the heat of embarrassment remaining permanently embedded in her neck. "Look, the guy you've been gossiping about isn't a boyfriend—"

"Boy toy, then. I approve," Janet said.

"You know what? I retract my offer to return to the photosynthesis study."

"No!" Carson jumped up and set a hand on her shoulder. "Let's not get carried away or make any rash decisions because one of us"—he peered down at Janet who had erupted into full-fledged guffawing—"is being presumptive. Elle, I don't care who this guy is. I need you in this study. *We* need you." He nudged Janet's seat with his foot.

"Okay, okay. I'm stopping." Janet cleared her throat and wiped her cheeks. "I'm sorry. I won't bring it up again."

"At least not until the project is over, I'm guessing." Elle couldn't stay mad at Janet or Carson too long. Because while they were wrong about the *who,* they were right about *what* might be partially driving her reappropriation of duties to Spencer.

As if on cue, the phone in her pocket vibrated against her hip. She jolted a bit. It kept going, which meant it was a call, not a text. She slid it out and, without looking up, told Janet and Carson she had to go. When they protested, she swore it wasn't them. She needed to take this call and head back to campus.

She answered the phone while still trying to jam her arm into the sleeve of her jacket.

"Hi, hang on." She finished dressing. "Still there?"

"Nope. I gave up."

"That's too bad. I sacrificed the rest of an amazing coffee to answer this call."

"Uh-oh. Don't ever do that, Elle. Not for me or anyone else."

She smiled and walked down the sidewalk back to work.

"So what are you doing right now? Besides not drinking good coffee."

"I'm on my way back to work. How about you? Please tell me you're not exercising again."

He chuckled. "No. I'm getting ready for dinner. I've got a long night ahead."

"Food good, at least?"

"It is pretty good. But the company could be better."

She stopped by the fountain in the school courtyard and sat on the brick wall. The water was turned off this time of year because it would freeze the pipes otherwise and destroy the century-old landmark of the university.

"Who's going to be there?"

"Ah, well, a king or two. A couple of prime ministers. Some princes and chancellors. A duchess. Another president."

"Another president?"

"Hey, don't sound so excited about that one. You're spoken for."

Her cheeks lit up. "Is that a fact?"

"Full disclosure?"

She gulped. "Full disclosure."

"I kind of have a serious crush on you. Like crazy. Like I can't stop thinking about you. This whole trip would be better with you here."

"Are you love-bombing me right now?"

"Uhhh..."

"Oh god, I didn't mean that as in love-love. Like you're saying or thinking that about me..." The blush in her cheeks washed away at the prospect of what she'd said.

"I don't know what love-bombing is. But if it means that I'm telling you I'm crazy about you and counting down the days until I get to see you again, then I guess I'm doing it."

She covered her face with her free hand. How was this her life right now?

"I have to run," he said. "Thanks for sacrificing your coffee for me. That speaks volumes."

"I do have a major caffeine addiction. So you're welcome."

They bid each other goodbye. She dropped the phone into her lap and tilted her head up to the sky. What would this be like if Ben was a regular guy she'd met at Pete's that night? Say, a construction worker or an accountant. It would change everything. They'd be able to go out. They'd talk on the phone the same, but she wouldn't need to do it from an encrypted device. She could tell Carson and Janet, appease Mom and Pete's curiosity. Though it had only been a month, she had an odd sense that she'd known him longer.

The wind shifted and the gray sky opened, trickling down fluffy snow flurries. Jim in meteorology was right. Again. She took the phone off her lap, snapped a selfie, then texted it to Ben.

If Ben was anyone other than who he was, things would be different. But not everything. The phone vibrated.

Just Ben: I wish I was there. I miss you.

She smiled at the screen. She felt the same, though it defied logic. They didn't know each other. How could she feel so much for someone who was still very much a stranger?

The phone buzzed again, this time with a picture. Ben in front of a mirror in a tux. One hand in his pocket. The other just off to the side of his face holding his phone. His eyes burned into her, even thousands of miles and six hours away. His smile radiated through the airwaves like a cosmic ray. He was a stunning human, inside and out. Her chest surged with that big feeling she'd buried a very long time ago.

Elle: I miss you too. Come home soon.

So maybe she had sacrificed the symposium applications to spend more time with a man she had no business being with.

NatU School of Science

Greetings Students,

Eight world-renowned scientists have confirmed speaking spots at the symposium. I'm also humbled to report that the list of sponsors is growing by the day, with thirteen tech, vehicular, research, and exploration companies confirmed. I expect that the exhibition hall will be packed with the best companies and research firms for space development by April.

The 52 student projects will be announced after spring break. This will leave those chosen a few weeks to finalize their posters. Consider preparing your full project to ensure you're ready if chosen. See Dr. Conroy during office hours if you require assistance.

Yours faithfully in science,

Dr. Lance Dunwoody

Department of Space Science and Aeronautics Chair

RESEARCH OPPORTUNITIES:

Interested in working on a four-department project about ozone repair and regeneration? Botany is looking for students in environmental, physics, chemistry, and space who are willing to get their hands dirty for the next three months. Email Dr. Pankowski and get on the list.

DEADLINES:

**The volunteer slots for the symposium have been created and assigned to those who signed up. Check out the symposium website to see what's left and email or message Dr. Conroy to be added.

**Just over a week left to nominate your favorite professor for the Worldwide Lecture.

CHAPTER TWENTY-THREE

The whiteboard Elle rolled into the middle of her office was full of lines and color-coordinated sticky notes. Her desk was piled with research on ozone molecules, sunspots, and other planetary stratospheres that might help the photosynthesis project.

In the past week, she'd used her spare time (courtesy of Spencer's preoccupation with the student symposium projects) to create a visual representation of her theory trail. She had dissected copious research studies down to the bare bones. She lifted equations, ran them herself with appropriate variables, and created her "if this, then" data points that she'd need to fill in when they started the test.

The greenhouse was about ready to be planted. But after visiting the site Friday, Elle had realized they needed extra help preparing the quadrants to simulate the various conditions.

She'd planned to ask Pete for help when they met Saturday for their now-standing 9:00 a.m. storage clean out. But the normal easygoing Pete had been replaced by sullen sourpuss Pete. The one who didn't have a sense of humor or crack a smile. The one who slammed boxes around and was much more apt to throw stuff out (she appreciated *that* Pete). She'd tried to engage him in chit-chat and to fall into their normal banter, even giving him a few openings to tease her, but each time, he shut it down with a sharp tone. After only thirty minutes of work, he moved the keepers back into the unit and locked the door saying he "had shit to do" and stormed off.

So the greenhouse had been delayed by a couple of days. She spent Sunday with Janet, Carson, Mortimer, and Greer (whom she'd been tasked to deal with) getting the walls reinforced and the refractory elements in place. Only the control section was a true greenhouse. The other three sections would be testing variables.

She and Ben had continued to chat when they could, and he still took her running at night. Her baking was replaced with research, and so she'd slip into her flannel PJs as soon as she could and get to work. She'd tucked herself in with articles, notes, and Ben.

He gave her some fun tidbits from the summit—nothing serious or confidential. He revealed which world leader chewed the loudest (France), which one had the worst manners (a prince from Dubai), and which one he thought would be fun to grab a beer with (Canada). She concurred that in her experience, Canadians were ultra friendly, but a Swede could be counted on in a pinch. He said he'd take her word for it because he hadn't met one yet that said more than four words to him. She argued maybe the two of them had diverging ideas of what constituted fun conversation.

Even with their late-night conversations and her research that went into the wee hours of the morning, she managed to arrive at her office early Tuesday to put everything up on her board.

"It's been a while since you've done one of those." Janet

strolled in, her puffer jacket announcing her arrival before her voice. "I figured you could use one of these."

She extended a coffee Elle was only too happy to accept.

"Definitely, thanks. Yeah, it was time to lay it all out."

Janet craned her neck toward different elements, reviewing things, furrowing her brow at some things, and nodding at others.

"I'll be honest. I don't recognize much of this, but then again, guess I don't need to."

"If you did, you wouldn't need me."

Janet patted her on the back. "I always need you, Elle. You're the nicest genius I've met. Don't tell Carson. It would break his heart if he found out he wasn't a genius."

Elle chuckled and went back to her desk to grab the box of muffins she'd made just for Janet. Her friend's face lit with joy as she accepted it.

"Don't let anyone tell you you're not doing the Lord's work." Janet left as Elle's phone buzzed from her pocket.

Just Ben: Good morning. Guess where I just woke up?

Elle: I'm guessing a bed of some sort.

Just Ben: You're too smart for me.

A picture popped up of Ben in a Navy T-shirt (yes, her eyes ratcheted to the way the sleeve squeezed around his bicep), messy hair, drowsy eyes, sitting next to an airplane window. Her heart rate doubled and it stole the breath from her chest.

He was coming back. All the chatting they'd done, all the insights she'd learned from the way he talked about people and himself, made her feel like they'd spent way more time together than they had.

Of course, it didn't hurt that the press covered him. She didn't watch much TV, but he'd popped up on her feed more and more. Usually video footage or stills of him with one world leader or another. He barely addressed the cameras with more than a wave and a smile. When he did give a statement, it was brief and all-business.

Her favorite footage was when he had "insisted" on visiting the refugees and asylum seekers at the Geneva University Hospital. It was his human side, the one she'd gotten to know. He was a man who cared enough about suffering to drop to a knee and comfort a child who'd lost his parents when crossing the border. The kind of man who had his chief of staff cut the video feed and instruct all media to wait outside.

This wasn't a show to him. It wasn't a game he cared to win by any means other than integrity and record of service. It spoke volumes about him without him saying a word.

Just Ben: I guess this means I won't be taking you running anymore. <insert sad face>

Elle: Not unless you're busting into my house to save me from some kind of apocalyptic event.

Just Ben: Is this your way of telling me I need to start paying attention to asteroids?

Elle: Oh no. Global warming will kill us way before that happens.

Just Ben: Great. Something I'm equally unable to protect us from.

Elle: Luckily, you know a scientist who knows some other scientists who are all working on it. With the scientist you know. Exhibit A.

She snapped a picture of her board and sent it.

Just Ben: ...was I supposed to follow that?

Just Ben: Is that a murder board?

She laughed and glanced back up at her work. Dad's influence on her methodology was now very evident.

Elle: I'll explain it to you the next time we talk.

Just Ben: In person?

A knock at the door startled her.

"Hi, Dr. Conroy can I ask you about something?" It was a student from 1101, someone who she'd learned over the past six weeks was considering delving deeper into the program.

"Come on in and have a seat. Let me finish this up."

Elle: I was promised a tour.

Just Ben: Tonight at 8:00?

Elle: See you then.

CHAPTER TWENTY-FOUR

History had not been Elle's particular forte throughout her educational years. She did enough to get the credit required for her degree, choosing to take scientific history and evolution classes over social history or world events. She wasn't incompetent and understood the ins and outs of wars and famines, colonization, and conquest. But none of that had engaged her as much as the way science had unfolded through time.

But roaming through the halls and rooms of the White House at night, led by its sole occupant providing her personalized insight, might change that perspective. Ben had been waiting in the Palm Room after Ted's now-customary handoff. Once they were alone, he wrapped her up with his arms, cocooning her in a warmth and comfort she didn't necessarily want to leave. He kissed the top of her head and slid her coat from her body before guiding her through the door.

"I figured we'd start down here on the ground floor and work our way up."

"Sounds logical."

He smiled and placed a hand at the small of her back, sending a wave of goosebumps rippling down her arms.

But before they went any further, Elle stopped. "Full disclosure?"

"Full disclosure."

She sighed. "I'm not a history person. I feel like you should know that before we begin."

His brows furrowed. He stroked his chin. "That might be problematic because I am."

"Does this mean you'll drone on?"

"Absolutely." He grinned and pointed to the door on the left. "We'll start in one of my favorite places." His eyebrows shot up as he pushed through the door, unleashing a sanitary lemony scent. They stepped into a large restaurant-type kitchen.

She gravitated toward the industrial mixer. "My mom has one like this in the bakery. But there's so much room to work in here." Rows upon rows of pots, pans, and sifters hung down over the stainless-steel prep tables. Everything glinted. "This is one of your favorite rooms?"

He shrugged and dipped his head slightly. "What can I say, I love to eat. And full disclosure, this is where our chicken parm came from."

"And here I thought your talent knew no bounds."

"I haven't shown you all my tricks yet. Just wait." He winked and Elle considered how long it would take Secret Service agents to show up if she hurled herself at him right now. When he pushed up the sleeves of his deep blue knit, the lines cutting both forearms dared her to do it.

Warmth spread through her chest. "Where to next?"

Room after room, Ben's historical tidbits (like how the Map Room was the original Situation Room and FDR used it during World War II) were interspersed with personal anecdotes (it also happened to be the first place he'd taken a nap, which he didn't recommend since the chairs were not comfortable). They went up to the State Floor next, the most recognizable part of the White House because it hosted most of the public-facing events outside of the West Wing. They moved through the entrance hall and passed under the Presidential Seal into the Blue Room (gaudy, but still rich with history), Green Room, and Red Room, (Ben's comment about naming conventions made her laugh) and into the East Room.

The portraits of the Washingtons watched over them as they drifted closer together, coming to rest beneath George. Ben postulated that the Founding Father would be disappointed in the direction the country had gone in recently.

Elle felt the weight of Ben's disappointment. She placed a hand on his shoulder and his gaze moved from the painting to her. Maybe it was the influence of the history tour or the portrait overlooking them, but she imagined Ben Foster was the closest thing to a present-day George Washington: a reluctant leader who put duty to country above even himself.

"Good evening, Mr. President. I heard you'd been spotted about the residence tonight." A man dressed in a navy-blue vest and pants called from the other end of the expansive room.

"Hi, Harold. It's good to see you." Ben moved toward the man and shook his hand. "How's Dolores? Is she feeling better?"

The jovial man nodded and his face lit. "Yes, sir. The doctor put her on some new medicine. She's got all her energy back, which means"—he leaned in close to Ben—"she's back to bossing me around every chance she gets."

"That's a good thing."

"For her, yes, sir."

Ben put his arm out for Elle to join him, which she did. "Harold, this is Dr. Ellery Conroy. She's never been on a White House tour before."

Harold dipped his head toward her. "It's a pleasure to meet you, ma'am. You've got a good host here. The best I've had the pleasure of serving."

Ben's cheeks flared pink.

"Thank you, Harold," Elle said. "And if this gig doesn't work out for him, maybe he can stay on as a tour guide."

The older man laughed. "Oh, I like you."

Four people dressed in matching blue vests and pants with various cleaning implements came in behind Harold. They stopped when they saw Ben and tilted their heads down in respect.

"We'll get out of your hair. Thank you all for making this place what it is."

"Good evening, Mr. President and Dr. Conroy," Harold said.

Ben and Elle left the East Room and came to the bottom of the famed red carpeted stairs she'd seen in photos and videos through the years.

"Any questions?" He stepped back and put his hands in his pockets.

"You kept my attention way longer than I expected. This is amazing. All of the history. Not to mention the art and architecture. It's beautiful."

He fanned his right hand over his heart. "That means a lot coming from a history hater such as yourself."

"I never said hate. I said I wasn't into it."

"Same thing."

She shook her head at his grin. "Hey, one thing. Harold said he'd heard you were around. I haven't seen anyone else."

"Cameras," he said and pointed up to the ceiling. "They're everywhere."

"Makes sense." She was nailing this genius label she'd been slapped with. Growing up, Pete had often chided she was all brains and no common sense. Which fueled Dad's insistence she keep a foot in the middle and see everything.

"So, you want to go somewhere there aren't cameras?"

Her stomach fluttered. "Absolutely."

He grinned and held out his hand. She wove her fingers through his and as he clamped his shut, excitement shot through her body, leaving her breathless before they started their ascent. She managed to make it up, keeping her attention keyed on the way his fingers gripped hers, the skin smooth with little rough spots. Permanent reminders, no doubt, of his former profession.

When they reached the top, he opened a door. She stepped into another hall that was a dressed-down version of the grandiose one beneath. They walked hand in hand past built-in bookcases and walls with simple art. The living room they ended up in was even more simplified. The glamour and history of the previous two floors had been stripped away, creating the private and cozy space of a simple man.

He opened a cabinet that doubled as a mini fridge and pulled out two beers.

"Thanks for humoring me tonight," he said.

"Are you kidding? I had a great time."

"Would you tell me if you didn't?" He cocked an eyebrow.

"I've been told that my face often speaks on my behalf. So I'll say, yes. You would know."

He laughed and she eased back into the cushions. She didn't have the incessant need to monitor or control her facial expressions with him. Though that didn't mean a whole lot since they'd spent most of their time together separated by an ocean. Now that they were in person, something she hoped would happen more often, she should probably start. Otherwise—

"Exhibit A," he said.

She shot her gaze to his grin.

"Your face was just speaking." He took a draw from the bottle while the red tide of embarrassment seeped over her face.

"You know what would be cool?" He slid an arm across the seat back behind her. "If you would just say what you're thinking with your mouth."

She shook her head. "That's an absolutely awful idea. The worst." She'd scare him off within minutes. Guaranteed.

"Try me."

She groaned and shook her head. "Trust me on this."

He sighed through his nose and shook his head. "I would love to know what's going on in that brain of yours."

"Don't assume it's anything extraordinary."

"It's not about that." He tucked a piece of hair behind her ear, running his gaze over her face searching for an answer to a question he hadn't asked. "I want to know the real you."

She shrugged. "What you see is what you get."

"While we both know that's not true, I'll drop it." He narrowed his eyes, his fingers lingering on her shoulder. "Full disclosure?"

She nodded.

"I've been dying to kiss you for, oh, I don't know. Forever."

Yes, she understood because...same.

His gaze dropped to her lips. "Mind if I do that now?"

"You can try. I believe we were interrupted the last time."

He took the beer from her hand and placed both bottles on the coffee table before sliding closer. His mouth was inches from hers and he ran a finger down her cheek to her chin. "No one's interrupting us tonight."

Her heart clapped against her ribs as his lips fused with hers. The reality of where she was and *who* he was melted away around her.

When she gripped him tighter, he pulled her up onto his lap

in one movement. It took her breath away when he moved his lips down her chin and lapped at her neck. This must be the true sensation an asteroid undergoes when it's sucked into the atmosphere and becomes a meteor: it burns from the friction.

He parted his lips from her skin.

"Full disclosure?" he whispered, gripping her hips.

She swallowed and nodded.

"I really want to finish what we started back on your couch. But I can't."

Oh. Her shoulders lowered and the excitement pulsing through her body disappeared.

"Of course." She made a move to slide off his lap, knowing damn well it wasn't physical on *his* part. That was very, very obvious.

But he stopped and held her hips. "This isn't about you. It's me. I want things to be different with you."

She curled her toes and tried to remain upright and present. She wanted to run away and never look back because though he said it wasn't her, she couldn't help but believe it was. What else could it be?

"Don't do that." He forced himself back into her focus. "Don't disappear inside your head. Let me in."

She gazed down into his stunning gray eyes. So pure, so magnetic, so sincere. He really wanted to know her, and that scared the hell out of her. The only other people she'd felt wholly herself with had left her. Though Dad would argue she'd left him first.

"It isn't anything major. I promise," she said. "And you don't need me adding to your weight."

His face fell. The hope ripped by her words. He closed his eyes and sighed.

"Okay, if you say so." He wanted her. His eyes made that clear. The way his fingers caressed down her back and pulled her back towards him. "But promise me if that ever changes, you'll let me know," he whispered inches from her mouth.

"As long as you let me know if your stance on doing more than this changes. Though this is pretty amazing." She smiled and hoped he didn't sense the hint of sadness beneath the mask.

He paused and grinned. "You'll be the first to know."

CHAPTER TWENTY-FIVE

In a matter of two weeks, the following things had happened: Spencer had only communicated via email, making his condescending tone more tolerable; the photosynthesis co-op project officially began after seeds were planted; thirty-six students signed up to help (sending Carson scrambling to figure out how to either whittle it down or use them all); and Elle had made out with the president of the United States not once but twice, and she was going back for thirds tonight, a rare Saturday date.

She was making him her three-chocolate chip cookies (she couldn't bring them since everything he ate needed to be tested for poison—no joke). She was secretly hoping he would be so turned on by her culinary skills, he would end her sexual drought.

"Your whistling is driving me crazy," Pete grumbled from inside the storage unit. Brooding Pete had shown up three Saturdays in a row. She'd kill to have regular Pete back.

"I've got to do something to fill the silence. Seeing as how you're not talking."

"Nothing to say." He slung an empty box out from inside.

"That's never stopped you before."

He huffed. "Fine. What do you want to talk about?"

She shrugged. "How's Brody?"

"Fine."

"The bar?"

"Busy."

"Tabitha?"

His face clouded over. Ah. Elle figured that's what it was, but wouldn't dare ask. Pete and Tabitha had their fair share of problems, and while he played things close to the vest, he had confided in Elle a time or two. He would again if he wanted to.

"I found this box of mini tapes," he said, evading the answer. She allowed it.

"Probably more case recordings."

He shook his head and withdrew a large manila envelope. "Maybe, but these only have years on them. And there's nothing else in here but these." He pulled another one out and then another. "Looks like they go back over thirty years."

"Odd. Put the whole box in the personal stack, and we can check them out later. We never did ask Mom if she has the recorder."

Pete moved them over to the side they'd designated as personal and put his hands on his hips. "We're almost all the way through. I can see the back wall."

She stood and moved over next to him. They'd done a better job at throwing things out and sorting through the leftovers. Pete had stopped taking boxes altogether, another sign he was suffering from some undisclosed issue. While she loved that he was throwing things out versus holding on to them, she worried when he did snap out of it, he'd be upset she'd allowed him to rage purge. Fine. She'd break the stalemate.

"Hey," she said while they were standing elbow to elbow. Or rather his elbow to her bicep. "If you need anything, I'm here."

"No, thanks. I don't need my little sister solving my problems." His jaw pulsed.

"I don't need to solve anything. I am capable of listening, you know."

"Pfft. Sure."

She reared her head back and turned to him. "What do you mean by that?"

"You can't hear a problem and not try to solve it. Especially when that something has to do with my wife..."

She opened her mouth to object, but his shoulders drooped and his eyes glassed over. She swallowed her unease that this was something outside the bounds of Pete's usual marital troubles, which contrary to his now-stance, she had listened to without interjecting (though maybe not now that she thought back). Either way, she would do whatever it took to get her brother back. Even if that meant reaching out in a way she hadn't before.

"I'm seeing someone," she said and cleared her throat.

"Yeah, I know."

"What you don't know is that he's been a good influence on me. Like he's patient and a good listener. He's challenging me, too."

Pete shifted beside her. "How so?"

"Like calling me out when I go dark in my head. Encouraging me to share more."

"Has it worked?"

"Not yet. But he's wearing me down."

He chuckled and a grin made a rare appearance across his face.

"That wasn't the point of this story," she continued.

He faced her. "It is. Because if that guy can get you to spill whatever's really going on in your world"—he tapped a soft finger to her head—"let me know. Then I'll tell you what's in mine."

This was irritating. She opened her mouth and huffed. "This isn't about me."

"It kinda is. You want me to share what's going on, and unlike you, I have."

"I just told you I'm seeing someone!"

He sighed. "You don't share the hard stuff, Elle. All you say is work is busy or you have a lot gong on. You don't say why or what."

She took a step back. "It isn't that simple."

"Why? Because I'm not as smart as you, I can't possibly understand?" The hurt slapped across his face tugged at her chest.

"No...I didn't mean it like that."

He crossed his arms. "Then explain. What did you mean?"

Her toes reflexively curled. She didn't like conflict or confrontation. It's why she'd let so many wrongs slip through the cracks over the years. The discomfort flooding her chest pushed against that wall she'd erected. She could give him a rundown about the events at work, but he'd know she was still not getting to the gray area. The hard part. The feelings those things raised in her. Edgar's departure had reopened the wound left by Dad's death, and her shame had come thundering back with it.

"Elle," he said. "I know you didn't mean it like that. Uncurl your toes. It's just... How can you help any of us if you don't let us help you?"

"I don't need help."

He shook his head. "If you say so." He reached up and pulled down the storage unit door. "I'll tell you this, little sister. You need to open up to someone because if you don't..." The corners of his eyes drooped. "You're setting yourself up for a lot more pain and loneliness."

He snapped the lock and walked away.

CHAPTER TWENTY-SIX

"Can I run something by you?" Ben asked, his long form leaning against the counter beside her. He had been quieter than usual at the start of their meal, and when she asked about it, he brushed the concern off his face and said there was a lot at work and left it at that. Then he asked about the photosynthesis project she'd teased. She had no problem chattering about that.

While he had cleaned up, she had busied herself with the cookies.

"Sure." She folded in the last of the chocolate—dark chips—one tablespoon at a time.

"I have a big speech, and I suck at public speaking."

She stopped stirring and gawked at him. "You're kidding, right?"

"Nope. Dead serious."

"But you kind of have to do it all the time." This made even less sense than his running habit. Speaking was an important part of being president.

He shook his head. "Not exactly. I'm fine in short spurts, like sound bites and whatnot. This is different."

"How?"

He sighed and brushed a hand down his face. "It's my first State of the Union. And, historically speaking, it's long and a lot of data. Everyone watches. Everyone criticizes. And I'm kind of a mess about it."

She put aside the spoon and bowl for the moment. She had a short window to get the dough in the oven before the butter melted too much and flattened the cookies. But judging by Ben's defeated appearance, he needed more than half of her attention at the moment. He reminded her of Noah when he'd come into her office yesterday and asked if his project was on the short list for the symposium. He had confessed how nervous and over-whelmed he was between the waiting and the prospect of actu-ally getting picked. Especially since he'd continued working on the project as she had suggested. He didn't want to feel like he'd wasted time on something that was never going to amount to anything. She had empathized and reassured him he was in the running (though she didn't tell him Spencer was doing the choosing). But she couldn't imagine his innovative take on vehic-ular movement on Mars not making the cut.

Ben shifted beside her.

"Is your unease more about the content or the audience?" she said.

His gaze slid to the side for a beat before he crossed his arms. "The content and my ability to present it effectively. I've gone over it all week with my speechwriter and staff. We've tweaked it a ton. The consensus is that the speech is appropriate and my delivery is effective."

She nodded and started dropping the dough onto the lined cookie sheets. She'd prepared lecture notes and talking points for others many times since her undergrad days. But never had anyone done the same for her. She'd had Spencer go through and do some mock-ups for the first few weeks (which he fought tooth and nail and never did get right) but that was so she could get a handle on how he would organize material to present.

He sighed. "I have the rest of the week to practice. Hopefully that does the trick."

She popped the trays in the oven and started the timer before spinning around toward him.

"You haven't practiced on me. Give me your best thirteen minutes."

He balked. "You're not serious."

She moved over and sat at the dinette and gestured towards him.. "You have the floor, Mr. President. Show me what've you got." She clasped her hands in her lap and waited.

"I don't have my speech…"

She shrugged. "Start with what you remember. And then make up the rest."

"You want me to wing the State of the Union?" He raised his eyebrows.

She looked around. "We're the only ones here. And I can't tell anyone, remember? Sworn to secrecy or else." She moved her finger across her throat.

He chuckled and then stood up straight. "Okay, I'll give it a try." He took in a breath and started talking and didn't stop until the timer went off.

She withdrew the piping hot trays and placed them down on the granite away from the heat to let them sit before she could move them to a cooling rack, something Ben hadn't known was in this kitchen until she'd dug it out.

"Don't hold back," he said, hands on his hips. "I can take it."

The cookies were dense and thick, not too brown along the edges and not too raw in the middle. The three types of chips ensured every bite had plenty of chocolate without making it too sweet.

"Before I start," she said, turning around to blow on a cookie. "You should try this."

"I like this ploy. Comfort me with a warm homemade treat before dropping bad news."

He sunk his perfect teeth into the cookie, the warm chips leaving a dot of chocolate on his lip. He closed his eyes while he chewed. "This is the best cookie I've ever tasted." He popped the rest in his mouth and groaned in delight.

"Good. Now, full disclosure?"

He swallowed what was left in his mouth and nodded.

"Your content is insightful. You give a lot of facts and figures. It's a good speech."

He reached around her and grabbed another cookie. "But?"

"It doesn't sound like you."

"That's what I thought. I knew something was off. Now if I can figure out how to fix it." He shook his head.

"In my limited experience as a lowly member of academia." She brushed her thumb across his lip to wipe away the chocolate. "It's easier to talk about something you're passionate about. Take me for instance. I love lecturing about every facet of space. I don't use notes, and I don't even look at the material anymore. I walk in and say what I think my students need to hear."

"I don't love the budget or any number of things in this speech," he grumbled.

She moved her gaze back to his. "But you are passionate about this country and helping it get back to a better version of itself. That tour you gave me, the excitement in your voice was palpable and intoxicating. Hell, it inspired me so much, I went out and bought a thousand-page biography of George Washington."

"That's a powerful sentiment from a history hater," he said, and his face lit with amusement.

"My point is, when you speak from the heart, people believe

you. So I say, find an angle that gets you fired up, and write the speech yourself. Then the audience will feel it, too."

Isn't that what space had always done for her? On her worst days, like when Spencer tested her, or she had opened a STAR rejection, or the day after Dean Piedmont had informed them of Edgar's departure. Even after Dad died. Talking about the thing that set her soul on fire always played some part in easing her.

Now if she could get into STAR, it would unlock a whole other level of happiness. Working alongside those scientists, gathering that kind of data, and taking her exploration of space to a whole new level would surely turn out to be the one thing she had been missing all this time.

"I would love to hear you lecture." His face beamed with admiration.

She shrugged. "You'll have to apply to the university."

He reached across and took her hand. "Thank you. This was just what I needed."

"You mean the cookies, don't you? It's okay, I understand. They are pretty amazing."

His face widened with that megawatt smile as he pulled her to him and wrapped his arms around her. "I meant you. *You* are exactly what I've needed."

Now he was the one putting the extra beat in her heart in a way she'd never experienced outside of space. Her chest swelled as it pressed up against his. As his lips drew nearer to hers, he stopped short and whispered, "And the cookies didn't hurt either."

CHAPTER TWENTY-SEVEN

The rows of little green sprouts springing from the ground gave the greenhouse some much-needed color on a Thursday night, especially with the sleet pelting the roof. No one had bothered to tell Mother Nature that spring was supposed to be right around the corner.

Elle perched on the bench at the far end of the control house while Carson and Janet debriefed the student volunteers who had measured each seedling with meticulous care. She pushed the earbud tighter in her ear so she could better hear Ben's speech. She softened her gaze and let the world in the greenhouse blur around her while he spoke about unity without trauma. How we should stop being so divided by personal choices that don't threaten others. That we need to stop catering to special interest groups that put their profit margins above public health and welfare. Protecting children in classrooms meant ripping the blinders off the fallacy that gun control meant gun removal. And that the responsibility for providing access to affordable health care should fall squarely on the shoulders of the pharmaceutical and insurance industries, and not the government or the people.

"The thing that made America is the very thing we've gotten away from: unity. It used to be us against the world because *we* were doing something no one else was. We respected people's rights to live as they chose instead of what was dictated by class, religion, and government. Too long we've allowed the interests of a two-party system, forcing us to choose along loyalty lines without regard for doing what was ethically and morally right. We have been too willing to discard basic human decency all because we're putting money and politics above humanity. That has to end. And it will. But we have to make it happen. We have to stop falling into the old ways of black and white, or blue and red, thinking. That you're either for or against. That because one issue is so important to you, you're willing to turn a blind eye to all of the bad. Let's stop the empty promises. Let's stop the divide. And for god's sake, let's stop the rhetoric, *really* stop it. And find the common ground to once again become one nation. Indivisible from the inside or outside, with liberty and justice for *all*. Thank you."

The applause and hollers echoed through her ear. Goosebumps prickled down her neck and her chest swelled with pride and—

"What are you listening to?" Janet said.

"Nothing." Elle hastily removed the earbud and put it back in its case. "How are things looking?" She dipped her head toward the plants.

"Really, really good. Two of the three experimental areas are growing substantially faster, and one is emitting more isoprene than the other three. Care to guess which one?" Her left eyebrow arched a little higher.

"The plasma generator, of course." Elle leaned back. "Black hole theory does have applied uses beyond wormholes in Marvel movies."

"Not so fast. We still don't know if the lettuce will continue to grow at this rate."

Elle stood. "It will. You'll see."

Janet shook her head and chuckled. "But will the radiation be lethal?"

"Not if we set it up right. And we won't know *that* until it's over." Her phone dinged, but it wasn't the one in her hand. It was the *other* one.

Janet's brow furrowed and she glanced around. "Whose phone is that?"

"I don't hear anything." Another ding. And then another one. Janet's head tilted down to Elle's bag on the bench. Luckily, Carson swept in and saved the day.

"I'm stoked about these numbers," he said.

"Me, too, but we can't get too excited yet. It's still early," Janet said.

"Pfft." Carson swatted the air. "We take any and all wins, remember? Progress is progress."

"Right but ultimately..."

Elle was happy to let her two friends continue their conversation as she quietly withdrew the other phone from her bag and dropped hers in its place.

Just Ben: Not sure if you saw the speech, but I kinda hope you did.

Just Ben: It felt so good. <insert huge smile>

Just Ben: And if you disagree just send me over a couple dozen cookies and we'll call it even.

Elle: You killed it. I got goosebumps and that never happens outside of a telescope or Stephen Hawking.

Just Ben: I never would have done it like that without you.

Just Ben: I owe you big time. <insert wink>

A heat pattered in her gut and fluttered up through her.

Elle: Anything in mind?

Just Ben: Plenty… Can you come over?

Elle: I'm on my way to dinner with friends. And aren't you a little busy?

She imagined something like the State of the Union didn't exactly end when the speech did. Surely he had to rub elbows and shake a lot of hands.

Just Ben: I'm happy to bail if it means I get to repay you.

She gulped and that flutter in her belly spread. He'd said he wanted to take it slow and sex was off the table. But that had been weeks ago, and maybe now that this was off his plate, he'd changed his mind.

Just Ben: But I don't want to make you change your plans. Plus you're right. I have more work to do. Enjoy your dinner and call me later if you can.

She pulled her bottom lip between her teeth and imagined him decked out in the navy blue suit he'd worn to the speech (she'd seen it online), hands swallowing the phone as he typed, a crowd of some of the most important people in the country gathered around him, all while he was...

"Do you think she remembers we're still here?"

Carson's voice threw water on the fire. She looked up from the phone and straight into the very curious and slightly judgmental (with a side of humor) gaze of her friends. She cleared her throat and put the phone in her pocket.

"Where are we eating?" she asked in her most nonchalant, I-was-not-maybe-on-the-verge-of-sexting-with-the-president voice.

"Uh, what was *that* all about?" Janet pointed toward her phone, eyebrows lifting.

This was the second time she'd gotten caught. She adjusted the strap on her bag and ignored the vibration in her pocket, though not looking was drawing out the heat.

"Nothing."

"That face was *not* nothing," Carson said.

"It was the hunk, wasn't it. I knew it!" Janet rubbed her hands together, joy at either being right or believing Elle had a social life beamed from her face. Or both, knowing Janet.

Elle inhaled and shook her head slowly. "You two are like teenagers." She curled her toes and plunged her hand in her pocket, her palm itching as it enclosed around the phone. She'd have to start leaving it at home because it was too hard to hide her face when she texted him. Hard. Like his body... every single inch of it.

"Let's go. Dinner's on me." She walked out before they could see the quiver that wracked through her.

ACCORDING TO MY SCIENCE
TENTH SPRING EDITION—MARCH 13TH

NatU School of Science

Students,

It is with great pleasure that I provide this update ahead of spring break. I have secured enough sponsorships and vendors for the event. There will be plenty of exhibits and networking opportunities throughout the day.

I'm privileged to announce that the last speaker is NatU's very own Dr. Edgar Linton. This is a special homecoming for Dr. Linton, and I know everyone will be as pleased as I am to see him.

All students whose projects were chosen will be informed the Monday classes resume.

Yours faithfully in science,

Dr. Lance Dunwoody

Department of Space Science and Aeronautics Chair

Dear Edgar,

I'm thrilled that you're speaking at the symposium! That little nugget in the newsletter made my whole day. Spring break is next week and I'll be buried under a ton of grading (every class has a test or paper due by Friday). Sound familiar? I guess old habits die hard. Unfortunately, I won't have a TA like me to help, but I guess I can't complain. Though you never answered when I asked if I was as difficult for you as Spencer has been. I'll assume your silence is a no.

The photosynthesis experiment is humming along. It's been kind of nice sitting back after making the initial contribution and letting other people handle it. But I do miss all the data collecting and the going back for more. The excitement of possibility. The letdown when it fails. Maybe this will finally inspire me to find another corner of the universe to explore. The man I'm seeing wants me to tell him about my work, but I don't see the point. My black hole theory is dead. It's time for me to let it go, I know.

I hope to see you before the symposium. Drop me a line when you're back in town. I'd love to catch up. I really do miss you.

All my love,
Elle

CHAPTER TWENTY-EIGHT

She'd like to think she didn't get hurt easily. Her skin had thickened from all the years of Dad reminding her she needed to be tough and not let things get to her. The longer she'd let things bother her, the deeper they would go, and the harder they would be to get out. Like a splinter not tended to right away becoming impossible to remove.

Even so, moments had arisen that would do just that, and Elle had let them fester until they raged like an infection. She shied away from discomfort at all costs.

Thirty-eight years of avoidance had resulted in a lot of splinters.

She'd been thinking about it since the newsletter Tuesday announced Edgar's return. She still couldn't help but wander back through, trying to extract the latest hurt.

"...Stephen Hawking was a madman who didn't do any of his own work."

The shock of the statement snapped her head around like an airbag.

"What did you say?"

Ben leaned across the table and laid a hand on hers. "Whatever I could to get you to come back. You've been disappearing more tonight than usual. I know I'm not the most entertaining guy..."

She slid her hand out from under his and sat back, putting them both in her lap.

"It's not that. Or you. I've got...a lot on my mind."

"I've got two ears and all night. So tell me. What's going on?"

She peered down at her hands. When was the last time she'd shared her feelings about something personal? She'd told Pete about Ben, sort of, but that was meant as ploy to get him to open up to her. It had failed miserably and only added ammo to Pete's arsenal of things she'd done wrong. She'd meant to apologize this past Saturday at the storage unit, but he spent the entire time pacing and on the phone. She tried to eavesdrop (she was human after all), but he'd managed to stay just out of her earshot.

"Elle?" Ben said. She gazed up into his eyes and slumped back against the chair.

"It's just—"

Someone knocked on the door.

Ben put his finger up as he rose. "Hold that thought." He jogged out of the room, shutting the door behind him.

She rolled her eyes. Of course, he'd get interrupted at that precise moment. She scoffed and cleared the table. The kitchen was still full of the spice of fajitas. The first time she'd ever tried them had been at a little hole-in-the-wall Mexican restaurant Dad loved. He'd surprised her when he picked only her up early from school. Not Pete. Though a few moments after that elation had come a wave of anxiety that something had happened to Pete or Mom, or someone. Dad had put his hand on the top of her head across the car and reassured her all was well. He had a hankering for fajitas and some time with her.

Elle had been skeptical of trying anything that sizzled and popped like that. Dad grabbed a healthy portion and plopped it on her plate. The spice and garlic tickled her nose. He narrated the process of creating the perfect fajita: Start with a soft flour tortilla, add a slab of refried beans and rice, then heap the peppers, onions, and chicken. He'd topped it with salsa, mild for her, hot and spicy for him, and folded it.

The first time she took a bite, half of the contents shot out the back. She froze, wide eyed, mouth full, the half-empty tortilla drooping in her small hands. Dad's face reddened, his eyes bulged, and Elle believed he was either mad or on the verge of death. Then he'd laughed, coughed and chugged water, alternating sips with outright guffaws. Whenever they ate fajitas after, he would beam and recount that first time with such sparkle and joy about his face, Elle couldn't help but exude the same.

Ben came into the kitchen with a similar sparkle that squeezed her chest.

"Leave all that," he said. "I've got something to show you. But first, you need this." He held out her coat and folded her into it before plunging his arms into that black fleece pullover he'd been wearing the night they met. She didn't bother asking questions or protesting, partly because his reappearance had jarred her from such a bittersweet place.

He reached for her hand and led her up a set of stairs to a gray steel exit door.

"Brace yourself for the blast of air," he said and knocked on the door. Ted opened it from the outside and the whoosh of chill was every bit as strong as Ben had warned.

"Trident is in the crow's nest," Ted murmured into his wrist. He looked over at Ben. "We've got you set up on the south side, sir."

"Great. Thanks, Ted." Ben slapped the man on the shoulder and took her hand. "This way."

"The crow's nest? Are you making me walk the plank?"

"Not exactly." He stopped and put his hands on her shoulders. "I know this isn't going to be too exciting for you, and it's not anywhere near what you're probably used to."

"If this is your idea of foreplay, it isn't working."

He smiled and turned her around. A soft fleece blanket had been set out next to a small portable fire pit. Rising out of the middle of it all was a telescope aimed at the sky.

"Better?" he whispered in her ear, his breath warm and tingling.

"Definitely." She shivered as his lips glanced her neck.

He guided her over to the setup and she noted the two bottles of beer open and waiting. He moved over to the telescope. "I was hoping maybe you'd give me a private lesson."

She caressed the cool metal of the optical tube and stepped behind it. The mount was stiff, so she turned the knob to allow for easy movement while still maintaining stability. She adjusted the height for both her and Ben and checked the finder scope for relative accuracy. It was off by a few millimeters, but she could easily account for that, and really didn't need it. It was a clear night with few low clouds. She swung the lens up and to the left, tracking the moon and knew before her eye peeked through the lens and sharpened it that she had aimed it at the perfect viewing spot.

She inhaled and indulged, losing herself in the gray craters juxtaposed throughout the silver haze of the sun's reflection. How many hours had she spent as a child before a scope much like this one, sketching and documenting every one of these pitted wonders, each of which she would go back many years later and view through a much more powerful lens. And still she'd get lost.

"My dad got me a scope like this," she said aloud as she continued to meander through the history of the solar system one crater at a time. "It's in my spare room. I haven't used it in forever."

The seas of the surface swallowed her back into the pit of the past. She'd packed that scope away when she came back on her first break from college, aggravated at Dad's suggestion they take it to the park one last time before she returned to the West Coast so much sooner than he'd thought.

"About twenty years. That's how long it's been since I looked through it..." She stood upright and stepped back. "Take a look."

Ben bent and hovered over the eyepiece. "That is so cool. It looks like the Death Star."

She chuckled. "That's the Copernicus Crater and the most famous part of the moon."

He moved his gaze to her. "How do I know that name Copernicus?"

"He first discovered that we move around the sun and not the other way around as everyone believed back then. Galileo doubled down almost a century later and got excommunicated for it."

"Tough crowd back then." He returned to the scope. She reached over and shifted the lens slightly. He jerked his head back. "It's looking at something else. I must have hit it."

"I moved it so you could see the Sea of Tranquility."

"Where Armstrong landed!" He went back to the eyepiece. His giddiness mirrored that which she had exuded so long ago when she'd watched the moon, the stars—anything really—from her window, or the park, or the beach with Dad.

Ben moved the scope and she'd peek and identify what he was looking at, what it meant (usually "sea of" since ancient people believed the dark patches were oceans), and if it had any significance (like the Ranger 7 crash site that resulted in the best images of the lunar surface at that time).

When they finished, they sat around the fire and drank their beer. He leaned back on his elbow and pointed out various things above, asking if she knew what they were. Mars was fairly high in the sky, and Jupiter's yellow hue was easy to spot. She helped him trace constellations and identified famous stars and clusters.

"You said you hadn't used your old telescope for a long time. I'm guessing because you have a better one?"

She shook her head and stared at the fire. "Not at home, no."

"You go to a fancy observatory probably."

"Sure." She absently sipped her bottle.

He chuckled. "I've lost you again. I'm starting to take it personally. Not that it would be a surprise."

She moved her gaze over to him. "What do you mean by that?"

"It means I have that effect on women."

"Losing them?"

"In a way, yeah." It was his turn to stare absently into the fire. "You once asked me why I was still single. The answer has a little to do with why I don't want to rush this with you."

Her attention ratcheted to Ben, pulling her away from the past drifting in her head. He was going to tell her what was wrong with him. Or reveal the secret that had hovered between him and Raymond the night she'd signed the NDA. Finally.

"Okay. Tell me."

"In my experience, women are usually only interested in me for two things." He paused and moved his attention to her. "My job, because it made me exciting and sex, because, well, not to brag, but I'm fairly good at it." He shrugged and took a swig of beer.

Interesting. She nodded dumbly and turned this all over in her head. So the big secret he'd been hiding was that he was a sex machine. But he didn't want to have sex with her. Maybe he was afraid he was so good at it, she'd magically forget how much she liked him as a person and they'd no longer do anything but that? This opened up a rabbit hole of questions she wanted to dive down, but before she could he continued.

"It was perfect when I was young. I had a job I loved, and when I had time, I could find a woman for a couple of hours. Any relationship I tried back then fizzled out pretty fast, I assumed, because I'd get called away at a moment's notice and be gone for anywhere from a week to six months. Life was too unpredictable for anything steady, and that worked fine for me. Fast forward to my mid-thirties, and my priorities changed. I realized there was a difference between alone and lonely. I wanted something more serious.

"So I shifted into relationship mode. I tried that for a bit, but nothing lasted more than a couple of months. When one made it to four months, I got my hopes up and asked her to move in with me. It was quick. And it wasn't the kind of relationship I dreamed about having. But it wasn't awful." He scoffed softly and tipped the rest of his bottle. "I thought maybe things between us would get better once I retired from active duty and became an instructor. I'd be around all the time, so we'd have more time together. And *that* move put the final nail in things."

Elle's questions only multiplied exponentially. First and foremost—who in her right mind wouldn't want to spend more time with Ben? She'd give anything to see him everyday like that. Unless SEAL Ben was a raging asshole, or maybe Instructor Ben was. Neither scenario was logical.

He sighed. "I asked what it was about me that she didn't like. Turns out I'm boring. She said the only thing that made me appealing was being a SEAL. Without that, I didn't have anything else going for me other than the sex." He shrugged.

"When I sat back and thought about it, any attempt I'd made at a relationship always died out. There wasn't much conversation or connection. I decided the common denominator was me. The real me beneath the job can't maintain a woman's attention. So that's it. That's why I'm single."

She turned this insight over in her head, like data points gathered during an experiment. She couldn't square the information she'd obtained through direct observation with what he was giving her secondhand.

"Are you...being serious, right now?"

"Afraid so." A faint blush flashed across his cheeks. "I've been nervous that you'll lose interest and that'll be that."

She sat up and swung her legs underneath her.

"I spent the past couple months waiting for you to wake up and see how far outside my league you are, and you've been worried that I would think *you* were boring?"

"Elle," he said, brushing his finger down her jaw. "You are so wrong. I wish you could see yourself the way I do. Because then you'd realize that you're the one outside of my league. And before you object, let me state the facts because I know you like those. You're the most intelligent person I've met, yet you never make me feel stupid. You explain hard things in a way that make sense. You're empathetic. You're funny, like smart and dry and dark funny, with the greatest laugh I've ever heard. Add onto that how absolutely beautiful you are, and I don't stand a chance."

She wanted to object. To remind him she was a lowly science teacher he met alone at a bar on a Wednesday. No research prospects. No personal prospects, either. Just her and a trail of broken dreams she'd left behind along the way.

"My guess," he said, "is that you're collecting data to mount an argument against all of this, but full disclosure: you won't win. And as far as I can tell, your biggest flaw is that you've protected yourself for so long against so many things that you can't or won't let anyone in. Well, I assume anyone. I hope it isn't just me, or else I'll really lose all credibility."

He was somehow able to read her, though she hadn't opened a single page of her innermost self.

"What are you thinking right now?" he said.

"Those women who thought you were boring. I can't wrap my brain around that."

"That's not what I meant and you know it." His face softened even more. "Let me in. Really in."

"I don't know how." Her throat squeezed before she could say more.

"Start by telling me what you were thinking about when you first looked through that telescope tonight."

She swallowed against the urge to unleash all she'd held so tightly for so long.

"How good it felt to be back up there," she said. It was true, but that wasn't all of it. Even here, on a blanket on top of the White House with the most perfect man she'd ever met, who opened himself up to her in a way she'd never experienced, she couldn't quite go to that place where she kept her deepest pain sealed away.

CHAPTER TWENTY-NINE

Elle returned to her office after 7:00 p.m. and dropped into her chair with a rather ungraceful thud. It had been a full day of tests and projects. Tomorrow would be more of the same. She had to remind herself she'd done this intentionally. With a full week off for spring break, she had more than enough time to grade it all. She and Ben had even more date nights planned in light of her week off. Of course, if something came up at work for him, that might change. He always said these things like he was talking about any old job, and not running the country.

She was packing up, her mind running over her schedule for tomorrow when someone pushed open her door without knocking. She lifted her head and met Lance's condescending gaze.

"I'm glad you're still here, Ellery. I've been meaning to catch you." He strode over and sat down without being invited. It prickled her spine and filled her chest with a groan she fought against by curling her toes tight. She was *always* still here, unlike him.

"What can I do for you, Lance?" She folded her hands on the desk and did her best to appear open, though her mind whirred with retorts and scoffs and eye rolls.

"I assume you saw the news about Edgar coming back for the symposium."

She tightened her legs under the desk in addition to her toes. That smug face was begging to be...

"Yes. It's great for the event and for us." Hopefully, she was turning her lips up in some semblance of a grin and not a snarl.

"I believe it is, too. I hope you aren't too cross with me for circumventing you and contacting him directly."

"Of course not. I'm glad he's able to make it." She gripped her hands together.

"Splendid."

Who said that in conversation? Rolling her eyes was getting harder to fight.

"Now, for the second thing," he continued. "An old friend of mine will be attending the symposium. You may have heard of him. Jasper Cunningham, from the Space Technology and Aeronautics Research Institute."

Her heart skipped several beats and the breath caught in her hollow chest.

"Really," she eked out and cleared her throat.

A spark of satisfaction danced across his face. "Ye—"

Her phone rang from her bag. She scrambled to fish it out, Pete and Brody's faces lighting across the screen. She declined it.

"Sorry about that. You were saying?" she said.

Lance opened his mouth, but Pete was calling her back. She sent it to voicemail and silenced it this time, so it wouldn't interrupt. But before Lance could start again, the screen lit back up with another call from Pete.

"Perhaps you need to answer..."

"One second," she said to Lance before picking up the call. "Pete—"

"Are you home?"

"No, I'm in a meeting at *work*." Her lips were tight against her teeth.

"Jesus, what is with you and that job?"

Irritation grated down her chest and she glanced at Lance's curious and impatient glare. "Hang on." She stood and said to Lance, "This should only take a minute."

He huffed and made a big show of checking his watch. She went into the hall and shut her door almost all the way.

"Did something happen?" she whisper-yelled into the phone.

"Elle—"

"Is it Brody? Mom?" A panic began to melt the frustration.

"Just call me when you're home."

"Pete, you are *not* doing this. I left a meeting with my *boss* to take this call. And I'm here because I *need* to be. Now tell me. What is going on?"

"They're fine. Everyone is safe. Nothing happened."

"Then why are you blowing up my phone?"

Silence hung in the air between the phone and her ear. Growing more and more impatient, she peeked through the crack in her door at Lance tapping his foot and shaking his head down at his phone. Damn it.

Pete sighed. "It's nothing. Forget about it."

Anger flared. "You're joking, right? You don't call me three times, and then not tell me what the hell is going on. That's an asshole, selfish move. Even for you."

He scoffed. "Whatever, Ellery. You've cornered the market on selfish."

"That's original. Especially since it's not close to the truth."

"Everything is about *you*. Your job that you hate. The new boss you can't stand. The old one you've been crying about since September. The stupid space place that keeps rejecting you. And don't even get me started on Dad..."

"You are crossing a line here that you won't come back from." She seethed between clenched teeth. "Considering you're the reason I got held back so much."

"What the hell does that mean?"

"Oh, come on. Dad couldn't bear to bruise the ego of my eternally golden, but academically inept big brother. *You're* the reason why I wasn't in college four or five years sooner."

"Fuck you, Ellery."

"No, fuck you, Pete. And let's not forget the phone call to beg me to come back when Dad got sick. I didn't want to be here, and now I'm stuck in a dead-end job with almost no chance of living up to *my* potential, all because of *you*."

Blinded and deafened, she was breathless, the rush of her anger pulling it from her chest. It was quiet. Too quiet. She assumed he'd hung up.

"Thanks for confirming how much of a loser and fuckup I am." The phone beeped with the ended call. She closed her eyes and leaned against the wall. She inhaled one, two, three big breaths, paying extra close attention to the pulling of her skin across her chest. The curl of her toes inside her shoes. The pain rattling loose from her heart.

"Ellery, is everything all right?" Lance stood in her office doorway.

She pushed off the wall and shook away the conversation. "I'm fine. Apologies for that. Shall we go back in and keep talking?"

He waved his hand. "I'm tardy for a personal engagement. All I really wanted to say was that I hope you're taking this symposium assignment seriously. If any of it goes wrong and makes this university and *me* look bad, I'll make sure Jasper and anyone else at STAR knows it was you." He ran his palm over the black strands of his combed-over hair. "And that will all but ensure you never get out of this dead-end job." He dipped his head before turning and waltzing away.

Spencer,

I need a status update on the student projects for the symposium. Come see me first thing in the morning.

Elle

CHAPTER THIRTY

Elle wiped the sleep out of her eyes and went back to her inbox. She'd arrived at work early, still agitated from the night before.

Last night, she'd picked up her phone a few times to call or text Pete, but had done neither. Every time she started, a new flourish of anger would flare and she'd shut down. How dare he say such insulting things and then expect *her* to apologize?

She'd jumped at the message tone before 10:00 p.m. But it was from Ben, bidding her goodnight and hoping she'd gotten through the meeting that kept her from their nightly phone call. She didn't bother sending back a message. She hadn't wanted to explain why she didn't feel like talking before, and certainly wasn't going to open that can of worms when he had to get up so early.

She baked a few batches of beignets in a lame attempt to quiet her mind. First Pete, then Lance, and on the spiral continued despite her efforts. Every tidbit drifted through her mind and led to an even bigger one, until she couldn't stand it anymore. She threw the dirty dishes in the sink, left the mess on the counter and darted upstairs. She threw on a pair of leggings and sneakers. Locking her door behind her, she did something she'd never thought she would. She ran.

It was hard to get going with the cold air slapping her in the face and her legs heavy. The entire activity was so foreign she stopped a block away. It was almost midnight, and the streets were empty. A misty fog descended from the streetlights. Her breath was already heavy and she tipped her head back to open her lungs. The sky was bright, the full moon laughing at how ridiculous she was. She started walking back home, but those thoughts bombarded her again: Pete, Lance, Pete, Lance, Pete, Edgar, Dad... Dad.

Before she knew it, she was plodding through the night, pushing her legs faster and faster, her breath igniting her chest. With each foot strike, she imagined stomping out the sparks of internal wounds threatening to ignite.

She collapsed into bed around 1:30 a.m., her brain exhausted and her muscles throbbing.

Even so, she was in the office before 8:00 a.m. booting up her laptop, hoping there would be an email reply from Spencer attaching the list of projects he'd chosen. She would casually review the list over break, familiarize herself with the ones she didn't know, and then shove it down Lance's throat. It would be glorious.

But there was no email from Spencer, and after a hefty sigh, she charged through her inbox.

The sharp rap at the door brought relief as Spencer appeared.

"It's so good to see you." For the first time since they'd met, she genuinely meant it. She winced and shifted in her seat, the muscles in her legs reminding her of how she'd punished them last night.

"Are you sick?" he asked. When she shook her head, he continued. "You look awful."

She'd missed that Spencer charm the past few weeks.

"That is a lovely thing to say," she snapped. But judging by the clueless look about his face, he didn't understand what she meant and perhaps believed she was being literal. She sighed and settled back as best as she could. "Do you have the list of projects?"

He dug the folder she'd given him out of his briefcase and held it fast. His nose crunched.

Oh no...

"Yes. These are the very best and worthy of a spot at the symposium." He held the folder out in such a confident manner it diminished the flash of dread.

"Excellent." She took it. "You scared me. For a second I th —" She flipped it open and blinked at the single sheet of paper inside. She turned it over and ran her gaze over it again before bringing it back up. "Spencer, there are three names on this list."

He nodded. "That's correct."

This must be some kind of a joke. Or at least Spencer's idea of one. "Where are the rest?"

"That's all of them."

Her chest raked with frustration. "There are supposed to be at least forty-nine more."

Nose scrunch. "Yes, but you said to pick the best. And I did."

"No, I said choose the *fifty-two* best from the 286 applications."

He shrugged, completely unbothered by the increasing volume of her voice. "There weren't fifty-two best. Just three."

Oh, god, oh, god, oh, FUCK. She let the paper go midair and it drifted to her desk. She stood abruptly, ignoring the muscles pulling from her heels to her neck.

"No, no, no, no," she whispered, turning her back to him.

She inhaled and exhaled, eyes closed. But all the breathing in the world wasn't going to magically fix this error.

"Dr. Conroy, surely you don't want to encourage erroneous conclusions and ill-reported data be displayed at the symposium."

She reeled around. "What do you mean by that? Did you try and disprove these projects?"

"Yes, of course. I put all 286 through my unique stringent process." He held up the iPad. "I've got the conclusions and data an—"

"Spencer! That was not your job."

"How could it not be?"

"Because these aren't *your* ideas or projects. You don't get to be jury and judge. The students who developed them have the right to draw conclusions using their methodology. Not yours."

Spencer blinked through his lenses. "That's inefficient. How will they learn if you let them go along the wrong course?"

"It's *their* course to traverse. Not mine. And it sure as hell isn't yours. They have to fail to succeed. We all do! It's *science.*" She exhaled and rubbed her temples. Almost three hundred applications to go through and vet properly. *Hundreds* of exams, essays, and reports to grade.

Ten days.

His tapping on the iPad acted like an anvil to her head. Damn this idea to pass things off to him. The fury directed at Pete sputtered back to life and she cursed his name under her breath.

"Fail to succeed is an irrational teaching implement and scientific assertion. I have never failed, and I've succeeded plenty. My methodology is accurate and the logical conclusion to your assignment."

The tone of his voice fanned the spark and ignited that fury. "Get. Out."

"That's an inappropriate reaction. He was right about your emotions getting the best of you."

Lance? That motherfucking asshole.

"Spencer." She seethed between clenched lips. "I need you to leave my office. Now. I'm not going to get any nicer the longer you sit and argue."

He opened his mouth, but she put up a hand. "Don't." She warned. She didn't try to hide her anger. The red tide broke across her skin from under her sweater and seeped up her neck to her face. He must have understood, finally, she wasn't going to react any other way at the moment. He quietly took his brief-case and iPad, along with his too-big-for-his-own-good ego and left.

CHAPTER THIRTY-ONE

The next morning at the storage unit, Elle waited until 9:15 before she put down her coffee and dug out the extra key Pete had given her. She unlocked the door and flung it open. The crash of it in the frame elicited the attention of a man down the aisle, but she only offered him a glance.

"If he wants to be late, then fine," she said to the boxes. "I can move this shit around without him. I don't need him." She grabbed a box out of the middle of a stack, which sent the four above it crashing to the ground. She jumped before they hit her.

"FUCK!" Her phone chirped. When she realized it was Ben's and not hers, she let it go and didn't bother looking. She'd been short with him the night before, ignoring the messages he'd sent throughout the day until that night while she sat at the greenhouse agonizing over the shitstorm of work she'd gotten caught up in. Only then did she tap out a succinct reply:

Elle: Been busy. Bad day. Won't have time for a while.

"Messaging your hunky boy toy," Janet had teased, but Elle being in no mood for chatter of any kind, tossed the phone in her bag and answered the question with a scoff and eye roll.

"O...kay," Janet said and went back to work, which Elle was only too happy about. She'd grabbed fresh readings from the plasma generator, looked over the lettuce billowing from the mounds of damp sand, and left for the night.

She hadn't looked at the phone again until she was headed out the door to run after 11:00 p.m.

Just Ben: I've been stuck in a meeting all evening, but I'm sorry you're having a shit day. Maybe you'll be able to call me tomorrow and fill me in. Anytime.

Just Ben: I miss you.

Now, as she sat back on the concrete amid the contents of Dad's boxes, more case files and Matchbox cars she had no desire to go through, she dragged out Ben's phone.

Just Ben: I'm really worried about you.

"Jesus." She hung her head.

"Everything okay down here?" A man's voice came from the door.

She lifted her head, the man's white wispy hair moving in the breeze.

"It's fine. Just having a moment." She began to clean up the avalanche, slamming scattered papers and folders into the closest box.

"Would you like some help?"

She stood, every muscle begging her to accept. "No, thank you. Sorry for the language."

The older man tilted his head, but he didn't move. "You're usually here with a man."

"Yes, my brother. But he stood me up today."

"He was quite upset last week. That phone call sounded rough." He blew air out of his lips like a horse. "I remember having knockdowns like that with my late wife. Man, that woman could fight. Sounded like your brother was going at it pretty good with his."

Yes, Pete had been on the phone in a heated and hushed conversation. And no, she didn't care so much at this moment. She was too mad.

"He's good at pissing people off lately." She gestured around. "Case in point."

"Maybe he's got more going than he lets on." The old gent picked up an errant piece of paper that had slipped out from the unit and danced in the breeze outside. He leaned in and offered it to Elle. "This is a cute one. Your kids make it?"

Irritation rattled her chest. This guy needed to go and stop interjecting himself into her business. Her gaze dropped to the paper. It was a crayon picture of a little boy holding a little girl with pigtails and a purple smile. Little boy printing, shaky with backward letters, scrawled along the bottom simply said, "Pete and Ellie best friends."

The heat dissipated from her body. She reached into the box she'd been shoving stuff into and pulled out a dozen more crayon drawings, all created by Pete of him and her.

"I'll leave you to it," the man said. She'd forgotten he was there.

"Thanks," she managed, her throat scorched with sadness and regret as time rolled back to a childhood before she was strange. Before she was put in a box. When it was just her big brother and her against the world. She'd idolized him and he took care of her. Always.

She wiped away the tears bulging at the corners of her eyes, scrambled for her phone and dialed his number. When it went to voicemail, she left a message. Then she opened their text string.

Elle: I tried calling. I'm sorry, Pete. I didn't mean to be such a bitch. You were right. I am selfish and I always have been. Please call me when you get this.

She paused, fingers hovering above the screen.

Elle: I love you.

She didn't do that, express her feelings. Not to him. Not to anyone. They were too big and too complicated most of the time and often laced with shades of shame and regret. But alone in this storage unit, a time capsule of sorts preserving Dad's life and legacy, all of it came thundering through.

She shook them off. Now was not the time to melt down. She needed to find Pete. Maybe he'd gone to the bakery at the last minute to help Mom.

Mom picked up on the third ring.

"Hey, Ellie. You coming by?"

Odd. "Should I be?"

Mom chuckled. "I figured you were going to swoop in and take Brody somewhere fun."

That alarm sounded inside Elle's chest again. "I didn't know he was there."

"Oh, yeah, Pete dropped him off Thursday night. Said Tabitha was out of town, and he had some things he had to take care of. Didn't want Brody to be with a babysitter. He didn't tell you?"

The energy flooding through her heart threatened to blow it apart. She grabbed her bag off the floor and jumped to lower the door. "He might have. I've been busy." Too busy to talk when he called Thursday night. Too selfish to notice how much he'd been hurting. Too chicken to insist he talk to her.

"When is Pete coming back to get Brody? You know, so I can plan some things." Elle crunched her toes and locked the unit, hustling down the aisle and out toward the street to hail a cab.

"Brody's got the week off for spring break, but Pete didn't

really say when he'd be back. Is there something wrong, Ellie? You're doing a lot of huffing and puffing."

"I'm, uh, out for a walk."

"That's the first I've heard of you doing that. Is everything okay?"

She waved into the street, and a yellow cab slowed to a stop. "Listen, Mom, let me get a few things done and I'll come see Brody. If not tonight, tomorrow."

"No rush. I'm enjoying having him all to myself for more than an hour."

The tone of Mom's voice supported her assertion. Even so, Elle might have to see Brody and ply him with ice cream. Get the little boy to talk about what was going on at home.

Elle hung up and slid into the taxi. She rattled off the address for the bar and immediately called Pete's number. Straight to voicemail again. She sent another message:

Elle: Pete, Mom said you dropped B off Thursday night. Please call me.

A message came in from Mom. A picture of Brody in his bakery apron with a small set of mixing bowls. A huge Pete-like smile on his face. Elle leaned her head back and said a silent prayer to a god she wasn't sure existed that her brother was all right.

CHAPTER THIRTY-TWO

The bar was locked and a sign in the front window indicated it was closed until further notice due to a family emergency.

Panicked, she rushed around the side entrance. She bent and counted the rocks in the bed, until she came to thirteen—her favorite number—and slid the false bottom to release a key. Nothing seemed out of place inside the bar, everything tidy. As if Pete closed it one night ready for the next and never opened it again.

She picked up her phone to call Mom again but didn't. Instead, she went to her contact list and called Tabitha.

After four rings, she was sent to voicemail. At least her sister-in-law's phone was on. Elle flipped the overheads off as she turned to leave, but a dim light filtering through the door of the back room caught her attention. She gulped away the fear and pushed it open. A cot with a pillow and blanket, all folded neatly. Clothes were hung from exposed beams in the wall where drywall had been peeled away. She recognized Pete's army jacket, the one she'd last seen him wearing a week ago at the storage unit. The wall next to the bed housed pictures of

Brody and Pete, Mom and Brody, Elle and Brody. Next to that was the picture of Dad and her, a copy of the same one that hung in the bakery.

Pete had been living here. Or maybe he'd just moved his things here Thursday night, though Elle recognized the stack of boxes he'd pilfered from the storage unit and a few case files scattered on the upside-down bucket next to the cot that doubled as a nightstand. It had been longer than a couple of days.

Her head spun. Mom didn't know. That was certain based on her excitement at having Brody and her cavalier answers about Pete's location.

What the actual hell was going on with her brother and why wouldn't he tell her? Her phone rang inside her bag, but it was Ben. *Her* phone was in her hand, trembling from gripping it so hard. She had to find Tabitha and get to the bottom of whatever was going on.

In the taxi, she tipped the Ben phone to her ear. His voicemail was an echo of her unease, only it was about her and not Pete. She thought about calling him back, but she didn't have time. She simply pulled up the text string and responded:

Elle: `I can't do this right now.`

Just Ben: `Thank god you're okay. I've been so worried about you. Did I do something to upset you?`

Elle: `I'm turning this phone off for a while. I can't have the distraction.`

The phone rang in her hand, and she sent it to voicemail. She didn't have the capacity to talk to him.

Elle: `Please stop trying to contact me. I have to focus right now.`

She waited to see that it had been delivered. Three dots appeared on his side, indicating he was answering back. But she didn't want or need to see it. She turned the phone off and put it into her bag while she waited to get to Pete's house and put an end to this mystery.

THE HOUSE HAD BEEN LOCKED up tight and the extra key was missing out of the rock. She knocked and rang the doorbell. She climbed the fence (which would have amused Pete to no end if he had seen it) and tried the slider. Nothing. The house was a good secret keeper.

She huffed and sat on the back stoop, running through her options. She considered breaking the bathroom window, but on the off chance something bad waited, she didn't want to find out that way.

Nothing happened. He was blowing off steam. So was Tabitha. Maybe they went away together to try and patch things up. That was the most likely answer. It explained why no one was answering, and why Mom wasn't worried.

Her only course of action was Brody. She needed to go over there, grab him, and pump him for information. When the sky overhead rumbled, she realized how dark it had gotten. The meteorology text thread had warned of late morning showers— and sure as shit, here they came. The rain was ice pelting her skin and permeated her jacket within seconds. She flipped up her hood and set off toward home. She'd have to change before she grabbed Brody, or Mom would ask too many questions. Instead of taking a taxi, she decided to walk. She was already soaked. Maybe she'd get pneumonia and be hospitalized, thereby getting her out of all the work she should be tackling instead of running around following Pete's nonexistent breadcrumb trail. If she wasn't so worried, she'd be furious with him for pulling this. Fine, she was furious, but worry definitely outweighed anger at the moment.

She ran through every scenario, including the one where Pete did something with Tabitha or rather *to* Tabitha, thereby forcing him to make a run for it. Leaving Brody with Mom all but assured she would get custody of him instead of Tabitha's alcoholic parents. If something had happened to Pete, though, Mom would never recover. Not even having Brody would replace her shining star.

"Pete, I swear I'm going to kill you if you did something stupid," she mumbled as she turned onto the walkway up to her home.

"I'm not the one standing out in the rain." She turned to find him under her front door overhang. He was dry as a bone while she was soaked straight through. "You're gonna catch pneumonia."

Shocked by his appearance, she forgot how to move. She finally shook the hood from her head and walked to her front door. When she stepped alongside him, she moved her head back to get a better look at him. No bruises. No cuts. No obvious signs of struggle. Her gaze traveled to his hands, his right plunged into his pocket, and his left holding his backpack strap.

"Why didn't you go inside? You know the code."

He shrugged. "I figured I should wait out here."

She nodded toward his pocket. "Show me your hand."

His eyes narrowed and he held it up, knuckle-side toward her without question. It was swollen and bruised, the skin broken in a few places.

"It's not what you think," he murmured and put it back in his pocket.

"It better not be," she said and pushed into the house. "Let's get ice on that." They moved toward the kitchen.

He dropped his backpack on the ground and peeled off his sweatshirt. "It's not that bad."

She tossed a bag of peas at him, and he took it into the living room. Before she could think of joining him, she needed to change. She closed herself in the laundry room off the kitchen, swapped her soaking clothes for warm flannel pajamas, and wrapped a towel around her hair. The change complete, Elle made a couple of cups of coffee and joined Pete. She offered him a steaming cup before curling her legs underneath her in the opposite chair. Sitting back, she sipped, letting the warmth work its magic.

"I guess I owe you an explanation." He cleared his throat. "I've been having a lot of marital problems."

No answer required. Just a nod to let him know she was listening.

"I know you're thinking it's nothing new, except this time it is." He sighed and let the peas slip from his hand. "We split up."

She sipped from the cup and held fast to his face with her gaze. So many things begged to be said, but she didn't dare.

"It turns out I make a better dad than a husband. So she replaced me with some government guy. An accountant. Been seeing him for a while apparently right under my nose."

That bitch. Elle was livid.

"I've been living in the bar for the past month or so."

Okay, now she needed to say something. "Why didn't you tell me? You could've stayed here."

He put his hand up. "Elle, I'm not taking charity from you."

"It's a room, Pete. I'm not giving you the house."

"It's not easy for me to ask you for help." The pain coating his face punched her square in the gut. "I'm a hypocrite, I know."

She let that comment go without a retort. "I shouldn't have been so vocal about her or your marriage. But..." She contemplated her cup for a beat. "I never thought she was good enough for you."

He chuckled and his shoulders rumbled. "*That* was obvious. Though I don't know why."

"You're the best guy I know. You deserve someone who's going to treat you like it."

"That'd be sweet if it wasn't coming from my little sister." He settled back into the couch and sighed. "Sorry about Thursday."

She stopped him with a wave of her hand. "No, that's on me. I'm sorry. I shouldn't have dismissed you like that. I knew something was wrong, but once again, I was too caught up in my stuff to think about yours. I never should have said what I did."

"Did you mean it?" He leaned his head back against the pillow, and for the first time in a while, his face appeared slack.

"No. I never blamed you for what Dad did, or rather didn't do."

"You really think Dad slighted you on purpose?"

She scoffed and leaned forward. "You're kidding, right?"

He shrugged and started examining the bruises on his hand before bringing his gaze back up to hers. "Thursday night, I went back to the house to grab more of my stuff, and the guy was there. Eating dinner at my table with *my* son. That was it."

Her nerves rattled and the anticipation clenched her chest.

"I took Brody and dropped him at Mom's. I didn't want him to see me like that." He went back to his hand, turning it over. "This was me versus the brick wall outside the bar. Ten out of ten, *don't* recommend."

She heaved out a heavy sigh and sat back. "I thought we were going to have to bury a body somewhere."

He smiled. "You'd do that for me?"

"If you think I wouldn't, I have failed as a sister." She shrugged. "Besides, it's the least I could do."

"For what?"

"Hold that thought." She dashed back into the foyer where she'd dropped her bag. She brought it into the living room and handed him the drawings from Dad's boxes. As he studied each one, his eyes filled with tears. She'd not seen Pete cry much. In fact, she could count the number of times on one hand. They weren't affectionate beyond hugs on occasion. But they used to be. Pete used to cart her around on his back and she'd plant kisses on his cheek, which he'd pretend to hate but loved. He'd brush her off when she fell. She'd hold his hair back while Mom patched up a gash on his head after he tried out a tree limb for Elle and it turned out to be rotten, sending him crashing to the ground.

"For you taking such good care of me." She settled onto the couch next to him now. They were thirty-eight and forty-two, but looking at those drawings, they were both transported back to simpler times when it had been the Conroy Kids against the world.

He settled an arm around her shoulders and pulled her in for a hug, and she wrapped her arms around him. His sobs against her shoulder caused her breath to catch, and her own throat burned against the grief. She hadn't been the best sister for a long time. But that could change. She would change.

After a few minutes, he drew back and wiped his eyes down the sleeve of his shirt. "I don't know how these aren't in a museum."

"Don't worry," she said, smiling and taking the pictures from him. "I'll display them on my fridge. Proudly."

CHAPTER THIRTY-THREE

It's amazing what one person can accomplish when there is so much at stake. Elle's brain was capable of astronomical feats when threatened with certain career suicide.

That was why, at 9:30 p.m. on the Thursday of spring break, only five days after she'd started, she fired off the list of fifty-two projects and four alternates for the symposium to her sniveling boss.

At what cost had Elle accomplished this? She sat back on her sofa and laughed hysterically, almost maniacally at the sheer insanity of the past five days. She hadn't even cracked her laptop until Sunday night, after spending the weekend moving Pete into her spare room. He objected when she bought a bed she said she'd been meaning to, but hadn't gotten around to. He insisted she keep her things stored in there, though she said she'd wanted to move them up into the attic for a while. He got choked up when the furniture was delivered, including a bed for Brody.

So Sunday evening, when Pete left to reopen the bar, she sat down and opened her laptop. When he tiptoed in after 2:00 a.m., she was in the very same spot.

Thus, the days went. She'd sleep here and there, but most of the time she worked with a manic rhythm, one that she hadn't fallen into for a very long time. Maybe during graduate school or her post-doc work. Even when she spent nights at a scope and days sifting through and analyzing data, her brain hadn't been in this kind of gear.

Pete came and went, bringing boxes from the storage unit and his garage, working alongside her some days sifting through the contents. He'd slide food in front of her she'd mindlessly pick at without realizing it. He'd cover her with a blanket when she passed out from exhaustion, and fold it forty minutes later when she threw it off and went right back to work.

This felt like an achievement beyond what she'd done before, and now that it was off her plate, she wanted to celebrate. But it was late and Pete was at work, so she decided to go see him and share the good news. She peeled the clothes from her skin and showered, because she also hadn't done *that* since Sunday—*gross*—and set out.

The night air was cool but steeped in humidity, the first inklings of spring. Greenery had started coming back to life in planters and along sidewalks. She wondered then, for the first time in a while, if the garden at the White House was also coming back to life. Her ribs panged like a tuning fork. She hadn't allowed herself to think of anything but student projects since Sunday, including Ben. And now, she realized how awful she'd been to him.

Pete's was way more crowded than she anticipated, but her usual spot hadn't been taken. She slid onto the stool, and spied her brother down the bar, a broad smile across his face. He was pushing the hair off his forehead while he talked to a trio of women. He glanced at Elle, excused himself, and trotted over.

"Are you finished or have you done something bad?" He raised an eyebrow.

"My dear, sweet brother. I have pulled off a near impossible feat with days to spare."

He popped the top off two beers and they toasted. "I never doubted your ability to do the impossible, Ellie."

She glanced at the other end of the bar where the women sat. That was where Ben and Ted were sitting that first night. She sipped her beer to keep the ache at bay.

"I see you're back to breaking hearts just like the good old days," she said.

"I don't know any other way to be." He smiled again, and it warmed her. This season of life had been hard on Pete and would continue to be for a while. But now, she could see shades of his old, more settled, more jovial self peeking out.

"So." He leaned his elbows on the bar. "Were you bullshitting me a few weeks back about dating someone?"

Ugh. "How about we not do this," she said and sipped her beer.

"Oh, we're doing it. Spill it."

"Don't you have customers to flirt with?"

He scoffed. "You suck at sharing, you know that? I literally cried on your shoulder and you still won't tell me."

He had a point.

"Fine. I was dating a guy for a while, but it's over." She shrugged and started peeling the label off her bottle.

"That your doing?"

She could lie and say the guy was awful and demeaning and took advantage of her.

"What do you think?"

He nodded and picked up the pieces of peeled paper off the bar, then plucked the bottle out of her hand.

"Hey," she said, "I wasn't done with that."

"You have a prior engagement." He leveled a serious stare.

She shook her head. "Oh, no, it isn't like that. He's...not

available." It was after 10:30, and Ben would be fast asleep. She hadn't dug the phone out of her bag since the weekend, so it was likely dead.

"If he's even half as into you as you are him, he'll make himself available."

"No, you don't..." But this counterargument wasn't going to work with Pete. "I screwed up. As usual."

"Yeah, I gathered. Which is why I'm saying you need to fix it."

"It isn't that simple."

"Ellery, you better not be shacking up with a married man—"

"Oh, my god, Peter, it isn't THAT!"

He tilted his head and brushed his hair from his forehead again. "Then you have a chance to change things."

Her shoulders slumped. "It's too late." It wasn't Pete's fault. He didn't know what she was dealing with. What she'd done, or rather not done, when she told Ben to leave her alone because she was too afraid of sharing her life.

"Ellie," Pete said, his voice soft, "if he's worth it, you have to at least give it a shot. And not a half-assed one. A real one where you let him in on all the messy bullshit swimming around in your head."

Yes, Ben was worth it. He was worth so much. But how did she tell her brother that *she* wasn't worthy of Ben?

"Why are you still here?" He cut through the quick of her thoughts. Maybe she could tell Pete what she was up against. Or rather *who* she was up against. Though really, it wasn't Ben she was talking about. It was herself and all the heavy baggage of her past.

CHAPTER THIRTY-FOUR

I t was strange having someone other than Ted walk her up to the Palm Room. But then again, it was after 11:00. Surely, Ted was home—wherever that was.

The guard escorted her into the elevator, where he scanned his card and stepped out. The ride was short, but it was the first time she'd done it alone.

The door whispered open to Ben standing down the hallway. His hair was tousled, hands pushed deep into the pockets of his gray joggers. His black T-shirt pulled against his chest.

She stepped hesitantly out of the elevator. Like she was walking out on a frozen lake on the cusp of a springtime thaw.

She stopped well short of his solid form looming ahead. He wasn't going to make this easy, and he shouldn't. She was the one who screwed up. Brushed him aside like he was a speck of dust. No gray in what she'd done. He was mad. Hurt. Betrayed. And she had done that.

"I didn't mean to wake you." She gathered her socks with her toes while the seconds ticked past.

His gray gaze pressed down, burdening her in the most

uncomfortable way. Burrowing in her chest, cracking through the last pieces of wall.

"Wasn't sleeping well anyway." His tone was flat. His face stiff.

Alright, Ellery. Time to see how much he's worth.

She inhaled until her lungs inflated and tightened the skin across her chest. He remained unmoved. She exhaled. "I'm sorry. About last week. About...a lot of things."

He slid his hands from his pockets, crossed his arms across his chest. Creating a barricade, a definite him and her.

She sighed and shifted her weight. Her skin crawled. "The last time we were together on the roof. You asked me what I was thinking about when I looked through the scope...and I lied. Kind of. I mean, it did feel good to be doing it again, but that wasn't all of it."

The pain thundered in her chest, then exploded through the wall with one big clap.

"I was thinking about my dad. It's hard for me to think about him because while he was my biggest cheerleader, he held me back. Taught me to hide what and who I really was, so people wouldn't treat me differently." She didn't have to live in the gray. She just had to see it. That's what he'd always said. The world was full of gray, so the more she saw it, the better off she'd be. The better she could get at protecting herself. So she'd intentionally seek the gray areas. Day after day, school year after school year. Until she existed so long in it her black and white brain no longer worked the way it once had.

"When I went to college, I met my mentor, Edgar Linton. He was the first one who encouraged me to be me. To not hide the science, but rather to embrace it. He made me realize how wrong my dad was for forcing me to change because"—she gulped because she had never admitted this out loud—"he was ashamed of me."

Edgar had helped her in so many ways. He had been more than a mentor, even back then. He'd been the father she'd needed. The one who encouraged her with more than silly fake interviews and trips to the beach to stargaze. Edgar had taught her to dive into her intelligence, rather than lock it away in a box.

So she had done what any other teenager would do in her situation: She distanced herself from Dad. When he'd call, she'd be short. When she came home to visit, she stayed in her room, head buried in work, even when Dad suggested they take the old scope out for a spin. She'd roll her eyes when he'd asked her to explain the latest thing she'd been working on, his little recorder in hand. He couldn't understand. He never did and he never would.

"I stayed away for years to avoid my dad. And then he got sick." Karma, Edgar had said when she called him. She'd winced, but secretly agreed because that was the person she'd morphed into.

"Edgar was at NatU by then and offered me a job. Said he'd help me get my STAR fellowship application prepared. Edgar was the only person who knew what I'd been working on, and he could help."

Ben shifted his weight, but his gaze remained glued to her. It felt heavy, pressing her to go on. Was it encouragement or judgment that tightened the squeeze in her chest? She gulped it back and plowed ahead with the worst of it.

"I took it and came back. But I didn't see my dad for a long time. I made excuses and kept myself busy so I wouldn't have to face him." One year. That's how long she'd waited before she saw him in the hallway outside the maternity ward the day Brody was born. It had been an awkward moment for her, that pause between their gazes locking and what happened next. It had been Dad who smiled and rushed toward her, arms open.

Elle had thought he didn't seem as sick as she'd thought he would and it irritated her that she'd given up the West Coast on the premise that Dad and her family needed her.

She cleared her throat. "I'm ashamed to say that I spent a lot of time avoiding my dad. I'd arrange to see Brody when my mom said he had doctor's appointments so I wouldn't have to try and explain..." Edgar had encouraged her to confront Dad and tell him how he'd hindered her. He'd even offered to meet with Dad and facilitate the discussion to put an end to this once and for all. But Elle knew Dad had never liked Edgar. Not since she'd stayed at Stanford during break to help Edgar prepare his final draft of a research paper. Dad had asked if she really knew Edgar well enough to do so much of the work for him. She'd been furious with Dad and hung up without trying to justify herself. After that, she started dodging his calls.

She blew the air out through her lips. "Then my dad fell at home. I couldn't avoid him anymore."

The first time she walked into that hospital room, she'd gasped at how this once larger-than-life force had shrunk. A dying star fizzling out one great gaseous layer at a time. That's when the doctor told them the cancer had spread aggressively through every major organ. She closed her eyes and even now was transported back to that room. The way Dad's exhausted eyes lit up at her. The shaky smile spread across his face. The rattled breath from the pressure of the tumors eating him from the inside out.

Her throat burned as the memories poured from her heart.

"He started asking me what I was working on. To tell him all about it. The project. Being a professor. He wanted to talk like we did when I was kid. Like there had never been this huge chasm between us. He even pretended to have his stupid recorder. And I decided that it was time for me to tell him all the things he'd done wrong. How he'd hurt me by holding me back with his shame." The tears stung as they slid down her cheeks. That anger back then was so raw and powerful, it shook her from head to toe.

She sighed. "But I couldn't do it. It seemed pointless by then. He was dying. So I did what I learned to do. I swallowed my pain and started talking to him again. Three months later, he was in hospice."

By then, she'd sewn those emotions into the wall of her chest. Edgar had helped, reminding her there was no emotion in space and science. Only what was and what wasn't. She'd focused on that: the work, the lessons, the research.

"That's what I was thinking about that night on the roof. How it all started with a telescope and my dad. It made me miss him. It allowed me to miss him. And I didn't like that feeling."

Her time with Ben over the months had softened the scabs of old wounds. The anger that had melted away and the regret that hardened in its wake. She'd come to terms with who Dad had been and what he'd done. He was a man who protected and served his whole life, and did whatever he thought was best for her. He was a man who took his last breath after she'd bent over his ear and told him she loved him and she always would.

"I guess I've been hiding it all for so long that letting it out scares the hell out of me." Like someone was cracking her open and digging her out piece by piece. There was veritably no end to the depths of her inner world. She'd tell Ben anything and everything right now to get him to understand it actually *was* her. Not him. She couldn't bear that he'd think she was like the women who'd hurt him in the past. He was so much more than they'd led him to believe, and she couldn't allow him to take on any of the blame in the demise of their relationship. It was all her doing—her undoing.

Ben dropped his head no doubt disappointed in who she was. How awful of a person she was. Good. That's what she needed him to believe. Because it was, in large part, true.

"Thanks for giving me the chance to apologize. I didn't bring the phone with me, but I can drop it at the guard house in the morning." She brushed the hair off her face, tears making the strands stick. "Again, I am so sorry."

He rubbed the back of his neck and brought his gaze back up to hers. It was softer, more like the Ben she'd gotten to know.

"Full disclosure?" he asked, his voice soft.

She nodded and scraped the tears from her face.

"I forgave you the second they told me you were at the guard house." He shrugged, the corner of his mouth lifting in an apologetic grin.

She shook her head, disbelief racing through her.

"So I just did all of that for nothing?" she said, only half kidding.

"Oh, no, it wasn't for nothing," he said, stepping towards her, brushing his fingers down the side of her face. "It was for everything. To me."

She took a minute to appreciate the way a few strands of his hair stood upright. The subtle creases at the corners of his eyes that deepened as he continued to stare. She inhaled wholly for the first time in a very long time, breathing in the gift Ben had given her. The compassion. The support. The courage to be herself and open up without fear or reproach.

She exhaled, releasing the burden of shame she'd carried all these years over the way she'd treated Dad. The regret that came with it seemed to unlatch itself from her heart and dissipate into the air between her and Ben.

The pulse his fingers caused shot through her skin and into her chest. He moved them around under her chin and tilted it up to him. "Thank you for trusting me. For opening up. Finally. It's all I've wanted you to do."

She hadn't come here for his forgiveness. She hadn't come here for his empathy. But the minute he folded her into his embrace, her face up against his heart space, the tears flowed again. And unlike any other time in her life, Elle allowed herself to remain in the pain because she was in the safest place to do it.

CHAPTER THIRTY-FIVE

"You have white knight syndrome," she said.

He lifted his eyebrow from the other side of the couch. "Is it terminal?"

"In your case, definitely."

He clasped his hand over his chest and pretended to fall back into the arm of the couch. She laughed when he kept taking breaths and coming back to life. He smiled and shot up, grabbing her empty glass.

"What does it mean to have white knight syndrome?" he asked from the water cooler.

"You have an innate need to rescue people. Like refilling their water glasses twelve times in an hour."

"I'm a big hydration guy."

She stood and stretched her arms over her head, finding her muscles stiff and achy in ways she hadn't realized. Probably from days spent hunched over her laptop with little else.

"Although, now that I think about it," she said, sliding her feet into her shoes. "White knights usually rescue people in unhealthy intimate relationships."

"That's not us," he said. "There's nothing unhealthy about

you needing to always come to my place. Or not being able to bring your phone when you do."

She shook her head. "The paradigm of healthy. Especially when you consider the non-disclosure agreement."

He winced.

"I didn't mean that in a bad way. It wasn't a big deal for me to sign it. I understand what all this"—she waved her hand around the room—"comes with for you."

He plunged his hands in his pockets again and nodded, his gaze glossing over. Unease flooded her chest. But then just as quickly, he was back and regarding her with all of his attention.

"Thanks, for understanding." That's not what he wanted to say, she could tell by the tone. It was more President Ben than Just Ben.

"I should go. I've kept you up way past your bedtime, and I haven't slept for days. So we're both due." Though, she wasn't tired at the moment. The gray sweatpants and T-shirt were doing things to her insides. Her eyes fell to the hem of his right sleeve and the points of the trident—

"You're really fascinated with my tatt."

A blistering heat rushed up her spine and into her face. She had no defense and thus didn't even try.

He flashed his megawatt smile and moved closer. The proximity of his body to hers. His fingertips traipsing down her jaw. The shivers clawed down her back.

"Full disclosure: I don't feel much like sleeping right now," he whispered into her ear, his breath caused a fresh rush of goosebumps down her skin. His lips barely grazing the skin under her lobe.

"Me neither," she whispered back. His lips hovered above hers. The limbo caused the pulse rippling down her body to deepen into a throb. She was at the event horizon, the last spot visible before a black hole. If she went any further, if *they* went any further, she might not have a way back. She might be so engulfed in his gravity, pulled into his orbit, crushed by his very essence she'd be unable to stop herself from feeling so much. From falling in love. From being in love. That was more terrifying than anything.

"Elle, don't disappear on me now. I want you here for this."

Body quivering, she gulped. "Me, too."

He threaded his fingers through her hair, cradling her head as he brought his lips down onto hers. Nothing in this world compared to this. Nothing anywhere would ever compare. Deep and tender, slow and sexy. The flutters in her stomach beat against her with such rhythmic patter, it reverberated up into her chest.

He moved his hands down her back and swept her up into his arms, lifting her. It pulled the breath from her chest.

"You're going to hurt yourself!"

"I spent decades carrying hundred-pound packs for miles and miles. Taking you to my bed isn't going to hurt."

She wrapped her legs around his waist and he groaned. He reached up and grabbed her lips with his, and they went back at it, lapping at each other's mouths while he carried her into his room.

The citrus and wood scent of him enveloped her as he laid her down and crawled on top of her.

He worked his hands up under her shirt, wasting no time, cupping her breast, moaning into her mouth. She arched her back when he brushed his thumb over her nipple and he dropped his mouth to her neck. They'd made out, but this was different. This was heat. Combustion. An absolute chemical reaction between her body and his. They melded. They fused. They were absolutely going to explode before the night was over.

She ran her hands under his shirt, first his back etched in

marble, up the rungs of the muscles climbing up his sides, to the cobblestone of the front. Until she hit an anomaly poking out of his skin.

"It's a scar," he said into her neck. "I have a few."

Didn't everybody? Only hers were much further underneath, where his hands would never touch.

"I want to see every single one." She pushed up the hem of his shirt. He sat up, straddling her, and pulled it off effortlessly. Every cut of muscle took the breath from her chest. Every line. Every burst of white scar tissue.

"Did you get shot?" she asked.

"Once or twice." He lifted her shirt. "Now it's my turn."

She let him strip her shirt. He smiled, his tongue pushed between his teeth. He bent and kissed her tummy, and she giggled.

"I've been waiting to get you naked for months."

He unbuttoned her pants and, standing at the bottom of the bed between her legs, he pulled them off. He dropped to his knees, kissing her inner thighs, the stubble from his face rubbing her sensitive skin. With each landing of his soft mouth, the heat heightened, melting her most sensitive parts.

She writhed on the bed as he worked his way toward her panties, and she swore she'd explode. Then he pushed them to the side and the heat of his mouth was there. Tears sprang to her eyes as he tickled and teased, licked and lapped, sucked and devoured her. Time didn't exist as she tumbled through space. Gasping with each brush of his tongue. Until she couldn't stand it anymore.

"I want you inside me," she whispered.

He sprung up and disappeared into the bathroom, emerging with a condom box. "I forgot Ted brought me these a while ago."

"Ted is your condom supplier?"

"I had him get them after you came for dinner that first night."

She stopped. "But you said you didn't want to have sex back then."

"No, I said I needed to wait. But I absolutely wanted to." He dropped his sweatpants and black boxers, and she forgot what they were talking about and no longer cared.

"Something wrong?" he asked, tearing her gaze away from, well, *that*.

She shook her head dumbly and licked her lips. He smiled and crawled back onto the bed, kissing her shoulder, sliding her bra strap down. He reached around and unclasped it in one shot, springing it open and sliding it from her.

He moaned and moved his mouth over one nipple and reached to stroke the other. She gripped his shoulders and tumbled back to that blissful edge. His hand fanned out across her belly as it moved down and tucked inside her panties, brushing his fingers over her most sensitive spot.

She cried out, which only made him work more to tickle and tease her with his hand, his tongue, his everything.

"I can't take much more," she rasped.

He moved his body back down hers, hooking his fingers inside her waistband and pulling her panties down her legs.

"But wait," she said and sat up halfway. He hovered over her. "Full disclosure?"

He grinned and kissed her belly. "Full disclosure."

"It's been a while. Like almost a year. Maybe longer."

He tilted his head and contemplated her, moving back up and planting a hand on either side of her shoulders. Bringing his lips down toward hers. "I haven't done this in years. And I promise I'll go slow."

Years? She might not survive. She grabbed onto his arms as he reached down and slid into her slowly, as promised.

He buried his head into her neck. "I could stay here all night," he growled.

She moved his lips over to hers and they kissed, moving together, like they'd been doing it forever. Like they were made for each other. She closed her eyes, and he whispered in her ear to let go. Let herself go.

So she did. For the first time in her life, Elle experienced true weightlessness and a freedom she'd never thought possible.

ACCORDING TO MY SCIENCE
FOURTEENTH SPRING EDITION—APRIL 17TH

NatU School of Science

Please join the Department of Space Science and Aeronautics at the 31st International Space Science Symposium this Saturday. Everyone who signed up to volunteer should have received your badges and maps via email. If you didn't, please contact Dr. Conroy. Report to the conference center one hour before your assigned volunteer time to get checked in and get to your designated area.

You're welcome to stay and attend the festivities after your volunteer time is over.

Please note that student posters will be displayed beginning at 9:00 a.m. All students are welcome to remain with their projects to answer questions.

Keynote speakers will take the stage every 30 minutes beginning at 11:00 a.m. Please check the symposium page and app for details on speakers. NatU's Edgar Linton is scheduled to speak at 2:00 p.m. Let's pack the auditorium and give Dr. Linton a warm reception!

SUMMER RESEARCH:

Stay tuned for information on summer internships and research opportunities.

CHAPTER THIRTY-SIX

She'd returned to school after the break, triumphant on every front. The students were notified about their projects, which sent a flurry of activity to her office hours. She'd graded all her tests and papers, and entered every single one before the deadline, all while lounging in various states of undress with the president of the United States.

When she'd peeled herself from him Friday morning, he'd made her promise to come back that night and to bring a bag. She needed to work, and he'd assured her he'd alert security and make sure she could bring her laptop.

Pete was in the kitchen, mug half raised to his mouth, when she came walking in. His hair was slicked back from the shower and he grinned as she passed. She took the mug from him as punishment and went upstairs to get dressed.

He didn't say a word, even when she sat opposite him and withdrew the stack of papers from her bag. He snickered like he'd seen something hilarious, and without moving too suddenly, she tossed a throw pillow, nailing him square in the face. They both devolved into laughter and went about their business.

"We going to the storage unit in the morning? We should be close to finishing."

"I can't," she said and moved another paper to the read pile. "I've got plans tonight. I won't be home."

"So you've got another unit you're working on instead."

She flushed, he laughed; she threw another pillow he caught and threatened to throw back, but she yelled and covered all the papers she had in meticulous piles between the couch and coffee table. He held back and instead left to get Brody.

She spent the night at Ben's, grading papers when he got called away during dinner, and then naked the rest of the night when he got back. He got up early to run and though she was exhausted, she dragged herself up and got back to work. He returned a little over an hour later and tossed her over his sweaty shoulder, then took her half protesting and writhing into the shower with him.

Yet, even with all the distractions (including sex so intense and fun and liberating she'd think it was all a dream if not for being a bit sore), she'd still gotten all of it done.

The first week after break passed without incident. Spencer appeared in the back of her lectures, quieter than he'd been before the symposium project, but tapping away on his iPad. Still casting judgmental glances at students. It didn't faze Elle in the least because she was on cloud nine with no chance of rain.

Then, four days before the symposium, Ben left for an emergency trip to Europe. And Lance called a department meeting where he dropped another bombshell.

"Edgar is no longer available to speak Saturday." The room gasped as a whole, but Elle felt a sense of relief. The more she'd thought about how Edgar had ignored her all these months, the madder she got. It was hurtful. She'd finally talked to Ben about it, and he suggested she try to contact Edgar one more time before the symposium so his presence wouldn't rattle or upset her at such a big event. She'd sent him another email and it went unanswered, like all the rest.

Her idea of Edgar, and the faith she had in him, had shrunk with each unanswered message. Short of something awful, like death, she couldn't imagine why he'd refused to acknowledge her...

"Ellery?"

She moved her focus to the outside, and noticed everyone was staring at her. She shifted in her seat.

"Sorry, I wasn't paying attention."

Steven cleared his throat to stifle a chuckle.

Lance was unamused by her honesty. He craned his neck one way and then the other. "I was saying that Edgar suggested you should take his place."

"Me? No thanks." She leaned back in her chair.

"Perhaps you'd like to think about it longer than five seconds, Ellery." Lance sounded scolding.

She shook her head. "Nope. I'm good."

Spencer's nose scrunched as he glowered at her from across the table. His eyebrows shot up. She shook her head and crossed her arms.

Lance leaned forward and folded his hands on the table as he addressed only her.

"Jasper will be very disappointed."

There was that. She curled her toes and sucked the inside of her cheek between her teeth. This was her opportunity to get her work in front of the head of STAR. No application to obsess over. No rejection letter to loathe. Just her speaking about her life-long passion project to the one person who could quite literally hand her the job of her dreams on the spot.

Lance didn't wait for her to answer and rose. "I'll give you until the end of the day to consider it. I'm sure someone else here would love the opportunity to present in front of such an illustrious and influential crowd."

When a few heads bobbed, Elle squeezed her toes harder. Spencer pushed up his glasses and put away his iPad. A few minutes later, she realized she was the only one left behind.

ELLE: Hey, Ben. I know you're insanely busy, but whenever you get a few minutes, could you call me?

Elle: If possible before the end of the day.

Elle: My day, not yours. I don't even know what time is it where you are.

Elle: You know what, never mind. You might be sleeping or negotiating a peace treaty or saving the world. Sorry for all the messages.

She dropped the phone on her desk and sighed. She was pretty sure Ben wouldn't even see those messages until Lance's deadline had passed. But between Edgar being a no-show and now this offer to take his place, she really needed to talk it over with someone besides herself.

Spencer rapped on the open door and didn't pause before sitting across the desk.

"Dr. Conroy, I don't know why you aren't preparing your speech for the symposium right now."

Her gaze slid to his and she again crossed her arms and leaned back.

"I'm not sure I want to do it."

"How is that possible? Dr. Dunwoody is giving you a fantastic opportunity. Why aren't you taking it?"

"Because I don't know why he's doing it." The words came

out without hesitation and surprised even her. Spencer jutted his head back and wrinkled his brow at the audacity of her statement.

"You're the obvious choice. Dr. Linton said so."

This all seemed hilarious coming from Spencer, who had spent the past three months second- and third-guessing everything she did. Undermining every decision she'd made. Insulting her methodology.

"Why do you think that is?"

He bobbed his head and shrugged. "You were second in the department after Dr. Linton."

"And yet Lance got the chair position." Another truth bomb ejected like it was on automatic pilot. She was on a roll.

"Which you don't want. You'd rather be at STAR, or you wouldn't have kept applying and getting rejected."

Fine. She didn't want the chair position, mostly because Edgar had sold her on it being beneath her, and it would only act to stall her on the way to her real goal. She didn't like thinking of his good advice right now; she was still mad at him.

"Spence—"

Ben's phone rang from her elbow. She stood and picked it up. "I need a minute," she said to Spencer as she walked out the door. "Take a look at the lecture notes you prepped for 3213 today."

She walked down to the end of the hallway. "Hi," she said into the phone. "I'm sorry for the fire drill. You didn't need to call, I'll figure it out."

"This is me ignoring you. What happened?"

She sighed and leaned against the wall. "Edgar dropped out of the symposium."

"That's a good thing, right? Unless it means something happened to him."

"No. Yeah. No, I mean." She grunted and rubbed her hand

over her forehead. "Nothing happened to him that I know of. But it means his spot at the symposium opened up and Lance offered it to me."

"And that's...not good, I take it?"

"It's an incredible opportunity. The head of STAR will be there. And maybe...I don't want to get ahead of myself."

"This would be for your super top-secret project that no one, including the person with the highest clearance in the world, knows about?"

She couldn't help but chuckle. Her shoulders relaxed.

"Hey, I get it," he said. "You never know what I'm going to do with that kind of information."

"You're ridiculous."

"Ah, but as I recall, you like my ridiculous."

Oh, yes. She more than liked Ben's *everything*. She shook her head. "I'm sorry I sent up that red flag to call. You should get back to work."

"Nope. Not going to let you pull back now, Dr. Conroy. You've made way too much progress over the last few weeks."

She smiled and leaned her head back against the wall. "I don't know what to do." The only other person she would've asked was the one who continued to ignore her. Well, him and Dad, once upon a time. An ache pulsed from her chest.

"Do you still want that job?" Ben asked.

"Yes, of course." There was, to her, nothing else she wanted more.

"Then you have to go for it."

"But." She gulped hard. "What if it doesn't work?"

"What if it does? The risk is worth the reward, don't you think? Nothing is guaranteed, even if we go all in on it. But not trying guarantees failure. It's better to take the shot and miss, than never aim."

"Did you just give me, like, three military or presidential sayings there?"

"I might have. Maybe a personal one mixed in there, too." He paused. "Look at us. I aimed pretty high when I took my shot with you, and now I'm on top of the world."

She could tell by his voice he was smiling and, damn it, if that didn't make her smile.

"I'm glad you did."

"Me, too. So why don't you do the same for your dream job. For yourself. It's what you've always wanted."

She nodded. "Thank you. For calling me back. For helping me."

"Thank you for asking. I'm sitting in my hotel room smiling like an idiot."

"I've seen that smile, and it definitely does not scream idiot. More like hot and sexy."

He chuckled in her ear and she set off for her office.

"Call me later," he said. "And tell me that you've committed to the symposium."

She rounded the corner. Spencer remained hunched over his iPad with the folder open on her desk.

"I will. I promise. Bye." She hung up and put the phone on her desk and sat. She didn't say anything to Spencer, just started reading through the notes he'd printed.

"What'd your boyfriend have to say?" he asked.

"Nothing that's your concern," she shot back, and his head snapped up outside of her periphery. She put the pages back in the folder and pushed them over to his side. "How about you look these over a few more times before class."

"For what purpose? So I can attempt to follow your illogical lecture?" Ah. He was back.

"No, so you can give your very logically ordered lecture."

She pushed her chair back and stood. "You can sit in here and work if you want. I've got 1101 in ten."

He was flustered. His nose twitched, his mouth itched to say something, but in the end, he was rendered speechless. Almost.

"Thank you." It came out in a half whisper before he grabbed the folder and turned his iPad back on.

She walked out of her office and diverted briefly to tell Lance she'd take him up on his offer.

CHAPTER THIRTY-SEVEN

The greenhouse was alive, each of the four quadrants popping with lettuce. Two thriving more than the others, but all in all, a beautiful sight. Elle had only had enough time to pop in here and there over the last couple of weeks, but each time, she was struck by how so much had grown in a space once so desolate.

"Janet left about five minutes ago," Carson said, slipping the gardening gloves off his hands. "I told her I'd finish the weeding for her."

"It's odd that you're weeding an experiment."

He shrugged. "Even the weeds can give us data."

She nodded. It made sense. They were still living and growing things.

"That, and I don't want them overrunning the lettuce. They'll choke out the good if they get a chance, since they grow, well, way better than almost anything else."

"Maybe next time measure weed growth and forget the lettuce?" She grinned.

That was never going to happen. Carson was a botanist, a garden enthusiast, the soil and its plants as equal in importance as space was for her. He spent all his free time cultivating community gardens around D.C. when he wasn't experimenting with his hydroponic setup on the terrace of his house.

"Nervous about Saturday?" he asked, his head tilted thoughtfully at her.

"Yes and no. More yes, though."

"Treat it like it's any other lecture and you'll be fine."

She laughed. "You've obviously never seen me lecture. If you had, you'd know what a horrible idea that is."

"I know you're a fly-by-the-seat-of-your-pants kinda speaker. But who cares. Do the same with this."

She shook her head. "This is too big for my normal repertoire. I have to deliver this like a dissertation."

"That means you have to break out all the big, spacey words."

She nodded. "Exactly. All the Latin. And quantum physics. I'm a bit rusty in both."

"I'll bring a thesaurus." He grinned. "Hey, you wanna grab a bite? I'm starving and haven't eaten since lunch."

"No, I can't." Her phone rang and she pulled it from her pocket to see it was an unknown number. She silenced it and put it back. But not before it started again. "I've got to get home and keep working."

The screen remained lit as another call came in. Something about the now four calls made her stomach turn.

She determined she'd answer the next call. It was Pete.

"What's wrong?" she asked.

"Are you home?" The noise around him was louder than his bar had ever seemed to be.

"No, but I'm on my way. What's going on?"

Carson gasped, and when his gaze came up to hers, she noted how pale he was. She opened her eyes wide to him and he shook his head.

"Where are you. I'm coming to get you."

Before she could ask why, Carson flipped his phone around to the breaking news banner splashed on his screen: *Meet President Foster's Secret Girlfriend, Dr. Ellery Conroy.*

PETE WAS WAITING outside the greenhouse when Elle and Carson walked out. Her head was swimming, wondering how this had gotten out. She hadn't said a word to anyone.

The shock was in full effect. Pete took her elbow and led her away. She ran through all the scenarios. It was a block before she realized they weren't going to her house.

"We're going the wrong way." She tried to turn back around.

"We can't go to your place. It's surrounded."

She stopped and ripped her arm away. "What are you talking about?"

"The press is camped outside. There and the bar."

The light swirled around. Her head grew heavy while her legs wiggled like jelly. Everything spun and she stumbled. Pete grabbed her under her arms right before she went down.

"I got you."

He led her over to a nearby bench. She trembled and hugged herself, leaning forward into a crash-ready position, even though the plane had already gone down and burst into flames.

"How did this happen?" she said aloud.

"It's true? The guy you've been seeing is the president?"

She drew her gaze up to where he stood. When she nodded, his brows arched high, and he pushed his hair away from his forehead.

"Holy shit. I honestly thought it was a mistake." He covered his mouth and paced along the sidewalk. "I mean, you realize how insane this is!"

No one understood this more than Elle. She'd been wondering when she was going to wake up from this fantasy she and Ben had curated. Her, a peasant, plucked by true American royalty. Spending days and nights a week in his castle, talking, laughing, teasing, whispering secrets across the pillow, her naked skin flooded with him. No one in the universe knew how insane this was more than she did.

"Yes, I know." She fixated on the concrete of the sidewalk around Pete's feet. The gray and cream pebbles embedded inside. The crunch of her toes. The breath burning her throat.

She moved her fuzzy gaze back to Pete. He dropped his head and sighed. The disappointment painted across his face was easy to read.

"I'm sorry." She hugged herself tight and rocked. It had to be someone from the White House. Maybe one of the guards. No, they wouldn't sell Ben out like that. A disgruntled staff member or aide? He did say something about needing to make hard choices and changes before leaving for Europe. Though they had gone about their relationship in secret, there were many people on his end who would know. Unlike her; she had no one.

Pete squatted down in front of her and placed his hands on her shoulders.

"Ellie, I don't know how you got yourself into this mess, but you don't have to go through it alone. I've got you, okay? It's us against the world, remember?"

The sincerity of his voice, the empathetic smile, those eyes so much like Dad's it panged her square in the chest. There was no one she'd trust more than Pete.

"Actually, it's kind of a funny story." She gave him a slight smile and fessed up to the big secret she'd been hiding for months.

ELLE: Hi. I know you're probably not even up yet, but the world is falling apart here. I don't know what to do. I'm staying at my mom's with Pete because my house is a media circus.

Elle: I'm hoping your end figured out who did this or at least has a good idea.

Elle: I feel so sick over this.

It was almost 10:00 p.m., and Elle sat back against the couch. Ben should be getting up to run any time, and she clutched her phone in anticipation of his call. His voice and his running cadence would calm her. Stop this spiral she was currently caught up in.

Mom was in bed at Elle's insistence. She'd have to be up at 3:00 a.m. to start work, and sitting here while Elle fell apart wasn't going to do either of them any good.

It didn't take too long for the shock and awe of the news to wear off. The numb turned to heat at the contents of various news outlets that claimed there were "sources close to the situation" who produced "evidence" of the relationship, none of which had been revealed to the public...yet. But it was compelling enough to report all about the president's "sexy scientist lover."

"Hey, they called you sexy. Not nerdy, like I would've," Pete had said, in an attempt to cheer her. It worked, and she swatted his shoulder.

"I can't believe he was at my bar. And I *talked* to him. The fucking president. A guy I have mad respect for."

"Don't forget the part where you let him walk me home."

He leaned back and covered his face with his hands. "This is fucking wild. You know that guy's my idol."

"I am aware."

"He's a military guy. But not a dickhead. He doesn't take shit, but he doesn't talk shit either."

Yes, she knew all of this about Ben. And much, much, MUCH more.

"I can't believe you didn't tell *me*."

She shook her head. "I couldn't risk it. The non-disclosure is no joke, and if anything came from my end of things, it would pretty much ruin me."

"I wasn't going to tell anyone. Obviously."

"I know you wouldn't. But to be fair, you were kind of checked out for a while with your own stuff. And I really didn't want anyone to find out."

"Ever? How far was this going to go if you could never tell anyone?"

She sighed. The truth was, anytime she thought about that, she pushed it out of her head. She would rather remain in the fantasy and pretend things were completely normal. Like they would go on under the radar, living their lives separately by day, and together at night. Sometimes.

The phone rang and Pete bolted upright, eyes wide and staring.

"Hey," she said, never taking her gaze from Pete.

"Sorry, this is the first chance I've had to call." Same Ben. So that was good.

"It's fine. I just... Do you know what happened?"

"Not yet, but Raymond is on it like a rabid raccoon. He'll find out what and who it was. I assured him it didn't come from your end."

"Definitely not."

Pete hadn't blinked in a solid thirty seconds. He did, however, keep leaning closer and closer.

"How are you holding up?"

"I'm, uh... well... Pete came and met me. The press was at my door."

Ben's sigh filled the space between them. "I'm so sorry. I never wanted you to have to deal with this."

"I know. I was woefully unprepared." An understatement if there ever was one. Though, again, what did she expect would happen?

"I guess your family knows now. Unless you'd already told them."

"No, I never did. And yeah, Pete's a bit..." His eyebrows shot up and he pointed to himself. "Starstruck."

That chuckle warmed her and she realized this was the first time she'd relaxed since Carson showed her the headline.

"You're kind of his hero," she continued.

Pete brushed her on the arm. "Don't tell him that," he whispered very loudly. His cheeks were a little flushed and he appeared nervous. This was very un-Pete-like behavior. Her brother always appeared cool and confident under most circumstances.

"Hang on, Ben." She pushed the phone at Pete who put up his hands like she had pointed a gun at his chest and was not handing him a phone. "Seriously? You don't want to at least say hi?"

Pete put down his hands and wiped one across his face before taking the phone. "Hello, Mr. President?"

She leaned back on the couch, observing her brother's facial expressions. He went from nervous to terrified (probably when Ben answered back), and then shocked. His end of the conversation was mostly head bobbing, followed by a few, "yes, sirs," and then, finally, by the end of the short interaction, a chuckle.

"I'm glad you weren't a serial killer, too." Second by second, Pete turned back into more normal, happy Pete. "Hey, drinks are really on me next time. Yes, sir. All right. Take care. Yes, Mr. President."

He handed back the phone, ran his hands through his hair, and collapsed into the couch cushions.

"I'm back," she said, smiling at her brother's excitement.

"I think he was still in denial until he heard my voice."

"Probably. But you should see him now."

"I don't even care that you told him that," Pete said, eyes closed, smile spread across his face.

A knock sounded through the phone. "Hey, I have to go. I'll send you news as soon as I have it."

"Okay."

"And Elle," Ben said. "I'm really sorry about this."

Without even thinking, she replied, "I'm not."

CHAPTER THIRTY-EIGHT

The convention center was not prepared for the president's alleged girlfriend to be presenting at an international space science symposium. The venue had spoken with Lance the day before to inform him they'd beefed up security and set up a press area. The science media was still going to be inside to cover the actual symposium, but the national press would be sequestered to the main lobby.

After news of her affair broke Wednesday evening, Dean Piedmont had agreed with Lance that she should not come to campus. She understood and threw her support behind Spencer, saying he was capable of handling the lectures in her absence. Elle was heartsick that she wouldn't be there to help the students counting on her moral support in the days before they were to present their posters at the symposium. But for the sake of the student body as a whole, her appearance amid the hailstorm of media was not for the best.

She consulted with students over video and phone. While many of them started off very curious about her relationship status (she told them all she wasn't talking about that), some, like Noah and Darsha didn't even bring it up.

Ben sent her a message Friday afternoon. He'd been in meetings pretty much every minute he was awake and was on his way to a black-tie dinner. No progress had been made yet on locating the source of the leak, but Raymond said he was getting closer to finding out and had a plan to deal with it.

Elle arrived at the symposium Saturday morning well before her slotted time and headed straight to the student posters section. She got emotional seeing the faces and works of the students she'd grown to know so well. Everyone was dressed to impress and doing their best to keep the jitters at bay. Noah was the first to see her and his face settled into a relaxing smile.

"Hi, Dr. Conroy," he said. He stood before his project in a pair of dark brown corduroys and a button-down maroon striped shirt. "Thanks for the last-minute advice on how to make it stand out." He gestured over his shoulder at his poster on the wall where he'd highlighted his data in different colors. Her heart squeezed over his meticulous presentation.

"I am beyond proud of you, Noah."

The young man reddened to match his shirt. "Thanks. I couldn't have done it without you."

"Nonsense. You did the work. This is all you."

"Well, I never would have had the guts to apply for this. So, thank you, for that."

They chatted for a bit. Elle moved the conversation away from her when three other students approached. They all expressed their appreciation for her guidance and support, and Elle reflected the praise right back at them.

After a bit of mingling in the student section, she moved toward the main presentation area. Dr. Belford Gruber was speaking about his groundbreaking mapping software being developed for deep space purposes. He was detailing how the newest exploration vehicle, Hipparchus, was being equipped with it, and Elle was immediately entranced by the data possibilities its success would provide. STAR would be the first to farm through it. A thrill shot through her, deadening her nerves until the end of the presentation cleared out a portion of the room.

That's when Elle spied Jasper Cunningham speaking to Lance on the other side of the stage. Lance was looking something over, blinking down at the page with folded brow. Jasper was nodding and pointing between what Lance was holding and something in his hand.

Curiosity was one trait she had plenty of (how else would she be an effective scientist?), but she couldn't become distracted with whatever that was. She had fifteen minutes before her presentation started, so she retreated to the restroom to freshen up and settle her nerves.

She washed her hands under the cold tap, taking time to focus on the water icing over her skin. The soap bubbles slipping between her fingers. The paper towel scratching them dry. She pulled the clip from her hair and let it flow down her shoulders. She finger-combed her tresses, still slightly damp from her shower that morning, before pulling it back and securing the twist. She smoothed down the silken midnight-blue blouse she'd paired with a black pencil skirt that dusted her knees.

The woman in the mirror was the epitome of a successful scientist about to take the stage and give the presentation of a lifetime, or at least one she'd been working on for almost that long. Her fascination with black holes had grabbed hold when she'd read Stephen Hawking, and it never let her go.

What happened in the next twenty minutes could dictate how the rest of her life went. Nothing meant more than this. Not the press throbbing outside to grab a picture or sound bite. Not the phones she'd left at Mom's with the sixteen unanswered voice mails and thirty-one texts. This was not about anything or anyone except her legacy and her future.

She nodded at the woman in the mirror and stepped outside.

ELLE WALKED on stage to a rousing round of applause. Carson and Janet clapped from the second row. Having them there took the edge off. The only other person who could have done more was half a world away and couldn't be in the audience even if he was closer. Spencer's awkward form leaned against the wall. The auditorium was packed, standing room only, and even that appeared to be at a minimum.

"Thank you for that introduction and welcome. Is it strange that I spent more time writing that bio than on anything else this week?"

This was met with a respectable flutter of chuckles, which helped ease her. The digital clock on the upper back wall was already ticked down to eighteen. It was time to begin.

She inhaled. "Black ho—"

"Dr. Conroy," Jasper Cunningham spoke from the bottom of the stage. He and Lance stood alongside three others she recognized from the space science circles.

"Is there a problem with my sound?"

Jasper climbed up the three steps and met her on stage. She glanced down at Lance, his pallor even more languid than usual.

"No. There's a problem with your work."

Ouch. He should have kicked her. It would have offended her less.

"Excuse me?"

He met her in the middle. "Do you mean to present the project you submitted the details for three days ago? Your theory about the death of black holes?"

She let out a nervous chuckle and nodded. "Yes, that was

my plan." She glanced back down at Lance who stared back, wide eyed.

"I can't allow it," Jasper said.

Whispers drifted up from the crowd. Metal scraped the floor as people shifted in their seats.

"Excuse me, Dr. Cunningham, but I don't under—"

"The theory has already been published."

Her heart stopped. "That's not possible. I haven't—"

"It is"—he jutted a paper at her.

The ripples from the crowd grew louder.

She took the paper from him. "This has to be some kind of mistake...." Her gaze dropped to the pages in her hand and a shock shot through her chest. She shook her head and blinked, believing this would clear up the hallucination, or wake her up from this obvious nightmare.

"Dr. Edgar Linton gave me this paper in August when he came to STAR for his final interview. It was published just yesterday."

Her eyes glazed over and the words on the paper jumped around. She flipped to the last page. His picture, his bio. Nowhere in it did he cite her. She had no attribution. No contributory credit. She wasn't even a thought.

"Oh, god..." she whispered and offered the pages back to Jasper with a shaky hand, a fraction of what was happening with the rest of her.

"Care to explain? Especially since what you turned in is almost an *exact* replica of part of this paper."

"I... I don't know why..." Her chest burned like she'd kicked back an entire bottle of scotch without taking a breath. She stumbled back on quaking knees that threatened to come out from beneath her.

"You took Dr. Linton's work and were attempting to pass it off as yours. This is a disgrace of unmeasured proportions."

"But... I didn't. That's *my* theory. My life's work."

Edgar had stolen it. The man she'd worshiped for over half her life. The one who she trusted with her most prized possession—her dream—had ripped it right out from under her.

No, that wasn't true. She'd *handed it* over. Served it up on a silver platter one data point at a time. All the while, she'd held back on applying for the fellowship because he'd drilled it into her that it wasn't quite ready. When really, Edgar had meant to take it the whole time.

The sounds around her grew in intensity. The voices, once hushed, now reverberated amid clicks and flashes. Jasper Cunningham droned on about something. Her name was being called over and over.

Someone took her by the shoulders. Her head swirled and her stomach roiled as she was guided away. Her saliva choked her. She cupped her hand over her mouth to stop the bile from shooting out on the floor.

"We're almost to the door," Carson said, his were the hands on her shoulder.

"Use this," Janet said and shoved her flowered silk scarf into Elle's face to catch whatever started coming out. "Jesus, the press wasn't supposed to be in here."

"Well, someone let them in," Carson said.

Elle breathed in the shea butter from Janet's scarf and willed her stomach to stop squeezing. The mucus to stop choking her. The nightmare that had become her life to stop gripping her, and let her wake up.

CHAPTER THIRTY-NINE

Elle clutched the coffee cup like her life depended on it. The heat scalded her palm while the bitter notes drifted into her nose.

She sat back on the bed of the hotel room where she'd checked in under Janet's name. Mom's house had become a hub of activity after someone reported Elle's presence on the neighborhood social media page. She didn't have a choice but to hide away after her newest debacle sent reporters scrounging up every bit of dirt on "the president's dirty secret."

Headlines were gradually becoming different. Today, in the Sunday sunrise, she was "enemy number one." Words thrown around like ping-pong balls branded her a liar. A cheat. A phony. A plagiarizer. A shark. Far too bad for the likes of President Benjamin Foster, the brightest light America had seen in decades.

The door beeped and the handle turned as Brody came in.

"Aunt Lelly!" he enthused, and hopped up on the bed next to her. She quickly put her cup down on the side table before she spilled it on him.

She wrapped her arms around his small form and let the

warmth of his little body ensconce her. She held him tighter than she had in a while. He must have known subconsciously how much she needed it because he didn't pull away. Instead, he patted her back with his tiny hand and pressed a candy kiss to her cheek.

"You're the best medicine, you know that?"

He craned his neck back, showing her a confused and screwed-up look.

"I'm not medicine, silly goose. I'm a boy!"

She smiled at his high-pitched giggles.

"How you doing, Ellie?" Mom appeared around the door. A bakery box full of goodies was tucked under her arm. Elle had told Mom she didn't need to come, but she'd insisted.

"I've been better." She stood and fell into Mom's cinnamon and sugar scent.

"I brought actual food." Pete held up a bag. "And all your stuff from Mom's."

Pete set her things on the bed, and Elle immediately searched for her phones.

"You shouldn't be watching this garbage," Mom said gesturing to the news.

"I know, but I can't help it."

Elle found both phones at the bottom of her bag while Pete set the table up for lunch. Her phone still had a charge, but Ben's was dead. She plugged it in and went about the unpleasant task of checking hers.

Sixty-eight missed calls since yesterday morning. Double that in texts. She scrolled through the missed calls, including six from Lance and two from Dean Piedmont.

Dean Piedmont: Ellery, I need you to contact me as soon as you receive this.

Lance: PHONE ME ASAP.

The rest were a mix of unknown numbers and colleagues,

both current and former. She put down the phone and slumped into the chair at the dinette.

"That bad?" Pete said.

Her forehead sank onto the table.

"I figured as much," Pete continued. "So, I brought you something else." He slid a bottle of Grey Goose from the bag, along with cranberry juice.

"You have my attention and appreciation." She folded her hands in prayer and he fixed two glasses.

"Make that three," Mom said. Pete and Elle exchanged little grins. Mom didn't drink at all; her cheeks reddened after half a glass of wine. But this was an extra awful occasion.

Once they all had their respective beverages (chocolate milk for Brody), Pete held up his glass.

"A toast. To my brilliant sister."

"You definitely have to stop calling me that after recent events." She groaned.

"I wasn't finished. To my brilliant sister, who doesn't always know what she's getting herself into, but who I trust will figure out how to get herself out of it."

They toasted and dug into the food. Elle pushed hers around the plate, her stomach not up to handling much. She sipped her drink, let the warmth of the vodka (a weak pour, but she excused Pete) trickle down and waited for it to dull her nerves. Maybe then she'd feel like eating. Maybe then this entire thing would be over.

Pete's toast had been sweet, but unlike times past, she didn't believe she'd be getting herself out of this. Edgar had waged a campaign and pilfered every bit of research she'd conducted, simply by setting up a shared doc—in the interests of being able to review it and assist "in real time."

One sticking point kept bugging her. She'd applied to STAR three times, (all against Edgar's advice), using some semblance of this same research. Granted, it wasn't written out in true paper fashion as he'd apparently submitted. But she wondered why his submission hadn't set off red flags, being so similar to her previous applications.

"Aunt Lelly is thinking," Brody said from next to her. She gazed down at him and he was rubbing his chin, also apparently deep in thought. It made her smile and she kissed the top of his head.

"Ellie, do you have any idea how this happened?" Mom's gentle voice was steeped in empathy.

"I do. That fucker stole her work." Pete shoveled in another heaping fork full of lo mein. Mom shot him a look and pointed down to Brody, slurping his noodles and lost in his own world.

Elle nodded. "That's one way to put it."

"But there has to be proof that it was yours, somehow," Mom said.

"You would think. But I was stupid. So very stupid."

Mom shook her head and sighed.

"What's POTUS say?" Pete said.

"Nothing. I haven't heard from him since Friday. He's been busy and his phone was with my stuff at Mom's." She gestured behind her to where she'd set it to charge. "I can't even begin to fathom what this is going to do..."

The news of their relationship was one land mine. But this was an entire field of them. She was smart enough to know Ben would have to tread lightly to make it through alive. The media had spent the last twelve hours branding her a "master manipulator." While that sent a rattle through her chest, she also knew Ben well enough to believe he'd have some kind of plan to get them through it. She'd love to hear it right about now.

"Look, Aunt Lelly, that's you on TV!"

She groaned as her university portrait flashed on screen,

next to a video of her on stage at the symposium as Carson led her away.

"I'm turning that off." Mom got up to find the remote.

Pete leaned over the table. "I'm sure POTUS will have some idea about how to fix all this."

"I wish I had your confidence."

She glanced over to the TV, still on even though Mom had the remote in her hand. The footage had shifted to Ben in a tuxedo standing next to some gorgeous young woman. Then it switched to video footage of the two getting into the back of a car. The headline at the bottom: *President Foster plays the field.*

"Turn this up," Elle said. But Mom remained unmoving. Elle got up and slid the remote from her hands, turning it up herself.

"White House sources have denied the allegations that President Foster has been dating Dr. Ellery Conroy, submitting as proof these photos and videos of his long-distance affair with twenty-nine-year-old Katarina Beauvoir, a duchess in Monaco and distant relative of Princess Grace. As recently as Friday evening, the two were spotted getting into the back of a blacked-out vehicle after a formal event. They were taken to his hotel where they were spotted in a very intimate spot at the hotel bar before retiring up to the president's suite."

Photo after photo displayed of the two together, including their close encounter in the bar, as grainy as it was.

"No fucking way this is true," Pete said.

"No fucking way," Brody echoed.

"I'm going to take Brody down to the playground," Mom said, swatting Pete's shoulder as she passed.

Elle dropped the remote and went to Ben's phone. Her stomach flipped and flopped as it turned on. She agreed all of the photos seemed convenient. But the way he leaned in close to Katarina, who was stunning, was unmistakable. Her hands shook when the screen flickered to life and the notifications indicated she had one new text message from yesterday.

7:04 p.m. **Just Ben:** I cannot continue with our relationship. Your scandal at the symposium is too detrimental to my reputation. I've also been informed that the leak of information about our relationship came from you. Our text message string, photographs included, were sent to the media. Therefore, you've broken the terms of the NDA and legal action will be forthcoming. If you attempt to come to the White House, you will be turned away. Do not try to contact me by any means. This phone will be remotely wiped and deactivated.

She sunk to the bed. Her entire life had unraveled in less than twenty-four hours. Her career was over. Everything she'd ever done was now going to be examined under the microscope of being a plagiarist. Edgar had stolen her identity as a scientist. And now Ben. Her amazing, unbreakable, kind Ben had not only disposed of her in the coldest way possible without hearing her out, he may have also been seeing someone else the whole time. How much betrayal could one heart take before it broke?

Heap onto that the fact that the NDA all but assured that she'd lose everything her name was attached to: her savings, her retirement, her house...because somehow her cellphone was the source of information about their relationship.

She saw no way around any of this. No way through it, either. Everything she'd worked for. Everything she'd wanted. Even something she didn't think she'd have or get, in Ben, had been ripped out from underneath her. And it was all her fault.

The scream came from elsewhere. It had to. It was too visceral. Too feral to be coming from a person. Too terrifying to be coming from her.

CHAPTER FORTY

Does someone marching toward certain doom bother to shower? Elle decided not to the next day when she reported to Dean Piedmont's office at 9:00 a.m.

The waiting area was silent as she walked in. Darsha was at her spot behind the desk, and the distress painted across the young woman's face squeezed at Elle's now hollow chest. She had no heart left to break. She'd gone through the stages of grief in quick succession. She'd accepted her life was over. She didn't need verbal confirmation.

Dean Piedmont stood in the hallway and nodded. His face was drawn, his eyes punctuated by darkening circles. He, no doubt, had also suffered from her swift fall from grace.

They proceeded to his office. Inside, the president of the university and two board members sat with Lance around the conference table. Elle's glazed over gaze fell to Lance, who quickly diverted his eyes. At least, she still had something going for her Lance never did: guts.

She sat and folded her hands in her lap. She didn't squeeze them or curl her toes. She had no more emotions left to hide. No more nerves to keep in check. No more gray area. She'd been peeled back and exposed.

Dean Piedmont started. "Elle... Dr. Conroy. Thank you for coming in so quickly. We'll keep this brief."

His posture remained rigid as he read the laundry list of her crimes. There'd be an investigation into the allegations of her plagiarism. The university agreed it was best if she left. She would be paid while they conducted their investigation.

Her gaze didn't divert from his, even during those times he glanced around at the others like he was looking for help. She wanted him, at least, to know she wasn't a coward. She'd accept her fate with the last tiny bit of dignity she had left. Though it was smaller than a few angstroms at this point.

"There's another development that's come to our attention," he said. "We aren't sure how to handle it, and we may have to defer to higher authorities."

Great. This was about her NDA. She hadn't been served yet, but expected the suit to come swiftly. She wouldn't even fight that when it did. What good would come of it.

"Apparently you were chosen to give the Worldwide Lecture in less than two weeks."

Of course she was. She fought the urge to laugh.

"The students—*your* students, present and past—launched one hell of a campaign this semester to ensure that you were chosen. The Universal Science Instructor Society is still deciding on how to proceed, but at last check, they were willing to honor the vote and allow you to speak."

What is the point? She wanted to stand on the conference table and scream.

"However," he said, then cleared his throat. "We'd like you to respectfully decline given the current climate and the bad light this would cast on the university. While we'd like to believe we'd have the results of our investigation by then, we won't know. I think you can agree that doing what's best for the students is paramount at this juncture."

Sure. *Whatever, Dennis.* She nodded.

She cast an apathetic glance around the table at the others, their gazes all bearing down on her. Their judgment was crystal clear. The suspension was a formality. The sentence was a foregone conclusion. She would lose the job she had never wanted. *How ironic.*

"Would you like to say anything?"

She scoffed. "Is it so hard to believe that *he* stole *my* work and not the other way around?"

Dean Piedmont shifted in his chair and his mouth opened.

She cut him off with a wave. "Forget I said anything. You're going to do whatever you want regardless of what I say."

Again, why bother? Like the shower and the lecture, they didn't make sense framed in this new reality. She had no defense to mount. No proof. She would go quietly into the night while they formalized things and made her departure permanent.

She shook her head and surveyed all the men, letting them know she was defeated, but not pathetic enough to beg for something she wasn't going to get. She didn't want it, anyway. She'd never wanted it.

Her gaze lingered on Lance a beat longer than the others. But unlike the satisfaction she figured she'd find, she was surprised to see concern, maybe a hint of remorse, ringing his long face. Nah, that couldn't be right. She was delusional. Obviously.

"We'll have to deactivate your I.D. badge. You won't have access to any of the university systems or resources. You'll be allowed to remove your personal items from your office before you're escorted from the campus."

Treated like a criminal. What a fitting end.

"We ask that you not contact students in any way. They're adults and we can't control what they might do. Obviously, they think very highly of you."

They used to. She should probably speak up and say that. But she didn't. Instead, she remained silent and nodded her understanding.

Dean Piedmont wrinkled his brow and cast a troubled glance around the table. The rest said nothing, but it was clear they echoed his sentiment. They wanted her to speak. Maybe they wanted her to explain. Perhaps even fight back? But again, what was the point? Edgar had her dead to rights.

"Very well, let's get this over with, shall we?" Dean Piedmont rose and showed her the door. Two security guards, Ron and Cyrus, waited in the hall to escort her through the ultimate walk of shame.

FOR SOMEONE who wasn't much of a drinker, Elle had become really good at it. The hotel made a great place to lock everyone out. It gave her plenty of time to drink, pass out, throw up, and start the cycle over again.

"What are you going to do?" Pete had asked Sunday after she'd agreed to go the university. After Ben's phone reset back to factory settings and wiped the entire history of their relationship away like it had never happened. After she'd screamed and cried in her brother's arms for the better part of the afternoon.

At that moment, though, she sat on the floor and leaned up against the bed.

"Nothing."

Pete didn't like that answer. He reminded her she was a Conroy. And Conroys were fighters. Dad didn't raise either of them to lie down and take a beating. He'd taught them to find a way out. There had to be something that could at least vindicate her against Edgar. Something she couldn't see right now because she'd been sucker punched. Blindsided.

When she returned from the university with her box of personal items tucked under her arm, she called down to the concierge to cancel all the room keys. She wasn't going anywhere, so she didn't need one. She ignored phone calls and texts, even from Janet and Carson. The concierge rang her a few times to let her know one or the other was downstairs looking for her. She never answered, just listened to the messages.

Only room service and Uber Eats were welcome. Both provided her with a little bit of food and a lot of alcohol. Pete had come by Monday afternoon to check on her, but she didn't let him in. He called and left threatening messages, but she knew damn well he couldn't kick in a fireproof door at the hotel. He did inform her the media had abandoned their post at her house, and he was moving all the stuff from storage there. She didn't care. Even when he said he'd let her rot in the hotel, she deleted the message and went back to doing just that.

She'd started watching *The Real Housewives* franchise. She considered taking up smoking to go along with the drinking. Maybe it would speed up her demise. What would drinking and smoking herself to death feel like, and how long would it take? She'd even gone so far as to order cigarettes along with her Grey Goose and cranberry juice. But as drunk as she was, she still didn't see the appeal. Though, the Marlboro Reds did bring back hints of Dad's smell. Those had been his brand of choice. Eventually, they led to the cancer that killed him.

She'd thought about him a lot while hovering in her alcohol haze between reality and sleep. Dad had worked his ass off to make sure this very thing didn't happen. To teach her people couldn't be trusted, especially with her gifts. Though she never saw her intelligence that way. It was more a curse than something to be appreciated. Especially since Dad also forced her so far out of her comfort zone all the time under the guise of acclimating her to the gray of the world. Would she not have these huge feelings if he'd let her exist as she should have? The way Edgar said? She felt so much more than others, an intuitive and an empath, Dad had called her. He'd wanted her to lean more into that to balance with the science. To see the gray. To separate the good from the bad.

Edgar had taught her to take those feelings and put them in a box, unless it came to him. She could emote all she wanted—when it benefited Edgar. But when it came to anyone else, her family included, he had turned Dad's lessons against him, hardening her heart to all the injustice Dad had done.

Injustice, indeed. If Dad had let her be what she was born to be, she never would have encountered Edgar. She would have been out of Stanford undergrad before he arrived. So really, as she'd always suspected, this was Dad's doing. His fault.

She thrashed in the king-sized bed and punched the pillows. The anger came in waves, aimed at eroding her sadness and shame. She aimed it toward Dad and Edgar and Ben... All three had let her down after they'd pried her open at the chest and forced her inner world out. They'd taken what they needed from her and when they were finished, they folded her heart between their hands and crumpled it like paper. Tossed it on the ground and walked away, leaving it to be trampled on by those who followed.

She'd eventually pass out from the combination of vodka and exhaustion. She'd have visions of her childhood, of the telescope on the beach, of Dad and his recorder. Of Edgar encouraging her to keep on track with her research. Of fleshing out more of the data, and spending time talking it through with him. Of Ben standing at the end of a tiled hall, hat pulled low on his head, sleeves rolled up to his elbows lighting her way with his megawatt smile. She'd get close to his arms before the vision changed. Then she'd be standing at Dad's hospice bed. He'd cry and beg her to come back to him. But she wouldn't. Instead, she stood there, watching him fade away until all that was left was his imprint in the bed.

There was no gray in killing a man—and she'd done exactly that.

CHAPTER FORTY-ONE

A beep and click sounded from somewhere. Voices. The slam of a door. None of it dispelled the veil that weighed her.

"Damn it, Ellie." Pete gripped her arms and shook her body. "Ellie, wake up. Come on. This ends today." Shake, shake, shake. "Damn it. God damn it." Rattle, rattle, rattle.

Her stomach clenched and she moaned. She reached up to swat at him, but he rolled her to the side of the bed.

"Throw up on my shoes and I will hurt you," he said.

"Move," she said, then opened her eyes. She threw her legs over the bed and stood. The dark room spun around her. She sank back down onto the mattress and put her hands down to steady herself. The door beeped again and closed.

"Help me get her to the bathroom," Pete said. "She's dead weight and with my back..."

"I got her." A voice came from the other side of her before a thick hand moved her arm across broad shoulders and lifted her like she was nothing. Fitting. She didn't feel like much at the moment.

Her feet dragged along the ground, and when they hit the cold tile she cried out. The squeal of a knob. Water smacked the wall.

"It's warm. Put her in," Pete said, and the very capable arms that carried her set her on the floor of the shower. The water pelting her back forced a sharp intake of breath. The fabric of her shirt weighed her down and she leaned back.

"No, you don't." Pete pushed her forward. The water drained down the sides of her head and face. "Come on, Ellie. Get it out."

She choked as her stomach contracted and spewed hot liquid out of her mouth. Over and over and over. She let it come out in waves. Someone held her hair back, a kindness she didn't deserve.

The liquid stopped and the dry heaving began, leaving her ribs sore. Her head throbbed with each empty ejection.

The water went off.

"Stay there for another minute."

She moved her hazy gaze toward the voice.

"Ted?"

"Good. She can still see." Pete crouched down next to Ted. She turned her head, but that made the room wobble.

"Whoa, take it easy," Pete said and wrapped a towel around her shivering shoulders. He popped some pills in her mouth and then tilted her head back and poured liquid in—ginger ale. She swallowed but kept her gaze ratcheted to Ted.

"I need a real shower," she managed to say.

"Okay, but neither of us wants to see you naked..."

Ted shrugged. "I'm good with it. She's not my sister."

Pete shook his head. "I'm ignoring that for now." Pete stood; Ted wrapped his hands beneath her arms and pulled her up.

"Hold on to us," Pete said, and they stood on either side of her as she stepped out of the shower. He held a bathrobe up to her. "We're going to be right outside the door. Holler if you need help and I'll send this brute in. Reluctantly, mind you."

"Not on my end it won't be."

"Seriously, man? This is my little sister. I swear, I don't know how I let you talk me into coming along."

"I'm the one who got us the key, remember?"

Pete huffed. "Fine, but I didn't have to let you come up to the room."

There was nothing that Elle wanted more than to know how these two came to be in her room, but her teeth were chattering too hard at the moment for her to think of another thing.

"Can you both actually leave so I can do this?" she managed. When they had left, she got back into the shower, naked this time.

The ginger ale bubbled in her stomach, but she willed it to stay down. After a proper shower, she dried off and slipped on the bathrobe.

"Ellie, are you okay?" Pete yelled in through the crack.

She opened the door to the two of them standing right outside, staring down at her.

"Aside from the pounding head and aching body, I'm fine." They'd opened the blackout curtains and she winced. "Jesus, are you trying to make my head explode? Isn't my public humiliation enough punishment?"

"Apparently not," Pete said. "Chug this."

The rotten smell gagged her again. "Dear God, what is this?"

"The only hangover cure."

"It smells like garbage."

He nodded. "Tastes like it, too. But it works. Now do it."

"Who said I wanted to be sober? What's the point?"

"Ellery Lincoln Conroy, if you don't willingly drink that, I am going to get this beast to help me force it down your throat. Now. Drink. It." Pete crossed his arms and she surrendered. She gulped and gulped. Even through the gags, she forced it down, tipping the cup until the disgusting concoction was gone.

She clamped a hand over her mouth. That was awful.

"Don't breathe through your nose for a while," Ted said.

Pete gave her a bottle of water and she stumbled over to the dinette chairs. She sipped while the two men went about her room, cleaning things up. Wrappers, bottles, cups, towels, an occasional pile of her vomit. Pete shook his head, mumbling the whole time about killing her once all this was over.

She shrugged and sat back, an observer in her own life. No action. No care. No concern. Except when Pete held up the half empty bottle of vodka and tossed it in the garbage.

"That was my last one," she said.

"And it will be. You're a very bad drunk."

She scoffed. "I'm a very bad everything, Pete. In case you missed the news." She turned to Ted. "Why are you here exactly? Because I'd like you to leave. Both of you and let me get on with it."

"With what?" Pete asked. Looming over her, his eyes narrowed, so like Dad's again. She shivered.

"Nothing." The shame of her desire to rot away until she disappeared gripped her. She clutched the folds of the robe across her chest.

Pete sighed and sat down opposite her. "I've been trying to get in here since you locked me out Monday. Then this guy showed back up at the bar a couple days later, looking for you."

"Why?" she asked Ted.

"Ben wanted me to—"

She put her hands up. "I don't want to hear anything about that. About him."

"Fair enough," Ted said. "I wanted to check on you. After what happened last week, I was concerned."

She sipped her water and rubbed her forehead. "The relationship leak? Why would that still matter."

Ted and Pete exchanged a glance.

"What?" she said.

"Ellie, he's talking about the symposium eleven days ago. You locked yourself in here last Monday. It's been nine days," Pete said.

Wow. She fell back against the chair. Nine days since she got suspended and left campus. Since she gave the directive to not let anyone up. Nine days since she'd started drinking.

"You can see why we've been worried. Mom was going to call the cops if I didn't get in here today."

Yes, that sounded like a very Mom thing to do. Elle immediately felt guilty about letting her get so worried.

"I'm sorry," she mumbled and moved her eyes to the hands in her lap. She'd tried so hard to shut out the world she'd also shut out the people who still loved her no matter what. There were only two of them—three with Brody—but they meant the world to her.

"I don't know what else to do. I don't have anything..." Her throat burned again. How was it possible to cry this many tears? "I lost my job. My students. My career. My reputation. Ben will probably live happily ever after in a castle with a duchess and forget I ever existed. It's all...gone." The tears slid out down her permanently stained cheeks. "I know you want me to fight, Pete, but I don't have anything to fight with or for."

Ted grabbed the box of tissues from the bathroom and set them down. He pulled a few out and handed them to her, his face the softest she'd ever seen it.

"I can tell you at least one of those statements is false." He leaned back and put his hands up in defense. "But I'm not allowed to talk about him. Your rule, not mine."

She wiped her face. She wouldn't allow herself to wonder.

"A lot of those statements are wrong, actually. Like that you don't have anything to fight or anyone to fight with." Pete said and put his hand on top of hers across the table. "In fact, what you don't know is how many allies you have right now."

CHAPTER FORTY-TWO

When Elle stepped through the door of her house, she was smacked by the musty smell of old cardboard. Pete had done what he threatened—cleaned out the storage unit and moved everything marked personal into the front hallway. She walked along boxes with dates older than her, on her way to the living room where the next thing surprised her even more.

Spencer and Lance sat at her coffee table hunched over the iPad, a laptop, and a bunch of paperwork. Elle stopped, dead certain she was in some kind of dream or nightmare. How were two of the people who had been the source of her stress these last few months somehow in her house?

Pete and Ted moved from behind her with her bags from the hotel. She couldn't move her feet or her gaze. She likely hadn't blinked.

"How's it looking?" Pete nonchalantly asked the two on the couch.

Maybe she was dead.

"We're up to 712 signatures and climbing," Spencer said, then his gaze landed on her. "Dr. Conroy. I'm happy you are safe."

Yup. Definitely dead.

"Ellery," Lance said, standing. He wore khakis and a mustard polo, his work uniform of old before he'd gotten that promotion. "Thank goodness they got to you. We were worried." He placed his hand over his heart.

Her only logical conclusion was the alcohol had left her with brain damage. Or she had consumed so much she'd simply slipped into a coma.

"I think she should sit down and you all can explain what's going on," Ted said, the remaining logical voice in her head.

"She does appear rather peaked," Spencer said and pushed his glasses up on his nose.

Pete moved a box out of her soft white chair, and Ted led her over. She didn't resist when his hands gently pushed her down to the seat. She didn't sit back, though. She was too afraid of waking up before she could find out where this hallucination was going.

"Right," Lance said, then cleared his throat. "There are a few things you aren't aware of, and you should be. You weren't the only one Edgar duped."

Strong and interesting start. She remained intrigued.

"Before he left, Edgar told Dean Piedmont to give me the department chair position over you. Dennis wanted you to have it, but Edgar told us both it wouldn't be in your best interest. That you would be lacking a certain oversight that you would need so you could eventually reach your untapped potential. He said you did your best work under pressure, and suggested I give you as much as I could. Including a mentee."

Elle shifted her gaze over to Spencer. He scrunched his nose as Lance nudged him with his elbow.

"Dr. Linton informed me that you only got better when you had someone who challenged you. When I reported back to him that you were not reacting the way he said you would, he told me it was because you had gotten too emotional since your father died. But that the more I fought you, the better you'd eventually be for it."

Ouch. That was another gut punch. Edgar not only stole her work but actively plotted to stress her out by aligning Lance and Spencer against her. All under the guise of making her stronger. She leaned back into the folds of her fluffy chair and gripped the handrest. This was a lot to take in.

"Tell her the rest, Spencer," Lance said and nodded to the young man who looked like a scared teenager caught stealing from his parent's liquor cabinet.

"First, I have to say that I always admired you. You were—are—a legend at Stanford. The benchmark everyone, myself included, held ourselves up to." He pushed his glasses up with a shaky hand. "Dr. Linton said you mentioned a boyfriend in an email. That I should figure out who it was and report back to him. You left your phone on your desk the day Dr. Dunwoody offered you the spot at the symposium. So I went through it and found out you were dating the president." His Adam's apple sunk. "I took pictures of the messages and sent them to Dr. Linton."

Her breath caught in her chest and she covered her mouth. The implications raked over her skin. All the years she'd looked up to Edgar. Put him on a pedestal. Believed everything he did was for her best interest. Only to have him scheme in a way that robbed her of everything she'd worked for. He already had her research and the job at STAR. Why go through all this trouble to disrupt her life...

"The theory," she said. She moved her gaze between Lance and Spencer. "He did all of this to discredit me, so when he published it, no one would believe it was mine."

Lance nodded. "I'm afraid so. When Jasper pulled me aside at the symposium and showed me Edgar's article and accused you of presenting the same thing, I was beyond shocked. I'm ashamed to admit I believed Jasper's allegations at first."

"Edgar did a great job of making me look bad."

"Quite so. But once I saw your reaction on stage when Jasper showed you, I had the feeling I was wrong. When I spoke with Spencer after, he said he suspected Edgar had lied. I realized then that Spencer and I had been pawns in this awful game."

"How did you know?" she said to Spencer.

"Dr. Linton's paper contained too many similarities to your methodology and presentation style. There weren't many frills or fluff. It was too conversational and easy to understand in most places. Dr. Linton does not write that succinctly."

Look at that. Spencer's methodology analysis actually worked in her favor for once.

"After your suspension, I informed Dean Piedmont that I believed you were innocent. He concurred, but said he needed concrete proof. I called and left you messages for days." Lance nodded to Spencer. "When you didn't return them, I gathered Spencer and came here. That's when we met your brother."

Pete stepped up. "And they've been here pretty much ever since, working."

Her mouth hung open. "On what?"

"Two things. First, we want to help you prove it was your work. Though Edgar was clever in covering his tracks. Right now, we're focusing on comparing your prior published works and Edgar's to this one to see if we can build the case from there," Lance said.

"As I previously stated, Dr. Conroy, your style is very different from his." Spencer's feather cowlick danced as he spoke and for once, it didn't make her want to scream.

The doorbell rang. Pete jogged to get it. "That's the second thing."

Elle confusion deepened as Carson, Janet, Darsha, and Noah filed in.

Carson grimaced. "You look like death warmed over."

Janet swatted his shoulder. "I told you to expect the worst and be nice." She came over and put her arms around Elle's shoulders. "It's good to see you. P.S. When can I expect some goodies? I'm in withdrawal."

"You're ridiculous," Carson shot back.

Darsha joined Lance and Spencer at the coffee table with her laptop. Noah waved at Elle from across the room, his cheeks reddening.

"What's the second thing?" She panned around the room at the very unlikely group.

"We're making sure the university lets you keep your Worldwide Lecture spot Friday," Janet said. "They want you removed, but we've been getting all the students who voted for you to bombard the Universal Science Instructor Society to ensure they rule in your favor."

"You'll be at 1,000 e-signatures by tonight," Darsha said.

"And we've got another 432 on paper." Noah held up a clipboard with several pages. "Don't worry, Dr. Conroy. We've got you. It's the least we can do to repay everything you've done for us."

Drop by drop, the situation sank in. The people in her living room were chatting and exchanging information like she wasn't there, though really, she wasn't. Physically maybe, but emotionally and mentally she was a galaxy away.

Ted tapped her on the shoulder. Offered her his phone and nodded. She took it, swallowing the lump threatening to burst through her esophagus.

"Hello?" she said.

A huge sigh flowed through the line. "Elle. Thank god. Are you hurt?" Ben said.

"I'm...okay."

"I've been so worried since the symposium. You stopped answering your phone, so I sent Ted back to check on you."

Everything was so weird right now. She swept her gaze over the room again before answering because things weren't making sense. Though had they ever? She was not a stand-on-the-side-lines-of-life person. Never had been. Never would be. But life was moving as if she wasn't even a part of it.

"I...uh... The news said you're with that duchess." She curled her toes and continued. "Then you sent that text..."

"Which one? I sent a bunch."

She shook her head like he could see it. "The one about how bad it was for you to be associated with me. That you were suing me. Then the phone was reset and everything was gone."

When she was met with silence, she moved her gaze up to Ted's. His eyebrows folded together.

"I never sent that... I couldn't—I *wouldn't*," Ben said. "That nonsense with Katarina was just that. There was never anything between us, regardless of what the press said. She was never in my room. I wouldn't have done that before you, and I sure as hell wouldn't do it now."

She uncurled her toes. In the aftermath of the symposium, the realization that Edgar had betrayed her had made it easy to believe Ben had done the same thing. Even though that text sounded nothing like him.

"You're too important to me," he continued.

She closed her eyes and allowed her memories of him to float back. She'd spent the better part of her time in the hotel banishing him and Edgar and Dad from ever reappearing in her thoughts and heart. But now she cracked the window and let Ben back in. The way he looked at her. The way he stroked her cheek. The way he kissed her forehead after he thought she had fallen asleep on his chest.

"Elle, I'm sorry, but I have to go. I promise that I'm going to get to the bottom of this. All of it. Then we'll talk, and I'll tell you everything, including the one thing I should have already told you... But don't give up on yourself. Or us. I haven't." His voice dropped so low it was like she could feel his whisper across the pillow.

Great. So Ben did have some super big secret. Perfect.

"I'll try," she managed.

"That's all I ask."

She handed the phone back to Ted, and instead of walking away, he placed a hand on her shoulder and bent so only she could hear him.

"I've never seen him so worried. Ever." He nodded, then straightened back up.

That was saying a lot, since Ted had been with Ben every step of his military and political career.

She surveyed her living room. So full of diverse and unexpected people, all talking and fighting. For *her*. Edgar's campaign had gone further than anything she could comprehend. But as the pieces of his deception snapped into place, the cold realization of the implications settled in.

"This is going to be impossible to prove." The words entered the world as a whisper. She let the weight of defeat send her head back into the chair and stared at her ceiling. Even with Spencer's analysis, it could be interpreted that she had spent her entire academic and professional career with Edgar. Adopting his writing style and voice wasn't unthinkable, though she didn't necessarily believe that was what she had done. When she'd written things on his behalf, like emails, newsletter postings, course syllabuses, research papers—she was intentional in sounding like him. But not with her own work.

"We're scientists," Spencer said, drawing her attention to him. "It's our job to prove the impossible."

The kid had a point. She silently chuckled.

The important part of it all was to remain curious. She'd told students that time and time again. Once they lost that wonder, that desire to discover or prove something, they were no longer in the right line of work.

She'd never lost her fascination with space. She'd had her fair share of highs and lows, but her curiosity remained. Especially when it came to the life cycle of stars and black holes. How something so wondrous could be born out of the death of something equally amazing still put an extra beat in her heart. Starting with that night on the beach with Dad when she'd spied a bright anomaly amid the folds of the dark sky. His face had been so lit with excitement. It was part of the reason she'd obsessed over figuring it out all these years. For him.

"Something will come up. Remember, Conroys aren't quitters." Pete nodded at her.

She was no stranger to discouragement. Frustration. Trying and failing. Trashing months and years of work. Starting over. Rinse and repeat until the outcome was different. Whatever happened with all of this, she wouldn't sit back and take it. She'd join in the fight. For everyone in this room. For those who had things stolen from them in the past. For Dad. And for herself.

CHAPTER FORTY-THREE

Tomorrow would be the Worldwide Lecture. The Universal Science Instructor Society had informed her only yesterday that they would honor the wishes of the students and let her deliver it. Apparently, she had received more votes during the initial rounds than anyone ever had. That was before the petitions and emails they'd received from students, professors, former colleagues, and current ones, all imploring them to allow Elle to keep her spot despite the plagiarism scandal. It was clear to them she had something important to say, a reason so many wanted her to do it on a world stage.

Shortly after she'd learned her lecture was on, she'd heard back from Ben. He was angrier than she'd ever heard him, but not about anything she'd done.

"Raymond. He's the one who sent that message. I told him I expect his resignation to be on my desk before we fly back—"

"Don't." She sighed. "He was trying to protect you."

"He knows I play by the rules and that underhanded moves like this are a no-go."

"You can't blame him. I don't. He cares about you and only

wants what's best for you. I could tell that from the night he had me sign the NDA."

"Which is another thing," Ben said across the line. "He assured me that no one is taking legal action against you. He knows the leak was Edgar. Regardless, I never would have let him take it anywhere."

It was a relief for sure, knowing that she wasn't going to have all her earthly possessions and assets seized in some sweeping government lawsuit. Even with that, as she hung up with Ben that night, with him promising he would see her soon to clear *everything* up in person, she still couldn't shake her concern over whatever his mysterious *everything* would be.

"Mom made you a crumb cake and already told me I can't have any," Pete said from behind the steering wheel, pulling her back to the present. They were dropping by the bakery before giving the storage place notice that Dad's unit was cleaned out.

"I'll share."

He popped his eyebrow. "I told her you'd say that."

She chuckled and went back to contemplating the city outside the windows.

Though she vowed to fight Edgar, she also could accept when the odds were well stacked against her. She'd have to start thinking about what she would do after her time as a space scientist ended. She'd need a job—her savings and investments wouldn't keep her afloat forever. Maybe she'd learn something new, like the violin. Or go into medicine. She didn't think keeping something tucked under her chin was appealing, nor was the sight of blood. So those two were eliminated and Elle was back to square one.

"It's time to put some meat back on those bones," Ida said from behind the bakery counter.

"That's what I'm here to do," Pete answered before she could, and Ida swatted at him with the towel.

"Your mom is in the back. She's working on a wedding cake. But she did volunteer you"—she pointed a bony finger at Pete—"to load up the van for the deliveries."

He slumped. "Of course she did."

"Guess the crumb cake is mine after all." Elle grinned and went into the back to find Mom.

She was sitting at her decorating station, swirling peach ribbons around the rim of a tier.

"There's my girl." She jutted her chin toward the cake. "I can't stop yet, but you can eat while I finish."

Elle sat on the other side of the table while Mom rattled on about work, the fun thing Brody did at dinner the night before, and how Dolores Cooper had been blocked from the neighborhood social media page (after outing Elle) for "being a nosy witch." Elle laughed so hard she inhaled a throat full of crumbs and almost choked.

"You have to stop making me laugh," she cried when Mom came over and beat her on the back with a very firm palm.

"Don't make me do the Heimlich, because I've been waiting since your dad taught me." She wagged her finger at Elle as she sat back on her side and returned to her work.

Elle composed herself and got up to grab a bottle of water. She paused by the photos on the wall, and that framed one of her and Dad from a lifetime ago.

"Did Pete ask if you have Dad's old mini recorder?"

"Not that I recall. But it has been a little busy lately." She finished off the last rose petal, purple this time, and got up to put the tier in the fridge. She dusted her hands on her pants. "And of course, I have it. It was more prized to him than his wedding ring. He lost *that* plenty of times. But not that silly recorder. I was sad when I thought it was gone, but then I found it packed in with his things from hospice."

"He had it there, too?"

Mom shrugged. "It was the man's security blanket."

Elle smiled. "He liked to pretend to interview me with it."

Mom laughed. "Oh sweetie, that wasn't pretend."

"What do you mean?"

"He recorded you. Every single time."

"Oh, come on, Mom. Why on earth would he do that?" Elle brushed at the air between them. It was insane to think Dad recorded her at all.

"He absolutely did. He said it was the only way he had a chance of understanding even ten percent of what you said."

No way. Not possible. Mom must be mixing things up.

"I can tell you don't believe me," Mom said, her hands on her hips.

"It doesn't make sense. He wasn't trying to understand me." If he could, Elle believed Dad would have hit the factory reset on her, so she would become a different girl. A normal one.

"He used to sit there at night with his earpiece, taking notes so he could look things up and get a handle on what you were thinking and talking about."

"But... he was ashamed of me. Why else would he want to change me so much?"

Mom clutched her chest. "Ellie, that's simply not true. That man worshiped the ground you walked on. All he ever wanted was for you to be safe and happy. He knew space made you happy. But he worried. We both did. Especially him. He'd seen so many bad things with his job."

Dad had lectured them many, many, *many* times growing up, all about things to do and not do in certain circumstances. All with the intent to keep them safe.

But this insight, that Dad recorded her? That he searched for ways to delve into the depths of her mind, didn't jive with the man she remembered. The one who always told her she was too black and white. That she needed to stop being so this or that all the time.

Mom ran Elle's ponytail through her fingers. "Ellie, your dad loved you beyond belief. It's why he fought so hard to make sure you were safe. You weren't like everyone else, and it scared him. Not because he was ashamed. He was worried people would take advantage of you. Your heart was always so big, and you had so much empathy. But you also had this scientific brain, and you'd lean more on that and ignore the rest. He wanted you to take it all into account—the way you felt and the way you thought."

"He wasn't trying to get me to stop being so scientific? I always thought..." Actually, that wasn't true. She didn't always think he was trying to do that. Edgar had told her that was Dad's intent. Before college, she believed Dad always had her best interests at heart.

"He wanted you to be both. To be the real you. But at the same time, he knew how some people, especially kids, might react. They'd get jealous. The manipulative ones would take advantage of you and trade their friendship for your intelligence."

It had happened. In third grade, the most popular girl, DeDe Boliva, invited Elle to her birthday party. She'd never been invited to one before, so Elle felt so happy. But before DeDe would hand her the invitation, she wanted Elle to fill in the rest of her math worksheet. Elle didn't feel right about it, but did it anyway, the prize too coveted to pass up.

DeDe gave her a fake invite. The address didn't exist. And Elle had done what DeDe wanted, but didn't get a reward in return.

This revelation turned the pain up in Elle's heart. The regret that sounded through her chest when she thought about

Dad past high school thrummed. It brought on another onslaught of burn and tears.

"Honey, what's wrong?"

"I... I was awful to him. Edgar made me think... He made me think Dad was so ashamed that he held me back on purpose. I believed Edgar over Dad. All those years. I moved back and still avoided him. I lost so much time... And then it was too late. I never got to apologize. To thank him." Elle started sobbing. The final crack in her heart had opened wide.

Mom took Elle's head between her hands. "He knew, Ellie. And he understood. You had to walk your own path and find things out for yourself. You always did. Even if he didn't like it, he loved you and was so proud that you did things your way."

Elle fell into Mom's arms and they sobbed on each other's shoulders. It released what was left of Elle's guilt. Once he was gone, she had put the shame and regret she carried for the way she treated him in a box and walled it up along with the others.

A box...

Elle separated from Mom. "Do you know where the recorder is now?"

Mom wiped her eyes. "It's in the nightstand on his side of the bed where he always kept it. Why?"

Her mind fired up in a way it hadn't since this whole debacle started. The depression over the loss of her life, the thing diminishing in the wake of all the people coming together to rally around her was finally pushed aside.

"I think I know what I'm going to talk about tomorrow at the lecture."

CHAPTER FORTY-FOUR

*Y*ou *don't have to live in the gray, Elle. You just have to see it.*

Dad had drilled those words into her head from the time the test results came back in kindergarten and explained everything wrong with her. From then on, he worked hard to remind Elle, while it was difficult for her brain to work in anything but absolutes, she had to remain in the middle of things and reprogram herself to not be so this or that—so *scientific*—or else she'd never survive in a gray world.

But there was no gray here. in the cracked and faded hunter-green of the lecture hall door, the very one she'd walked through hundreds of times over the last five years she'd taught at NatU. Though this was the first time she'd been back since campus security escorted her out almost two weeks ago.

After guiding space science students forward in the universe, it had taken the recent unraveling of her life to discover she'd stopped moving. Though Dad had trained her to remain present by focusing on things like the scuff of her feet across the concrete, or the warmth of the August sun washing over her, Elle had still managed to miss what was right in front of her more times than she cared to admit.

The chatter and creaking of risers leaked out from the door seams. The lecture hall wasn't occupied by her students today, but a hundred-plus strangers and thousands more streaming live beyond its walls.

One last lecture. A final shot to impart some bit of wisdom and share her excitement about the possibilities that existed beyond the atmosphere. Elle acknowledged she'd done at least one thing right since she'd been at the university. Her students respected her enough to orchestrate this Worldwide Lecture. Without it, she might still be in bed, hungover or drunk.

Will he be inside?

"Of course," she said to the door as a wave of anger scorched her throat.

How did she ever let herself get so wrapped up in him and give away so much of herself?

There was no gray in trusting someone. You either did, or you didn't. You either put too much faith in others—like her mom and brother did—or you learned not to trust anyone. You took the stones of past betrayals and regrets and built a wall to keep others out and yourself tucked inside. Fortifying it, adding layers of brick and mortar every time a new crack appeared. All in an effort to protect yourself, because at the end of the day, you were the only one who could.

It was a process Elle had stopped ever since Dad's last rattled breath grazed her right cheek. His death had made her weak and vulnerable, two things he'd fought to protect her from being.

She swallowed the lump rising in her throat as the door handle jiggled and turned.

The world changed when someone you loved left you.

The world changed when someone you trusted betrayed you.

And the world changed when you decided to do something about it.

"HELLO, ELLE."

Edgar stepped out from the lecture room door. His eyes looked beadier and blacker than she remembered. The fluff of white hair across his head had been cut and combed over to try and cover the scalp poking through. His mustache appeared more painted on than dignified.

"Edgar." She hoped he could see and hear she was talking through clenched teeth. That her jaw was set in a solid line.

"You look well. I wasn't sure what to expect after your absence the past couple of weeks."

"I'm glad I disappointed you. This time."

He scoffed and clasped his hands in front of him. She used to find it endearing. Now she found it infuriating.

"You always did let your emotions get the better of you. I warned you bad things would happen when you did."

She nodded. "Oh, I remember. You made it seem like everything I did outside of what you expected was bad. Including applying for grants, or even that fellowship at STAR. Funny how those were beneath me or, in the case of STAR, I wasn't ready."

"All of that was true. You still aren't ready for STAR."

The anger rippled under her skin, but she concentrated on the ground beneath her feet and her toes curling in her shoes.

"But it's good enough for you. Using *my* theory. My work to get in."

Edgar swept his gaze over her and tapped his temple. "You don't think that's going to work, do you?"

"What are you talking about?"

He inhaled. "You must think I'm stupid. You're obviously trying to catch me on some kind of recording saying something that would cast me in a very bad light." He leaned his head toward hers and whispered, "It won't work. Once again you let your emotions get the better of you."

The director poked his head out of the classroom door. "Excuse the interruption. Dr. Conroy, we go live in two minutes."

She nodded. "Thank you."

He disappeared back into the room and Edgar again tilted his head toward her.

"Well, I suppose that's my cue to leave you to it." He moved toward the door, but she stopped him before he could open it.

"You thought Spencer would remind me of who I could have been if my dad hadn't dummied me down."

"Very good. I'm impressed you still have your wits about you enough to figure it out. Between your career humiliation and your personal life. That duchess is really quite a beauty and a full decade younger than you. There isn't a man alive who would pass on that."

She chuckled. "Oh, Edgar. Is that the *best* shot you can take? I mean, you already robbed me of my dream job and my lifelong project. I feel like there are other things you could pick to get to me."

His brow wrinkled a pulse. He was trying to figure out what her next move would be. But she didn't give him much time.

"You really should go get seated. The show's about to start. I'd hate for you to miss it."

"Well." He cleared his throat and once again grasped the classroom handle. "Good luck."

"I won't need it," she shot back without a millisecond of hesitation. She bored her gaze into the back of his head as he disappeared. Then she counted the time down to when it was her turn to go.

CHAPTER FORTY-FIVE

She stepped out to the podium. The lights briefly blinded her, making it impossible to clearly see the setup. Once it resolved, she found three cameras, each capturing an angle and broadcasting live into classrooms around the world.

They'd told her to act like she was in front of her class giving any old lecture. But she'd seen enough of these to know the producers expected her to use the teleprompter and stand behind the podium.

She did neither. Her eyes had adjusted enough to find the university's bigwigs in the front row alongside Dean Piedmont, Lance, and Edgar. She needed to take the advice she gave Ben in March: talk about something you're passionate about and it will come through.

"As scientists, there are only two factors we know for certain. Everything has a beginning and an ending. Nothing is infinite. Nothing lasts forever.

"Our universe is no exception. It too has an ending. It won't happen for billions and billions of years, so no one watching this will be around. Which is good since this planet has about another five billion years before the Sun runs out of hydrogen and starts to die. I mean, *I* wouldn't want to be around to personally witness the star at the center of our solar system dying. It won't be pleasant." She grimaced and shivered, eliciting a number of chuckles.

"And that's if global warming doesn't get us irradiated first."

An "amen" and a few claps rang out from the gallery. Now Elle at least knew where Carson and Janet were seated.

"I digress. Which my students will tell you is not unusual." She moved about the front of the room as she always did. Though she did miss her usual audience of students.

"So everything eventually ends. There are no exceptions to this." She stopped and arched her eyebrows high, sliding to the left and waving her arm in the air. "'But Dr. Conroy, that's not true. What about black holes?'" She mimicked a student question.

She slid back to the middle. "Ah yes. You're right, Tommy. Black holes are infinite and everlasting. There has never been an end to any black hole that we've ever documented or witnessed. Or wait...has there?"

Faint whispers floated up to the front of the room. Lance and Dean Piedmont shifted in their seats; Edgar remained steadfast.

"Black holes are the top of the food chain. They feed off everything that gets even remotely close. And that's a lot of shit. I'm talking particles, planets, stars, meteors, comets, entire galaxies. They're the universe's Dyson and serve to take out the trash, so to speak.

"Did you know there's a black hole at the center of our very own Milky Way? It's just hanging out, luring unsuspecting space matter in with its beautiful and alluring event horizon. A veritable siren of space. Everything it swallows disappears and never resurfaces. Trapped in an infinite free fall that never ends. Except, according to my idol, Stephen Hawking, it has to.

"He presented this radical notion back in the seventies that black holes essentially leak radiation until they fade away and die." She pulled a red balloon from her pocket and held it up. "Imagine, if you will, that this was once a beautiful, massive red supergiant that suffered the most stunning death and subsequent collapse. All of this"—she pulled on the bulbous end—"represents the black hole. I know, you're thinking that's not a very impressive black hole at the moment. But remember, size doesn't matter."

A ripple of snorts and laughs moved through the lecture hall. The energy of the crowd bounced back and increased her confidence tenfold. She loved every minute of this.

"This part here with the opening is the event horizon. And as things come near that opening, they get sucked in and the black hole grows"—she blew into the balloon and inflated it to a reasonable size and tied it off—"and there it is now all trapped. Obviously black holes don't have a tie and the event horizon remains open, so I'm taking some liberties here."

She held up the balloon and moved it from one side of the room to the other so everyone had a look at it.

"As of now, this balloon has already started leaking minuscule amounts of air. I've got it tied, nothing should come out, and yet, if I set this balloon in a corner of my office, over time, it will eventually shrink down to almost nothing. This is the Hawking radiation theory. It has never been proven because no one has ever observed the moment a black hole dies. Or even the aftermath. So how do we know it happens?"

She stopped and put her finger to her chin. "Everything else in the universe has a life cycle, why not a black hole? Are we too afraid that it'll destroy wormhole theory and screw up intergalactic time travel?" She cupped her hand on one side of her mouth. "Spoiler alert—it doesn't exist."

Another ripple of laughter interspersed with a cry of

"That's not what Tony Stark said" emanated from the back of the room. The creak in the wooden risers told her people were turning around to see who'd said it.

"What if I told you that there is incontrovertible evidence that black holes die just like everything else in existence? Except, it doesn't have to happen like Hawking radiation suggests. What if I told you it can also happen like this." She withdrew a safety pin from her pocket and without warning, pushed it into the balloon. A massive pop was followed by a shower of white powder mixed with glitter exploding and drifting through the air.

"That was awesome," someone shouted, and the crowd clapped their agreement.

Elle wiped her palms together to rid them of the powder and smiled out to the crowd.

"You might be asking the question all scientific minds must ask to be any good at this job—'how do you know that's how it happens?' Is it because I spent decades researching it and poring over the data? Or did I simply read one published paper and adopt it as fact?" She cast her gaze at Edgar who remained ramrod and unmoving.

"Maybe, I made it all up and no such thing exists." She shrugged and walked back to her desk, sliding her last prop into her pocket. "Before I tell you the answer, I need to take you back in time to when I was eight years old—so three whole decades. I know. Ancient.

"My dad loved to take me to Sandy Point State Park to watch the stars. He'd throw me and my telescope in the car after dinner, totally ignoring my mom's protests that I couldn't stay up so late on a school night.

"One night we're out there. My scope is lined up perfectly with Andromeda. I've got my notebook and cool pen with a flashlight built in. I put my eye to the lens and bam"—she clapped her hands—"I see this bright flash. It was gone before I could blink, but it left a faint white hazy glow in the night sky. My dad asked me if I'd seen it too. He'd been looking through his binoculars.

"Now, I don't pretend to believe I knew right then it was a black hole dying. But in the days and weeks and months that followed, I formed this theory that it was. I called it a white hole because of that glow that hovered in the sky. I started doing research, as best as an eight-year-old with dial-up internet could do. My dad took me to bigger scopes on the weekends." He toted her around so many times. Even when he was exhausted from work. Three new cases and fourteen open ones. A trial, a hearing, a parole board to testify at. He still rallied and took her out. Her throat constricted, and she squeezed her toes to pull herself back.

"Recently, my longtime mentor, Edgar Linton published a theory about white holes being the real marker of a dead black hole. You won't see my name on there, and that's fine. None of us *owns* a theory, but it does help if we can prove where the data points came from and sometimes more importantly, when and how they were collected."

The cameraman closest to Elle craned his neck over to the producer standing nearby. The man ran his finger in a "keep rolling" motion. She withdrew Dad's black mini recorder from her pocket and turned it over in her hands.

"This was my dad's recorder. He was a detective and used it for everything. Even when I didn't know it, he was recording things. I'd like to play you a little snippet."

She punched the button, sending a hum of feedback surging through the speakers Spencer had set up in the corners of the room.

She inhaled sharply and closed her eyes while the cassette crackled and broadcast her memory to the world.

"THIS IS Jack Conroy interviewing the future Dr. Ellery Conroy. We've just returned from our fifth beach run in six months. So what theory are you working on proving tonight?"

She paused, looking up at him from her bed. "Dad, do we have to do this every time?"

"Yes. Scientists need to keep backups of their data in case something happens to one thing, they have another way to memorialize it. Like I do with my cases."

"You're silly," she said.

"Yes, well that's fine. I'll be plain ol' silly Dad, and you be brilliant future space scientist, Dr. Ellery Lincoln Conroy."

She giggled and sunk deeper under her constellation comforter.

"So tell me what you think is going on?" he said.

"Well... According to my science, I think there is a black hole that died and turned white. We saw a flash, and now six months later, there's a teeny speck of light floating around nearby. I think it's whatever popped out of the black hole."

He grimaced. "Things come out of black holes?"

She nodded. "Uh-huh. When things die, the stuff inside comes out. Like when stars die, they spurt out iron, carbon, and all sorts of chemicals into space. It makes sense a black hole would, too."

"Interesting. So what else do you need to be able to further prove this theory?"

"Lots of things. Like a super big telescope."

Dad cupped his chin with his hands. "Hmmm. I don't think we can swing that."

"You don't have to. Santa will bring it. It's the only thing on my list." She clapped her hands in delight.

Dad chuckled nervously. "Good point. Listen, I've got to tuck you in before Mom finds us talking and expels things at me that won't be very pleasant."

She closed her eyes and welcomed his warm kiss on her forehead.

"You are the brightest star in the whole universe, Ellie Belly. I love you."

"To PC 1247 and back," she whispered.

He smiled and tapped the tip of her nose. "Even beyond that."

SHE PUSHED THE STOP BUTTON. *Thanks, Dad. For everything.* She took a breath and again peered out into the silent crowd.

"I don't know if it's enough to prove that one data point—the original one in Dr. Linton's paper—is ironically the very one I collected with my eight-year-old eyes on the beach with my dad over thirty years ago. But I do hope that in concert with these"—she walked over to the brown box she'd slid behind the desk and pulled out envelope upon envelope of mini cassette tapes labeled by year, the ones they'd discovered in the storage unit months ago—"data points collected over the subsequent years, might satisfy any question as to whether the white hole theory Dr. Linton published is mine. I'm happy to share these with anyone who wishes to vet my work."

A lightness overran her body. With Dad's help, she had freed herself from a burden she never should have been carrying. What might have happened if he hadn't spent years connecting with her? If he had simply agreed with what others suggested back in kindergarten and let her accelerate. Leave the safety of his wing at a very young age. She never would have spent all that time building the skills he'd taught her. She never would have lived in the gray or felt all that came with it. She shuddered to think about where or *who* she'd be right now.

Rounds of applause roared through the room as did the boom of feet on the risers as people stood. Hoots and hollers bounced around. Lance was one of the first to his feet, and Edgar just about leveled him with a dirty glare. Elle nodded to Lance, then to Dean Piedmont, who appeared quite confused as to what had happened.

She dipped her head as the overheads came on, illuminating the packed lecture hall. Pete whistled from the back and Mom pumped her fist and wiped her eyes. Brody waved from Pete's arms and Spencer engaged in some kind of awkward hop. Janet and Carson waved furiously and hollered.

Everyone was celebrating except the one trying to slip out, hoping no one would notice his cowardice exit. Elle stepped right in front of him.

"Was that scientific enough, Edgar? Or was it watered down by too much emotion?"

Edgar huffed and leaned in close, snarling inches from her face. "You were a *child*. That recording doesn't prove anything except you were an entitled brat who happened to be born a genius. I worked my ass off. I *deserved* that theory. You don't."

She nodded and let a smile overrun her face a beat before stepping back and tapping the microphone still affixed to her collar. "Thanks for that last data point, Dr. Linton."

Face red, eyes bulged, Edgar never looked back as he hustled his way out of the classroom.

CHAPTER FORTY-SIX

The peace with which Elle walked out of the lecture room followed her through the afternoon and into the night. She was accosted in the hallway by, well, everyone. Her friends and family, those who had spent the week working so hard on her behalf. They hugged and high-fived her. Noah introduced her to his father, who couldn't stop expressing his gratitude for all she'd done for his son. He also offered her a job on the spot; she blushed and promised to consider it.

Dean Piedmont pulled her aside and apologized for not advocating for her more. He vowed to do his due diligence to ensure she'd get a fair inquiry. Spencer asked if she could meet with him the following week and go over some research he'd been putting off since coming to NatU. Lance shook her hand and told her how he was sure her dad was beyond proud of how she'd executed her career and fought for what was hers.

When things finally died down, she enjoyed the wine Janet and Carson had brought and listened to their update on the photosynthesis project. It was no surprise that the plasma generator was still in the lead, and they all got teary when Carson reiterated his gratitude for her contribution to the team and his pride in knowing her as a friend.

Elle was the last to leave the building, declining several offers of a ride home. She wanted to walk and enjoy the evening, something she hadn't done in what felt like forever. Beyond the courtyard, the air filled with gardenia, and she noticed Ted's blacked-out Charger parked at the curb ahead. Odd that he hadn't said anything about being here. But the passenger door opened, and Ben emerged. Ted stood from the driver's side long enough to wave and smile before ducking back inside.

"Hi," Ben said as he stepped closer.

"Hi," she said. It was the first time she'd seen him since all this began. That familiar warmth filled her, but she needed to keep it in check. His presence didn't mean they were picking up where they'd left off.

"Your lecture was beyond amazing."

She smiled and dipped her head. "Thanks."

"And I didn't even need to apply to see it."

"You can thank my students for that. They pulled this off."

He shuffled his feet and buried his hands deep in his pockets. He moved his head one way and then the next, like he was searching for something or someone. He appeared nervous, the very opposite of the way she'd seen him. This did not bode well.

"I haven't decided what to do about Raymond. I'm still really pissed about what he did. Even if you are right about his intentions."

She nodded and curled her toes, waiting for the bottom to drop out.

"It's extremely complicated. With him. And with me. My situation. No one knows about it besides Raymond. I couldn't even tell Ted, which has been hard."

Great. This was the part where he finally revealed he had a

secret wife. Maybe a husband. A kid he'd stashed away to maintain his good-guy image. A criminal record. A rubber band of nerves snapped against her chest, stinging her insides.

"There's a group of powerful people that knew I was considering running for president. They vetted me, like this was any other job. When they liked who I was and what I stood for, they offered to help with the campaign. But I had to make one concession. If I got elected, I would have to stay single the entire time I was in office. They felt like the country needed someone dedicated solely to it. No spouse. No kids. No distractions.

"It wasn't a problem because by then I had accepted that I would always be single."

Oh. Though this wasn't exactly what she thought it might be, it still kept her toes firmly curled inside her shoes. It still wasn't good because it meant—

"I've spent my life preparing for worst-case scenarios," he continued. "Something like meeting the love of my life at a bar after making that agreement had never entered the realm of possibility. And yet, that's exactly what happened."

Stunned didn't begin to describe the rake against her chest. The way his words settled into the last piece of her heart that remained bruised. The one that missed him when she thought he'd left. The one that broke when she thought he'd never really existed as she'd believed. She inhaled the air of spring swirling around her. All of it to remain here and not get drawn into her head.

"I had to be cautious. I needed to know that you felt close to the same way as I did. Because if you didn't, and I gave this all up for you, well, I'd feel like a real idiot then." He smiled and moved a step closer. "But then you finally opened up to me. You trusted me. And I knew. Raymond knew it, too. So when the news of our relationship broke, he concocted the duchess story to throw the press off your trail. He wanted my supporters to think I was a playboy taking advantage of my situation, and not the lovesick man I actually was. Especially after what happened to you at the symposium sent me over the edge."

She choked back the burn crawling up her chest. The pain of that moment on stage. The aftermath. Then, as easily as those bad memories had come, the goodness of the ultimate end result washed them away. She was not alone. Ever. She had Pete and Mom and Brody. Carson and Janet. Even Lance and Spencer. So many people had reached out and supported her when she was at her lowest.

Not to mention the man standing before her whose face was rimmed with what looked like uncertainty. He wore his heart on his sleeve and his vulnerability like a badge.

"I wanted to come back that night to be with you and help you figure out what to do next. To tell you I believed in you and"—he shrugged and then exhaled a huge breath that sent his shoulders sinking—"tell you I loved you. Which I guess is what I'm doing now. In a very rambling and roundabout way."

Her heart overflowed, not with shame or anger, but with love. She no longer worried about black or white or gray. Whether she was too this or that. She was just her. Ben, for reasons science could never explain, was able to see the real her and loved her because of it.

She cleared her throat, staring into his expectant face.

"Well, that's a lot to take in," she said.

He nodded but didn't make a move to say or do anything else.

"This is it then," she said straightening up, letting her toes uncurl and relax.

His face fell. "I guess so." A sad half smile formed over his handsome face.

She nodded and tilted her head to the night sky, bursting with the full moon. She'd spent so much of her life looking up, wanting to know everything about the universe. Getting lost through the lens of her scope. Some of it had been to avoid what was going on around her. She understood that now more than ever.

Her gaze floated back down to Ben.

"So no wife or kid hidden away?"

His eyes narrowed for a beat, confusion clouding his face.

"Your secret is that you're supposed to stay single," she said. "Not that you have a family in Canada you're keeping under wraps."

Realization lit his eyes. His left brow lilted, and he nodded. "That's correct. No secret family in Canada or anywhere."

She took a step forward. "And then the other thing you said. About your feelings. For me. That's also true."

"Correct. I am madly and hopelessly in love with you."

She raised her eyebrows. "That's pretty big."

He shrugged. "Maybe I say that to all the sexy space scientists I meet." When her mouth fell open, he leaned closer. "You're the only one I've ever met, by the way."

Joy flooded her chest, and she moved toward him. He met her halfway and they stood staring at each other. She was afraid to go further. She'd never actually been in love before, which is how she knew she was now. This felt different. It was scary and exciting. It was crushing and all encompassing. It was a free fall she didn't want to end. A black hole, that, hopefully, would remain infinite.

He took the final step. But before she could let herself go further, she needed one more answer.

"What are you going to do about your supporters?"

He brushed his fingers down her cheek. "Tell them I'm not letting you go now that I've found you. The voters can decide whether I get another crack at this job in two and a half years. Not them."

She tipped her head back up, moving her gaze across the sky. She used to hope beyond hope to find something extraordinary up there, a missing piece to the cosmic puzzle that would make her heart pound and her mind hum with purpose and hope.

"Dr. Ellery Conroy," Ben whispered. "What theory are you working on proving tonight?"

She moved her gaze back to his beautiful gray eyes and smiled.

"According to my science, the thing I've wanted most is right here."

ACCORDING TO MY SCIENCE
TWO AND A HALF YEARS LATER

Tenth Fall Edition—November 6th

ELECTION DAY EDITION

I am proud to announce that the Department of Space Science and Aeronautics is now ranked second in the country. I'd like to thank the faculty and staff for working tirelessly to ensure that NatU provides a wide range of space science offerings that entice students of all capabilities. Enrollment is up, advanced studies are full, and more students are changing their major to a space science field. I'm pleased to report that construction on the property acquired by the university last spring to expand the program will be completed by next summer. Keep up the good work.

 Dean Dennis Piedmont

ANNOUNCEMENTS:

**Congratulations to Dr. Spencer Draisson for the successful launch of his new app that breaks down ultra scientific methodology making complex theories and practicums more accessible to students at every level. Dr. Draisson credits his mentor, Dr. Ellery Conroy, for her assistance and support over the last two and a half years.

**Dr. Lance Dunwoody has opened additional spots for his spring seminar on ethical dilemmas within science including the perpetuation of misogynistic practices. Any student who wishes to participate should apply no later than November 13. After that, there will be a waiting list.

RESEARCH OPPORTUNITIES:

Dr. Janet Gibbons and Dr. Carson Pankowsi are recruiting for their spring growing project The wHole Ozone. This will be the third year they'll use a variety of scientifically engineered enhancements to find the best ways to accelerate photosynthesis to repair the ozone. Their prior findings have led to federally funded greenhouses in Arizona and Washington State. They expect a waiting list, so don't delay in applying!

REMINDER:

Today is the Presidential Election and the Student Union is a designated polling place. Polls close at 8:00 p.m.

EPILOGUE

"We really need to go if we're going to make it back in time."

"One more quick second. I need to finish this email and then... just... hit... send." Elle jumped up from her desk. "Okay, now I'm ready."

Ted checked his watch again. "Why don't you accept that you can send an email from anywhere. A car. A plane..."

She threw her laptop in her bag. Ted met her at the door and slid her coat over her shoulders.

"Because I don't like it when people are hulking over me and I'm trying to respond to a student. It doesn't make me go quicker."

"I wouldn't hulk over you, if you didn't insist on cutting it so close all the time."

She huffed out in the hallway and threw up her arms.

"I have a job, Ted. Outside of"—she flailed her arms wildly between them—"this."

He sighed. "And if you don't start walking to the car, I'm going to lift you up and carry you there. Because that's *my* job."

She narrowed her gaze. *He wouldn't.*

But he wasn't budging. Between the pop of his eyebrow and the way his jaw set, she knew without a shadow of a doubt he would.

"Fine. I'm moving. Go ahead and tell whoever needs to know." She marched down the hall toward the back door.

"Andromeda is a go. ETA thirteen minutes."

That code name was her choice. Obviously. The head of her security detail was not. Exactly. Ted had requested to be reassigned to Elle, and though Ben pretended he was hurt, she knew it was a conspiracy between the best friends.

"Dr. Conroy, do you have a minute to sign something?"

Noah jogged up alongside her. Ted flashed her a don't-even-think-about-it look, but she shrugged and stopped.

"It's the final vendor list for the Girls STEAM the World conference in January," Noah said, handing her a folder.

She ran her gaze over the page. She had been surprised when Noah returned last spring to start his graduate work. He didn't enjoy the job at his father's company, opting instead to pursue a career in education. She got emotional when he credited her for the decision.

"Thanks for staying on top of that." She scrawled her signature and handed it back.

"Sure thing. I gotta run. I'm late for a meeting with Dr. Dunwoody about the spring seminar. He's letting me lead a few sessions!"

"That's an excellent opportunity for you. Remind Lance I won't be in tomorrow and that he and Spencer are covering for me."

"Will do. And hey, good luck to your husband tonight. I voted for him, well, obviously." Noah trotted away, his raven hair flopping in the wind.

She turned back to Ted, who was shaking his head.

"Well, are we going or not?" She lifted her chin and marched forward toward the waiting car. He opened the door and she slid into the back.

It was odd to think she detested Lance not long ago. But when things unraveled, their relationship shifted to one of mutual respect and understanding. He'd resigned as department chair in the aftermath of Edgar-Gate (Janet coined the term). When Dean Piedmont and NatU's president came knocking, all but begging her to come back after the Worldwide Lecture, they offered her the department chair position at Lance's urging.

She made them wait a while before she accepted. Though she always believed she needed to work at STAR to fully realize her dream, Edgar-Gate helped her see that her real life's work was teaching. It wasn't because her Worldwide Lecture attendance exceeded the previous four *combined* (and remained the most-streamed event for the Universal Science Instructor Society). Or because Jasper Cunningham from STAR never apologized for overlooking the fact that she had submitted three prior fellowship applications that contained similar data to Edgar's. Jasper did, in fact, apologize. Profusely. He even offered her a permanent position, with a team she could pick and oversee, to conduct any kind of research she wanted anywhere in the world.

It was the opportunity Elle had always dreamed about getting. And it took her a whole thirty seconds to slam the door in Jasper's face. Literally. Ben had been impressed she let him get out an entire sentence.

When it came down to it, she finally embraced her role as an educator. She loved helping others sort out complex concepts by making them understandable. Remaining at NatU would allow her to do that and mold the curriculum to draw the most enthusiastic space-science students.

She continued to lecture at NatU and other engagements

when her schedule permitted. This semester she'd taken on six classes, four of which were lower levels. It gave her time to get to know the students and guide them down the path that best suited them.

NatU and STAR sued Edgar for breaching his ethics contracts at both places. They wanted Elle to join the suit, which she did on one condition: that they utilize any award they received to start a program encouraging more girls to choose science, technology, engineering, art and math careers.

"We're in on State," Ted said into his wrist.

Elle turned her attention to her *other* job. Throngs of people had gathered outside the barricades of the White House, waiting for updates on the election. She'd never seen the grounds so crowded. Especially not on their wedding day when she and Ben had exchanged vows in a very private ceremony inside the portico on the East Lawn. They'd invited thirty people; Elle would have married Ben in front of thirty million. She didn't care.

His reelection wasn't a foregone conclusion to many analysts. The people who had funded his first campaign made good on their promise to withdraw support from Super PACs. But Ben wanted a second term to continue the work he'd started. He'd already done so much good. The economy was booming, social programs were flourishing, and morale was at an all-time high. She couldn't imagine either of the other two candidates continuing that upward swing.

The car stopped and Ted jumped out to open her door. Before he got a chance, Ben was there, helping her out, sweeping her into his arms like they hadn't seen each other that morning for breakfast.

"I figured you were standing me up." He stepped back and looked at his watch before cocking an eyebrow at Ted.

"Your wife is stubborn," Ted said.

"Your best friend hovers." She straightened Ben's tie, which was askew, a sign that he had either been running his hands over it obsessively or burning anxiety by doing any number of pushups. He wasn't often nervous, but she'd learned some of his tells over the last two and a half years. Like the way he drew a very slight corner of his bottom lip in when he was worried. Or the rhythmic tap of his foot on the floor as he read something he didn't like.

"You doing okay?" she asked.

He exhaled and shrugged. "Yeah, you know. The results are finally starting to roll in. Raymond has been following me around spouting statistics and early reports."

"What a very Raymond thing to do. Did the family get here?"

"Oh yeah. Your mom's been dusting sugar over pastries. And Pete's been in the State Room chatting with your artist friend from New York."

"Cassie? I'm so glad she came!" Last year after a lecture at NYU, Cassie Reynolds had approached Elle, eager to get involved in the Girls STEAM the World initiative. Elle was impressed by her passion for art, her desire to help people, and her genuineness. They chatted for hours (much to Ted's chagrin, although Elle suspected he didn't mind that Cassie was tall and strikingly beautiful), about all things science, art, and life. A few weeks later, Cassie sent her a gift. Elle gasped at the canvas, a swirl of purples, blacks, blues, and silvers of a starry night sky melting down to a beach, a little girl, a man, and a telescope. The two became fast friends and kept in close contact ever since.

"And Brody brought his new puppy." Ben raised his brow. "Which I know you told him to do to distract me."

She affixed her most innocent look on her face. "Is it working?"

He crossed his arms, putting on a tough front that lasted about five seconds.

"That's not the point. You don't always have to be right."

"I'm not. Well, not about everything. But when it comes to you, I might be right more times than not."

He shook his head and unleashed his megawatt smile as he pulled her to him.

"I'm so glad you're home. You're the only thing I want or need. No matter what happens tonight."

When he kissed her, it still made her head swim and reminded her she'd done something she once thought impossible: she was living her dream alongside the man of her dreams.

"It doesn't feel good to be replaced, I'll be honest," Ted said.

The interruption separated the couple and set off a ripple of laughter through the three of them.

"Where we go, you go. Always." Ben clapped Ted on the shoulder. Elle knew he meant that, too.

"Good. Could you go inside so I can? It's a little cold and I'm starving."

The three of them made their way inside. Elle paused before she stepped through the door and looked up as a shooting star arched overhead. She smiled and knew unequivocally they'd be living in this house another four years.

The End

THANK *you for reading According to My Science. I appreciate that you chose to spend your time with my book. If you enjoyed it, please consider leaving a review. Even a sentence about some-*

thing you liked can help the book get noticed by others. Sign up for my newsletter at jensinclairwrites.com to stay up-to-date on all my events and upcoming publications. Check out my other book, There's Always a Price and continue reading for a sneak peek at my newest book, Stages out now.

STAGES

Three lives entwined by one shattering truth.

At thirty-eight, Cam has built a career fixing companies while never letting anything or anyone break her. As she's about to battle her workplace rival for a coveted promotion, she inherits an estate from a grandmother she believed died decades before.

Sixteen-year-old Josie is struggling to make it through high school. Between her father's drinking and her mother's prolonged absence, she's desperate to stay invisible. When a school essay contest exposes more than she intended, her father reveals a truth that shatters her world even more.

Sophia is a twenty-four-year-old who has learned that nothing pays the bills quite like a rich married man. After years of saving, she finally has the money she needs to start over. But just as she's about to walk away, a message forces her to face a past she's been trying to forget and a future she isn't sure she can have.

As the losses pile on, each will make choices that ultimately lead to the untangling of the thread that binds them together.

Stages is a powerful story about how buried secrets, inherited pain, and unresolved loss mold us into the people we become.

Get *Stages* anywhere books are sold.

When I was young, I wanted to be an astronomer. I loved all things NASA and space and begged my mom to send me to Space Camp. I never understood why she didn't. Decades later, when I looked at the price to send my youngest son, I finally got it. (Sorry, Mom).

Having said that, I am not a scientist or an expert on space. I am certainly not brilliant like Elle. I've done my best with space terms and concepts, but that doesn't mean I got them right. White holes are a hypothetical concept believed to spew matter out versus trapping it like black holes. I did not find uncontroverted proof that white holes exist; however, Stephen Hawking's theory about black holes fading away (Hawking radiation) is real. Elle's theory is a mix of half truths, facts, and hypotheticals. In short: I made it up because it seemed like a cool thing for her to discover. Plus, I happen to think stars and black holes are fascinating.

I've also never been to the White House. I wouldn't know the first thing about how the president would move through it except what I've found in my research. If the Secret Service bangs down my door based on all of my Google searches, at least I can present them with this book as evidence in my defense.

ACKNOWLEDGMENTS

I've been working on this story in some form or fashion for five years. Writing for me is a lot of working on something and putting it down. Picking it up. Changing it. Putting it down. Starting over. Repeat and repeat.

The easiest and most challenging part of this book was Elle. I was a space nerd (see Author's Note) and so creating her gave me a way to live the alternate version of myself where I was scientifically inclined and could, in fact, entertain the notion of being an astronomer. It was also tough because I am not. Thus began the multiple starts and stops and start-overs. I have more drafts and versions of this manuscript than any other so far.

What got me through was a lot of research, persistence, and support. A big part of that has to do with three women who agreed to meet on Zoom monthly so we could help each other brainstorm stories, marketing, cover design: You name it, we've done it. At some point, we deviated into something far greater and fun than what we even expected. So to Sara, Julie, and Marina: Thank you for helping me kickstart my creativity. Our group is my favorite way to spend an hour every week. I hope to continue our shenanigans for as long as possible. I love you all.

Two people worked real magic to get this book ready for readers. To my copyeditor, Lara Zielinsky and my proofreader, Kate Underwood, you are both amazing at what you do. I appreciate your shine!

Again I thank the Women's Fiction Writers Association, my local Writer-Hiker pals, the Write Inmates, the Early Birds, my amazing critique partner and award-winning author Rachel Stone, and my ever-supportive writing sister, Marta Lane. I wouldn't be this far without you.

Aimee Van Alstyne moved up from beta to alpha reader with the most recent draft of this book. Her opinions and insights helped me understand what wasn't quite working from a reader's perspective. Everyone should be so fortunate to have an Aimee for so many reasons.

My family showed up for my debut and they haven't quit. Mom, Kathy, Laurie, Ethan, Tim, Peggy, Kelli, Jodie and everyone in between. Please accept this as a collective thank you that will never express how much it means that you always make me feel supported. I love you so very much.

My daughter, Kaylee once again helped out a lot with this book. Her genuine obsession with American History provided the model of the president I most wanted to fashion Ben after. He had to be successful, quiet, humble, and possess an unassuming ability to lead people simply by being genuine, loyal, intelligent, compassionate, and courageous. Thank you, Kaylee. I love your adventurous spirit and you so very much.

My youngest son, Maddox is all over this story. His creative and scientific brain provided the inspiration for the way Elle innately views the world in very black and white ways. He helped me come up with Janet and Carson's photosynthesis experiment, and he pointed me in the direction of white holes. He'll only be 16 by the time this book is published. But I still think of him as the little boy who would spout off semi-factual tidbits or things he wished were true by declaring, "According to my science," beforehand. Maddox, I love you no matter what you do or who you become. I am simply honored to be your mom.

ABOUT THE AUTHOR

Jen Sinclair pens personal essays and contemporary fiction that explore complicated relationships, love, loss, and all the messiness of life. She uses humor, heart, and compelling plot elements to explore what it means to be human. Her stories often follow women who must fight to overcome tragic circumstances and loss to discover who they are and what they want.

There's Always a Price and *According to My Science* placed second and third for best Women's Fiction at The Florida Writers Association 2025 Royal Palm Literary Awards. They were both also named Best Books of Fall 2025 by Pencraft. Jen also collaborated with three other writers on the dark friendship fiction book, *The Accidental Life of MF Ascher* under the pen name Ivy H. Booker.

Visit jensinclairwrites.com to learn more about her.